# The Quest of Eight

## Part one:
## The Return of the Fury

I0547925

### Richard Reda

# Dedication

This book is dedicated to our first eight grandchildren:

Summer

Lochen

Solveig

Sean

Natalie

Stella

Quinn

Liam

# ACKNOWLEDGMENTS

A special thanks to my wife, Karren for her editing and support, and to my daughter, Jill Fox, for her editing.

Cover art: Mike Reda and Richard Reda

i

# Prologue

The time was right.  He could feel it.  The planets were perfectly aligned and his powers were at their peak.  He had been preparing for this moment for quite some time.  Everything he had learned, everything he had practiced had been dedicated to this moment in time.  His army was well trained and organized.  His diversion was carefully planned and ready to execute.  And the sky was blackening.  Only recently had he understood the connection between his own powers and the ominous clouds that filled the horizon, flashing lightning and booming thunder.  He had not yet realized the full potential of these clouds, and wouldn't until much later.  For now, though, he would use what he did know about them to his advantage.  He would need every trick he had and every bit of experience he had learned in his attack on the witch's fortress.

She was very cunning and not to be underestimated.  He would have just this one chance to obtain the talisman locked inside her secret keep.  He was certain she had cast a number of spells to protect and keep it hidden.  In spite of this, he had already discovered the location, but had never dared to remove the token.  Now was the moment for him to make his move.  With the talisman in his possession, he would be able to free himself from her dominion over him.  She had been his teacher, but she had kept much of her knowledge back; only allowing him glimpses of what could be.  That time would soon be over.

When he was certain she was away, he put his plan into motion.  He began the assault with a diversion in the event that her apparent absence was merely a ruse.  The diversionary forces crashed through the portal and into the citadel, drawing attention away from the real goal.  His own army added a secondary diversion while he moved quickly and stealthily to the target.  There was no sign of the witch.  Even though he had chosen a time when he expected her to be absent, but he knew that could never be trusted completely.  She came and went like a ghost, letting him know when she left, but never announcing her returns; instead, she just appeared.

Eventually, he made his way through the labyrinth to the keep where the talisman was hidden.  There it was, just as he remembered – resting on a pedestal in the center of the chamber.  He looked around furtively.  Still no sign of the witch.  He crept towards the talisman, picked it up and placed it around his neck.  He was momentarily distracted by the heightened sounds of fighting.  Something or someone was battling with the diversionary forces.

Before he could react to the shift in the attack or make any move to escape, she appeared.  He was caught with no support, with no protection but his own powers, which he knew could not match hers.  He was certain that the talisman had been the source of her power, and now that it was in his possession, it would enhance his own.  He had made a fatal error in thinking that.

She approached him with recriminations.  He had betrayed her, she claimed.  Finally, she screamed at him, hurling incantations as she thrust her arm forward.  He was unable to react fast enough, even though everything happened as if in slow motion.  She had snared him in her web.  He could see her outstretched arm coming down in his direction.  He could see the waves of energy billowing like heat waves, distorting the air in a circle emanating from her hand.  The wave increased in size as it slowly expanded and enveloped him.  He had been trapped.  His mind was filled with a raging fury.  No matter how hard he concentrated, he could not overcome her spell.  He knew he was doomed, which only enraged him even further.

He could see the flash of light in the center of the wave as it shot forward, coming directly at him until it struck the talisman, just over his heart.  The blast tore the token apart, sending pieces in multiple directions.  The band that surrounded the talisman flew upward, spinning slowly in the air.  As he felt himself thrown backwards by the blast, his eyes locked onto it.  He reached his hand out in an attempt to grasp it.

His last image was his fingers slowly closing around the spinning band as his body seemed to dissolve.  All the sounds around him, including his own screams, blended together into a single roar.  The room stretched as if it was being pulled at the top and bottom and then twisted.

And then everything went black – and cold.

# Chapter one

**D**ark clouds were beginning to form on the horizon. They had been taking shape for several days, moving slowly and heavily across the sky from one area to another in no particular direction. Booming thunder could be felt coming up from the ground and shaking the trees, even though it was far off in the distance. Flashes of lightning could be glimpsed between the clouds. It had not yet reached its way to land, but that would be happening soon. The air was warm and thick, though the wind blew, coming in ahead of the clouds as if announcing their arrival. This was no ordinary storm approaching. It was a force of evil; what the faeries called, "The Fury."

Summer sat on the edge of a leaf of a Banchu Tree watching the twin suns slowly fade behind the encroaching clouds. She had heard stories of The Fury, but always thought that they were made up to frighten the little ones to make sure they never wandered far from the safety of the village. The clouds often took the shape of an angry dragon, black and menacing. She herself had never seen anything like the images now before her. She was a hundred and twelve years old – still quite young for a faerie. The village elders were almost three times that age, and she was sure none of them had ever witnessed this, either. It was time to gather them once more and convince them to send out a scout to see which way the clouds were coming. Normally, a scout would not be needed. One could simply look up and observe the direction they were taking. These clouds were different. They just seemed to form, and then evaporate, only to reappear in another area of the sky. They didn't move so much as – what, she wondered? Appeared – that was the only way she could describe it.

She thought that the village should move away from the shores of the Cerulean Sea and into the forest. The elders disagreed. No surprise there. Even though she was Princess of the Faeries, the elders often didn't pay any attention to her and easily convinced the rest of the village to follow their lead. Well, if they wouldn't send a scout, she'd go herself.

She took a deep breath, stretched her arms and stood up. She was three inches tall – one of the tallest faeries in the village. As she stood on the tip of the leaf, the wind blew through her long hair, lifting it in the air, and then letting it float back down to the backs of her legs. It was the same russet color of the Banchu Tree in which she lived, but it was streaked with gold that would glisten in the morning sunlight. Her clothes were spun from the feathers of a peacock and her wings looked like a silver mist. She had the ability to transform herself when she needed to into the form of a butterfly. When she did this, her wings could change colors to match her surroundings, making her almost invisible. Around her neck she wore a locket that had been given to her by her mother. There were rumors that it had magical powers, but, like the stories about The Fury, Summer thought they were just stories, and never really believed it was anything more than a locket.

The village in which she lived sat in the small trees and bushes on the shores of the Cerulean Sea. Like its name the Sea was a deep bright blue. It was never turbulent; its waves always provided a gentle, soothing backdrop to the peaceful life of the faeries. The plants along the shores were dominated by Banchu Trees, which had natural hollows that the faeries used as their homes. The trees were surrounded by a variety of low lying shrubs and plants which were covered with flowers in every color of the rainbow, and the sweetest fruits and choicest nuts and berries for miles around.  As Summer flew over the village on her way to the elders, she understood why they were so reluctant to leave.

But it wasn't always this way.  Before Summer was born the faeries had lived far away from the shore, in the giant forest which they had shared with the forest creatures.  The ancient lore of her village told of a time when the faeries and the forest creatures lived side-by-side, sharing everything.  And then something changed.  There was no indication in any of the folk tales as to what the reason was, but something caused it.  This change took place further back than anyone could remember or identify. It didn't happen all at once, as far as anyone could tell.  It just seemed to creep into their way of life.  And then it took root.

For the last several centuries the faeries and the forest creatures fought over just about everything: food, water, the trees, and the plants — whatever there was to be shared was fought over.  The faeries accused the forest creatures of destroying their homes, eating their food and kidnapping the little ones.  There was no real evidence of this, other than the unexplained destruction and disappearances.  When confronted with these events, though, the forest creatures never denied the allegations, and, instead, became extremely defensive, which further convinced the faeries of their guilt.

The forest creatures accused the faeries of using their powers of enchantment to perform jinxes and to put hexes on them.  None of them could explain exactly what jinxes and hexes had been cast, and, in reality, the power of the faeries to do such things was very limited.  However, like the accusations made against the forest creatures, the faeries never denied the complaints lodged, only convincing the forest creatures of their truth. Being of a superior size and strength, the forest creatures finally drove the faeries out of the forest to the shores of the Cerulean Sea.  It was the fear that the forest creatures had of the Sea that kept them from driving the faeries any further and destroying them all together.

The wars between the faeries and the forest creatures were terrible and left deep scars. The village elders would tell stories of those wars and the horrors that the forest creatures committed against the faeries. No one ever challenged the accuracy of these stories, even though there was no evidence to support them. They were all assumed to be true. As a result, entry into the forest was forbidden. Any faerie that broke the laws of the village would be banished to the forest and never seen again.

Of course, in all of Summer's life, she had never known or heard of anyone breaking any faerie laws. She never heard of anyone getting banished to the forest and disappearing forever. She thought the stories about the forest creatures were probably a lot like the stories of The Fury – made up just to scare the little ones; but now she wasn't so sure. She studied the clouds for a while longer and watched the flashes of lightning. She was puzzled by the fact that the lightning seemed to hover in the clouds, but the thunder seemed to touch the ground. She had never seen lightning like this, nor experienced thunder so severe. She would definitely have to use all her powers of persuasion on the village elders. She wondered if the forest creatures were watching the sky as well.

When Summer was a little one, before she became Princess, she had been playing by herself at the north end of the village along the shore. On one particular day, she spotted a small crab scampering along the sand. She flew down to get a closer look, but the crab buried its head under its one large claw and pretended it couldn't be seen. Summer started to flutter like a butterfly and just floated around nearby. Eventually, the crab came out from under its claw and scuttled further up the shore. Summer followed along wondering where the crab was going. After a while the crab ducked beneath an old log and disappeared from sight.

Just as Summer became bored waiting for the crab, she spotted a large grasshopper and jumped on its back to go for a ride. The grasshopper jumped like a bucking bronco. It sailed over fallen trees and bushes. It splashed into small puddles of water, landed on branches and plummeted to the ground, all the while trying to shed itself of its rider. After a while it finally managed to throw Summer off its back. She landed unceremoniously on her butt in the middle of a small puddle of water. What a ride! She was laughing so hard that she failed to notice that she was deep into the forest. She began to look around and suddenly the warnings and taboos of the village elders shouted inside her head. "Stay clear of the forest! Beware the forest creatures – they eat the little ones for lunch! It is forbidden to go into the forest."

Her heart started to hammer inside her chest. She jumped up and quickly looked around. The trees here were enormous. They were nothing like the low-lying Banchus of her home. These almost touched the sky. They were also much closer together and covered with thick vines and heavy with leaves. How had she gotten so lost? How had she been so careless?

She became very frightened. She didn't know which way to turn. She couldn't fly high enough to get above the treetops. The thick and leafy branches blocked her way. She heard screeches of large birds. These birds could fly very fast and had sharp beaks and claws. She had been warned that some birds were big enough and mean enough that they ate faeries. She didn't know which to fear more – these birds or the forest creatures. She didn't know what to do. She was so afraid that she might never get home that she began to cry.

She didn't think she could be any more frightened until she heard a voice behind her almost shout, "Why are you crying?" She spun around and found herself staring into the gigantic face of a forest creature boy. He really wasn't that big, but compared to a faerie, he was enormous. Without looking where she was going, she flew backwards to escape and immediately got tangled in the web of a dragon spider. She was stuck and the more she struggled, the more entangled she got. The forest creature was as startled as she was and seemed to be unsure of what to do. In a few quick seconds, she had wiggled so much that she was wrapped tightly in the webbing. That was when she felt the web being moved by something else.

She moved her head as much as the webbing would allow and saw the owner of the trap slowly crawling down, one strand at a time, from a far corner. The dragon spider began to look at her as if she was his next meal. He was very large, had deep red eyes and long, sharp fangs. As Summer struggled, the spider began to inch its way towards her.

Her fear of the spider took her mind off her fear of the forest creature just as the boy reached into the web, brushed the spider away, and freed her. He held her gently in his hand, but still had it closed around her so that she couldn't escape. His fingers wrapped around her legs and came nearly up to her waist. She flapped her wings, but his grip was too tight for her to pull free. He moved her closer to his face and looked at her curiously. In an amazed voice he asked her, "Are you a faerie?" Before she could answer, he asked her if she was all right and why was she crying. She was too frightened to answer. The way he was holding her, she expected him to bite off her head. She didn't know which was worse – to be poisoned and eaten by a nasty dragon spider, or to be gobbled up quickly by a forest creature. What would her parents think?

As unexpectedly as she had been grabbed, she found herself staring into his face as he examined her closely, smiling broadly at her. He was sitting on a log with his arm resting on his knee holding her gently but tightly in his hand and close to his face. He had large dark eyes, dark hair that looked like a mop on the top of his head, and his face had a splattering of freckles across it. He was about three feet tall – not unusually large for a forest creature, but still more than ten times Summer's size.

"What's your name?" he asked.

She was still too stunned to answer, and a little uncomfortable in his grasp. That didn't seem to bother the boy. He immediately introduced himself. "My name is Sean. I live in this forest. Where do you live?"

He didn't wait for answers to any of his questions, shouting one right after the other. His voice was so loud that Summer had to cover her ears.

"Oh. Sorry," he said when he saw her blocking her ears. "My mother always says I'm way too loud," he continued in a much lower voice. "She always says to use my inside voice. I don't know what voice that is, exactly, since I talk the same whether I'm inside or outside. What about you? Does your mother complain about how loud you talk?"

"No," Summer said, finally finding the courage to speak. "And my name is Summer."

"Hi, Summer," he said with a wide grin. "I'm Sean – oh, yeah, I already told you that. Are you a faerie? I've never seen a faerie. My parents warned me about faeries. Are you going to jinx me or put a hex on me? I hope not."

When he took a breath, Summer quickly spoke up, lowering her hands from her ears.

"Yes, I'm a faerie, and no, I'm not going to jinx you or put a hex on you. I don't even know how to do those things. Besides, who is holding who captive?"

She spread her arms and motioned to his hand, which was still closed snugly around her legs and waist. He looked at her warily, and then smiled even more broadly as he opened his hand so she could sit on his palm. She thought about flying away, but was intrigued by him, so she sat cross-legged on his hand.

"That's better," she said. "Why would you think I could jinx you or put a hex on you? What is a hex?"

"What's a hex?" he asked in disbelief. "Are you telling me you don't know what a hex is? A hex is a ...well, it's a...it's sort of like...I don't know. A hex? You know?"

She propped her elbows on her knees and held her chin in her hands as she cocked her eyebrows and shook her head. Sean knitted his brow, trying to come up with an explanation.

"Well, you must know about the wars between the faeries and the forest creatures," he said when he decided he couldn't explain what a hex was.

"Oh, yes," she said with certainty. "I know all about them. Every faerie does. It was when the forest creatures destroyed our homes, stole our little ones – probably to eat them – and drove us from the forest."

"WHAT?" he shouted in amazement. "No way! We NEVER destroyed anyone's homes; we never stole any little onions. I don't even like onions. I'd never eat one."

"Little ones," Summer corrected him, "not onions! Little ones – faerie children."

He looked at her in horror. "Children?" he said, completely stunned. "We LOVE children. We'd never steal them, and we'd never eat them. How could you even think that? You're recollection of the wars is all wrong."

"Really?" she said a bit defiantly. "Then why don't you enlighten me."

"All right, I will. The faeries started the war by jinxing the forest creatures and casting hexes."

"Even though you don't know what a hex is," she interrupted.

"Maybe I can't explain them, but I know them when I see them."

"And when was the last time you saw one," she challenged.

"Well…" he hesitated. "OK, I've never seen one, but I've heard all about them. You put us into trances; you made us break out in boils all over our bodies; you made our food go rotten; you killed trees – you KILLED trees!"

He was getting agitated just at the thought of it. Summer fought her initial instinct to argue back or to fly away. She took a deep breath and collected her thoughts.

"I believe that's what you think happened," she said. "I believe that's what's been told over the centuries. Look at me and listen to what I'm telling you right now.  No faerie has the power to jinx anyone or put a hex on anyone.  Not now; not ever.  The only thing we can do is flap our wings and wave our arms to sprinkle a little faerie dust.  All that will do is to lift you into the air for a little while or to generate light.  It might make you a little sleepy, depending on how big you are, or it might just make you sneeze.  It can do a few other things," she added, a bit vaguely, "but it can't do anything like what you said."

Sean thought for a minute before asking, "Then why would those stories have been passed down over the centuries?"

"I think they might have happened," Summer answered, "but I think maybe the faeries and the forest creatures might have been the victims of someone else's magic."

Sean gave that idea some careful thought.  He didn't immediately agree with Summer, but she certainly gave him something to consider.  He decided to trust her – for the time being.  Once they got beyond their respective questionable histories, they began to ask and answer one question after another; their curiosity growing with each answer.  Sean usually would ask three or four without apparently needing an answer to any of them.  Summer waited patiently for him to take a breath so she could answer at least one of his questions and insert one of her own.  He was quick to answer, but then would pepper her with three or four more.

Summer had wandered to the edge of the forest creatures' village, although they called it a lodge instead of a village.  Sean was one of their little ones, but didn't know how old he was because the forest creatures didn't keep track of their ages.  In addition to his short, but very unruly, dark hair, he had a round face with a big smile, and small pointed ears.  He was dressed in a mixture of fur and leaves that seemed to be woven together and cinched around the waist with braided vines.  He also wore an odd looking band around his arm with a curious design in it.  Summer thought it might be a symbol of his family's rank in the lodge or their wealth.  Sean told her that lodge members didn't have any kind of rank and he didn't know what she meant by wealth. He had worn the armband for as long as he could remember.

The time passed quickly as they talked on and on. She described her village and he talked about his lodge. He went on to tell her that the lodge homes were built high in the trees. Sean could climb to the treetops with lightning speed and see across the tops of the forest. He could also jump from branch to branch very quietly and hide almost immediately. To her delight, he gave her a quick demonstration, climbing with incredible speed to the top of the nearest tree. He was nearly out of sight when he shouted down to her to watch as he literally flew from one limb to another on a nearby tree and scurried down.

He told Summer this was the best way to grab eggs from the nests of the Blue Falcons. She was shocked that he would even go near the nest of a Blue Falcon. They were the most dangerous birds in the forest. Sean then pulled a slingshot from his belt and told her that this was all the protection he needed against Blue Falcons or any other danger.

She looked at him a little skeptically.

"Oh," he said. "You don't believe me?"

He took a stone from a small pouch tied to his belt.

"Watch this," he told her, and with one fluid motion he pulled the stone back in the sling shot, spun to his left and let go. The stone flew through the air and sailed off into the distance. Summer looked at Sean and wondered what she was supposed to have seen.

"That's really ...good, I guess," she said. "You shot a stone into the woods. Wow."

Sean looked at her, slightly puzzled.

"Didn't you see where it went?" he asked.

"Yeah. Into the woods. I was right here, remember?"

"Follow me," he told her, running off in the direction the stone had been shot. She fluttered her wings and quickly followed after, nearly losing sight of him in the low lying brush. She realized how easily he could hide in the dense foliage.

After a minute or two they came to a tall tree with the stone imbedded into the side of the trunk. Summer was still not very impressed. With all the trees around it wouldn't have taken too much to hit one. Sean could tell she still didn't see what the big deal was. He began to pry at the stone, finally pulling it free from the tree trunk. Underneath the stone was a claw from a poisonous tree grub.

"That was a lucky shot," said Summer in amazement, although she had to admit to herself that it was really a very good shot.

"What do you mean, lucky? I was aiming for it."

Summer looked at Sean in disbelief. "Yeah, right. How do I know that?"

"Look," Sean replied. He then routed around in the leaves and undergrowth near the base of the tree, pulling up a tree grub that was missing both claws. It was plain to see that one missing claw was the one stuck behind the stone from Sean's slingshot.

"I shot the other one off about ten days ago."

Summer was speechless. Once she regained her composure, she asked him how he could have seen that tree grub from as far away as they were. He explained to her that he could see the smallest objects from miles away, even in the dark of night.

They continued to talk and regale each other with stories from their respective villages until nearly nightfall. Reluctantly, they said good-bye, but agreed to meet again the next day. Sean showed her the way back and pointed out that she hadn't been as lost as she thought. They agreed to meet again as soon as possible – in no more than a week. Summer would find her way into the forest where they had first encountered each other.

That first meeting had happened several years ago.  Ever since that time, they had both arranged to meet secretly at the same spot, which was far enough from Summer's village, and from Sean's lodge, for them to remain unseen and unnoticed by anyone.  Over the years they had become close friends, telling stories and sharing adventures.  As time went on they thought it more prudent to keep their friendship a secret and to find another meeting place.  Summer had suggested something closer to the Sea.

As a child, Sean had been warned about venturing too close to the shores of the Cerulean Sea.  He recalled being told about the hexes and jinxes the faeries could put on the forest creatures, and about the evils that lived in the Sea.  The more he got to know Summer, the more he began to disbelieve the stories about the wars, and now knew that the stories of the jinxes and hexes were false.  He still wasn't too sure about the evils of the Sea, though.  Summer told Sean that there was nothing to fear about the Sea, but Sean was not convinced.

Sean had suggested finding a place deeper in the forest.  She told him about the stories she had grown up with about spells and curses that the trees could place on faeries, but Sean told her those stories weren't true. Like Sean, she was not convinced – at least not at first.

When Summer told Sean that she was the faerie Princess, he asked her who the King and Queen were.

"We don't have kings or queens, just princesses."

"What about Princes?"

"No, none of them, either."

Sean was puzzled.  How did someone become a Princess?  Were they elected?  How many of them were there?  Why was Summer a Princess?

Over time she answered all of his questions. And over time, he answered all of hers. She was delighted when he told her one day that he had been made a lodge "Dozor". She asked if this was because he liked to sleep so much. He just laughed and said, "Dozor, not dozer!" Was this like a princess, she wanted to know. He explained that the forest creatures didn't have princesses or princes, or anyone else like that who was in charge. Decisions were made by a council, but no one had to follow their orders, even though everyone usually did. As a Dozor, he was more like a protector.

"What do you protect? And from what – or whom?" she asked.

He explained that the lodge Dozor was expected to make sure each member of the lodge was safe and taken care of, whether in times of danger or not. Being selected as the lodge Dozor was a great honor. It meant that everyone looked up to him and trusted him for their well-being. He would make sure that there was always food and shelter available, that the lodge was alerted to any dangers and was well protected, and if there were any arguments between lodge members, he would be expected to step in and settle them. His father was a Dozor; his grandfather was a Dozor, and his great grandfather had been a Dozor. A look of sadness crept over his face at the mention of his great grandfather, but it quickly passed.

"As far back as anyone can recall," he said with pride. "And it's not something you get just because your family has been Dozors for centuries. You really have to earn it."

"I'm sure you did," Summer said with a wide smile. She was very impressed and could feel his pride. She had no idea that Sean was such an important person to the forest creatures. She was glad he was her friend.

Over the years they continued to meet at the edge of the forest where they first saw one another. They debated regularly about finding another place, but were never able to agree on something suitable. The faeries and the forest creatures were still not very friendly towards one another, so Summer and Sean were able to agree on that matter, and they continued to keep their meetings secret.  One day, when Summer had continued along the coast instead of turning into the forest for her meeting with Sean, she had arrived early and decided to do some exploring.

Very near the edge of the forest along the shore of the Sea there was a small cove surrounded by a steep cliff.  Hidden in the cliff side was a ledge cut deep into the rock.  It was barely visible from the shore, since the bottom jutted out like a pouting lip.  And it was impossible to see from the forest above because of the loose rocks and boulders along the cliff's edge.  Summer was easily able to fly up to it.  When she met with Sean she took him to the base of the cliff.  He was a bit uncomfortable being so close to the Sea, but, being as nimble as a monkey, was able to climb down to it from above.  He agreed that this was the perfect place to continue their meetings.  Here they could sit and talk without worrying about any of the other faeries or forest creatures accidentally discovering them. It became their secret hideout.  They called it their fortress.

When The Fury first began to appear, Sean was the first person she looked for. He initially dismissed her worries saying it was just an ordinary storm.  However, as it became evident that this was not like any other storm, they agreed to meet every day at the fortress to share any information they could gather.  Summer asked the elders in her village what they knew about this storm.  None of them had ever seen it before, but they all had stories to tell.  She couldn't decide what was made up and what was real, especially in light of what she had been learning about the forest creatures and how wrong the ancient lore of the faeries had been about them.

Some of the elders claimed that The Fury was a demon come to life in order to destroy the world.  Others claimed that it was a force of evil in search of some mysterious key to unlock the gates of the underworld where all sorts of goblins and other evil creatures were imprisoned.  Who imprisoned them, she wondered.  No one knew for sure.  None of this really helped her. As she had grown to learn more about Sean and the forest creatures, she had become more and more certain that the ancient stories were wrong. What did that mean, then, about any information the elders had on the Fury. She was more confused now than she was before.

Sean wasn't able to learn much more than Summer. He had asked the same kinds of questions of the lodge chiefs. What the faeries called The Fury, the forest creatures called Vieldume. It was a word that was forbidden to speak, although a few of the forest creatures ignored the taboo, but said the word only in a whisper. After persisting to the point of being obnoxious, two of the oldest lodge chiefs finally consented to talk to Sean about Vieldume. They told him of stories that had been kept secret by the lodge chiefs for as long as anyone could remember. Even though Sean was not a lodge chief, they felt he should be told since he was now a Dozor and responsible for the protection of the lodge; that and the fact that he had pestered them nearly to distraction.

Over a thousand years ago the creatures of the world lived together in one place. At some time in their history one creature among them ventured off to the far reaches of the land and sea. He was an explorer named Ena Ray. He traveled to places that no one had ever gone before, finding all sorts of treasures and wonders, many of which were magical, but some of which were cursed. Over time he became very well known and very powerful. Eventually he tried to control all the creatures of the world, using the mystical forces he had accumulated in his travels. However, the mystical forces began to control him instead and the world was nearly destroyed. A tremendous storm raged; the ground shook as mountains erupted from the underworld. This was what the lodge chiefs called the Vieldume. Lands became divided by seas that boiled, and then froze solid. Then as suddenly as it had begun, it ended. Ena Ray had vanished. His powers had been broken and the creatures of the world were divided – forced to live in separate areas.

Sean had never heard of Ena Ray. He had never heard of anyone trying to control all the creatures of the world. And he had never heard of the lands of the world being divided by a tremendous storm. He wondered if these two old lodge chiefs were right in the head. He decided to press some of the others.

Some of the lodge chiefs who eventually opened up to him believed that the wars between the forest creatures and the faeries were part of the Vieldume, but others believed those wars were separate from the Vieldume. No one was certain, but the one thing they all agreed upon was that the approaching storm seemed to look like a return of the Vieldume, and the lodge members were becoming frightened. None of this really helped Sean. As he had grown to learn more about Summer and the faeries, he had become more and more certain that the ancient stories were wrong. What did that mean, then, about any information the chiefs had on the Vieldume. He was more confused now than he was before.

# Chapter two

Summer had told the village elders that she was going out to the edge of the forest to scout out the direction of the approaching storm. They had refused to admit that it was a return of The Fury, and dismissed her concerns. She thought they were denying what was more and more obvious. They warned her not to go into the forest, but none of them agreed to accompany her. Their warnings were so old and so unfounded, she began to wonder if the elders were in touch with reality any longer. OK, she thought; don't come with me. This was all right with her. She would rather have no one with her, since she was actually flying off to meet Sean. She wanted to see what information he had been able to pull from his lodge chiefs

As they had done so many times before, they met at their fortress high on the side of the cliff. Neither of them had anything new to report. The elders dismissed Summer, calling her a worry wart and a trouble maker. The lodge chiefs were a little kinder to Sean, but still could not come to any agreement on what to do other than to stay put. They were certain that Vieldume was only a myth and that the coming storm, though somewhat frightening, would turn out to be like any other.

Once they were securely hidden in their fortress and had told each other all there was to tell, they sat in silence pondering what to do next. They were both discouraged by the lack of reliable information they could glean from their respective elders. Summer finally said that they'd have to travel towards the storm to get a better idea of what it was doing and exactly which way it was headed. Sean stared at her with his mouth open.

"Go towards the storm?" he nearly shouted. "Are you crazy?"

"It's the only way we can see what's really coming. Do you just want to sit around with your head under a leaf waiting for it? This way at least we can get prepared. I would think that as your lodge's Dozor you'd want to be prepared."

This stung him. He took his responsibilities as Dozor very seriously, and was embarrassed that Summer, a faerie, had to remind him to do his duty. He swallowed hard, and then told her she was right. As much as he felt shamed by her bravado, he was reluctant to rush into the unknown. He thought of what he could do to stall their journey, hoping that they could get confirmation some other way. He suggested that they spend the next few days storing up some supplies for their journey. They would need to be properly prepared for a journey away from their homes that could take several days. They would need to gather things very slowly and very secretly. That way no one from her village or his lodge would know what they were planning and wouldn't be able to stop them from going.

"We'll have to work fast, though," she said, dismissing his attempts to delay. "It's hard to tell if the storm is just getting bigger or headed our way. If it's coming our way, we may not have a lot of time."

Sean grumbled under his breath, but had to admit she was right. Over the next three days they both snuck food, water, and blankets into their fortress. By this time at least one of their questions about the storm had already been answered. It was definitely headed their way. Even though it seemed still to be moving erratically, the overall direction was towards them. What they didn't know was how much damage it was doing along the way.

On the afternoon of the third day they were sitting in the fortress discussing which path to take. Summer wanted to follow the shoreline, but Sean, who was terrified of the Cerulean Sea, wanted to travel through the forest. They each argued the merits of their preference, without coming to any conclusions. Their debate was interrupted by a noise that kept getting louder.

"What's that sound?" Summer asked. It reminded her of the sound of a waterfall. At first it was gentle and soothing, but eventually it began to get so loud she had to shout just to hear herself speak.

"It sounds like the wind," said Sean. It reminded him of the breezes as they whipped through the treetops, shaking the leaves in the fall.

Then, without any warning, the floor of the fortress began to shake and wind blew into the cave. The gush of air pressed them against the back of the cave. Summer was pinned halfway up the wall as she had tried to fly up to the opening. Sean ducked his head and raised his arm to shield his eyes. The wind was so strong, that it filled his lungs and made it hard for him to exhale. Before either Summer or Sean could react it seemed as if both suns had disappeared from the sky. The darkness dropped on the opening with astounding speed, and was followed by an even louder roar. They looked towards the front of the fortress only to find it was filled with rocks.

"The boulders at the edge of the cliff above must have fallen onto the ledge and blocked the opening," Summer shouted.

Once the entry had become plugged with rocks, the wind inside the cave stopped as if someone had turned off a switch. Summer flew to the opening and saw that there was just enough room for her to squeeze through.  Just as she was about to do this, Sean reached out and grabbed her, pulling her back into the darkest corner of the cave.

"Don't go out there," he shouted.

"What are you doing?" she demanded.  Even though they were friends, she didn't like to be held captive in his large hands.  It reminded her of the fright he had given her the first time he grabbed her.  "I won't leave you behind.  I'll go for help."

"That's not it.  Listen to the noise.  It's more than just wind."

As he released his grip on her, she inched her way closer to the opening and listened closely.  Mixed in with the sound of the wind and rain, she could hear a wailing noise.  At first it was low and faint.  It quickly grew louder and more distinct.  She couldn't specifically identify it but it sounded like someone screaming in anger.  What was worse was that this someone sounded very big and very, very angry.  She couldn't make out any words.  It just sounded like howling.  She could also hear loud crashes and bangs.  The keening was accompanied by another frightening sound.  It was more than the sound that lightning made when it struck trees.  It sounded like explosions.

Just then her body went rigid.  She felt the pain and agony of hundreds of faeries.

"Something's happening to my village," she screamed.  She turned to face Sean.  He was shaking uncontrollably, and was unable to answer her.  She was torn between taking care of her friend and flying out to see what was happening to her village.  Although her heart told her to go to her village, her mind told her she couldn't help them, but she could probably help Sean.

She placed her tiny hands on his forehead and commanded him to lie down.  He was in the throes of some kind of seizure, but he turned his glassy eyes in her direction.  She could see a glint of understanding in them, and he lowered himself to the ground.  Once he was on the floor of the cave, she began to chant an ancient faerie remedy to ease his mind. It took a while, but he finally stopped shaking; he seemed to be in a deep sleep, although his eyes were wide open. All the while, and in spite of her worries about her village, all she could think about was if he would consider this a hex or a jinx and would he trust her afterwards.

She managed to get him to drink some water, and continued to soothe his forehead. Hours passed as the storm outside the cave raged. Sean remained in a trance but began mumbling words Summer couldn't understand. She continued to stroke his head and to chant. Eventually, overcome with exhaustion, she fell asleep.

It was the morning of the next day when she awoke. The noise outside had gone and Sean looked like he was sleeping peacefully. She called his name and he awoke with a start.

"What happened to you?" she asked.

"I don't know. That's never happened before. I saw all sorts of images floating in the air. I think it was just a dream, but I'm afraid something terrible has happened."

Summer told him about her fear that her village had been harmed. "I have to go see."

"It might be dangerous out there. You may not be safe." Sean was clearly worried about her.

"Come with me," she said.

He thought about the history of war and distrust between the faeries and the forest creatures, but he knew she needed him. He was also aware that she had stayed with him when she could have easily left him behind. "Of course," he said.

He then put his shoulders to the rocks blocking the entrance and began to shove them with all his might. They slowly began to move, and then gave way letting the morning sunlight pour in. More rocks from above slid down. Some of them rolled down the cliff and could be heard landing on the shore below. Others filled the gap. It seemed to take forever. Each rock removed created a small landslide of the dirt and rocks from above. Finally, Sean was able to remove enough to create an opening large enough for him to fit through.

Summer, who had waited patiently for Sean to clear a space much larger than she needed, flew to the shore below and waited for Sean to clamber down. He gave a wary look towards the Sea and kept as close to the inside edge of the cove as he could. The rocks were loose and his footing was uncertain. Inch by inch he worked his way down the cliff. A number of times the ground gave way and he avoided crashing to the shore by leaping upward or to the side and fortunately landing on more secure ground.

"I could sure use some of that faerie dust now," he joked.

Summer had been too fraught with anxiety even to have thought about that.

"Oh, my gosh," she said. "Of course. I'm sorry."

She shot over his head, shook her wings and waved her arms. A fine glittering powder appeared as if from nowhere and descended on Sean's head. He didn't feel any different and just clung to the rocks waiting for something to happen.

"What now?" he asked.

"What's wrong with me?" Summer shouted in frustration. "Just jump."

Sean looked at her skeptically.

"Trust me," she said. "You'll be fine."

He closed his eyes and stepped away from the cliff. Expecting to drop like the rocks he had been climbing, he merely floated down to the sand. As soon as he landed, Summer shot off like an arrow. He had to run to keep pace with her as she flew back to her village.

Although the Sea was calm, the shoreline was littered with rocks, branches, leaves and other debris. As she approached her village, many of the trees were uprooted and had fallen helter-skelter. Some of them were floating out in the water. Others were rocking back and forth on the shore, carried by the tide. She heard no sounds at all coming from where her home had been. Sean slowed down as he caught up with her — on the alert for any attack from the faeries, or from whatever had caused all the damage he was seeing.

Summer flew in and around the Banchu trees, looking into nooks and knolls where she would often sit. She saw nothing. With her anxiety mounting, she flew into the main village area, her eyes scouring her surroundings until she thought she saw some of the elders. A tentative sense of relief washed over her. As she got closer she realized that they were what looked like stone images instead. She didn't remember ever seeing any statues like this before. They looked so real that she forgot about the surrounding damage and looked at the fine craftsmanship that was able to duplicate such detail in stone.

Where did these come from, she asked herself. She had only been gone over night. How could so many statues have arrived in such a short time? They looked so life-like. Even the faces looked real, except that no one was smiling. In fact, their expressions were more like fright. She wondered why a sculptor would carve expressions of fear in the faces of the statues.

Suddenly a horrible thought came to her. These weren't statues. These were the elders. They had been turned to stone. She immediately backed away in panic, screaming. In spite of his unease about being in a faerie village, Sean came running to the sound of Summer's scream.

"What's wrong? Is someone hurt?" he asked.

Summer began stammering, "They're stone; the elders are stone; they've been turned to stone.  Where are the rest of the villagers?"  Without waiting for an answer Sean would not be able to give anyway, she flew to her home in the Banchu tree just south of the village center.  There she found her family: all turned to stone.

"No!" she screamed as she began to cry.  "This can't happen."

Sean wanted to console her, but as he started towards her home, he looked around and saw more stone faeries.  He began to look under leaves and into holes in nearby Banchu trees.  Everywhere he looked the faeries had been turned to stone.  When he met up with Summer he told her what he had found.  Together they quickly checked into every household in the village.  It was the same in each instance.  The entire village had been turned to stone.

"Look at the expressions on everyone's face," Sean said.  "This didn't happen quickly.  It looks like they knew this was happening.  Who would want to do this to an entire village?"  As he said these words two thoughts immediately crossed his mind.  The first was of the centuries of war between the faeries and the forest creatures.   But he knew that the forest creatures could not have done this.  His second thought was about the safety of his lodge.

"I have to go to my lodge," he shouted.

Summer didn't have to ask any questions or wait to be asked to go with him.  She followed right behind as he ran deep into the woods.  He ran up the shoreline and then cut into the woods, hurdling logs and ducking branches.  Summer flew with all her strength to keep up.  No words were exchanged along the way.  Each hoped they would not find what they expected they would find.  Within minutes they had arrived to a scene very similar to the faerie village.  In the center of the lodge sat several council members, frozen in place.  At the edges of the lodge Sean saw several Dozors with raised clubs and spears – also frozen in stone.  After a quick inspection they discovered that everyone in the lodge had been turned to stone. Sean was distraught.

"I'm supposed to protect them," he wailed.

"If you had been here you'd be stone, too" Summer pointed out. "You couldn't have done anything to stop it."

Sean knew she was right, but he found little comfort in her words. They looked at each other feeling completely hopeless and lost.

"What are we going to do?" Sean asked.

"There have to be other creatures that are all right. We have to find them. If they haven't been ...affected the same way," she couldn't bear to utter the words, "turned to stone," – they sounded too final. "We have to warn them. We have to find a way to change them back."

She gestured around her at the lodge and looked mournfully back towards her village. She was fighting hard to maintain control.

"What's on the other side of this forest?" she wanted to know.

At first Sean didn't answer. He was too deeply troubled by the events. Summer resisted the temptation to interrupt his thoughts. When the silence pressed in on him, he forced himself to push his recriminations and fear behind him.

"I don't know," he eventually answered. "No one ever traveled to the other side. At least not as far as I know."

"Someone did," answered Summer. "Remember those stories about Ena Ray. He must have gone to the other side. And how did anyone know where he went or what happened if they didn't go there, too?"

"Those were just stories. Besides, he disappeared. I don't think following his example is such a good idea."

"Anything is better than sitting around here waiting for whoever did this to come back. Besides, we have to get help and we have to find out if there's a way we can change everyone back to normal. And, if we can't," she hesitated, "we have to stop whoever did this from doing it to anyone else."

Sean knew she was right, but he was torn between leaving his family and friends behind – even though he knew he couldn't help them – and venturing off into the unknown. He finally gave in. This time he had no desire to delay their departure and was ready to leave that instance. Summer convinced him they needed to go back to their fortress and collect the supplies they had gathered initially. They also needed to rest and get a fresh start. Neither of them had any desire to linger in their respective homes, so they decided to spend the night in the fortress, and early the next morning they headed towards the opposite side of the forest.

At first their journey wasn't too bad. Sean was at least a little bit familiar with some of the surroundings. He had traveled this way on some scouting expeditions with other lodge members. But soon that familiarity vanished. The forest in many places was so thick neither he nor Summer could see the sky. He relied on her to fly above the trees to see where the lead sun was so that they kept headed in the right direction. She could fly to the treetops a little faster than Sean could climb, although several times her way was blocked by vines and branches. She fluttered around looking for an opening. Other times, she was confronted by strange and dangerous looking predators. She had to quietly blend into the background and wait until they left, or until Sean noticed their presence and placed a few carefully aimed shots at them, scarring them off.

When she returned from one such foray she told him she could see the storm clouds far off to their left. It didn't seem to be headed in their direction, but she told him she'd keep a watch on it. They still appeared to be moving randomly from one side of the horizon to the other, but in the same overall direction.

Fortunately, the weather was moderate. Normally this far into the forest, the air could get thick and heavy. There was no wind at ground level to cool things off, but it was as if the roaming clouds had drawn all the heat and humidity out of the forest to add to its power. Even the nights were comfortable; except that it was too quiet. There were no sounds of crickets, or frogs, or birds. Summer didn't notice the sudden lack of predators until Sean had commented on it one evening, when he also pointed out the usual nighttime sounds were absent.

Sean had never felt he was in danger whenever he was deep in the forest. However, the quiet was unnerving and he suggested that they take turns standing watch. Summer agreed, wishing she had the sort of powers Sean had earlier thought she possessed. A nice hex or spell of some kind to protect them, or to at least warn them, would come in very handy about now.

After four days they came to a large gorge that stretched for miles in each direction. It was much too far for them to change course and go to the left or right. It was too wide for Sean to jump over, and he was too heavy for Summer to carry and fly over. He asked if she could sprinkle some faerie dust to make him float across.

"Sorry," she said. "I wish I could. It's just not that strong, and I don't want to take a chance. If you didn't make it all the way across, I don't know if it would last long enough for you to reach the bottom safely, and even if it did, what would we do then?"

He didn't say anything, but inwardly, he was glad. He wasn't thrilled about the thought of flying. It was second on his list of things he really, really hated – right after water. There had to be another way. Sean started routing around in the bushes. After a short while of searching up and down the edge of the gorge, they came across an old tree that was covered in vines. It was leaning precariously over the edge of the gorge. Half its roots had broken through the ground and trailed down the side of the cliff. They cleared away all the dead branches and the vines that were too thin to support any weight and discovered one long, sturdy vine hanging from one of the top limbs that Sean thought could support his weight.

"I can get a running start and swing across," he told Summer.

She looked a little uncertain. She didn't think the vine would reach all the way across the gorge, so she asked him, "What if it doesn't reach all the way?"

"Well, I guess I won't let go then. I'll just swing back to this side."

She still wasn't too sure, but there really wasn't any other way for him to get across.

"What about our supplies?" she asked.

Sean had wrapped everything they had stored, and still had  much of it with them after nearly a week, stored in a pack and strung on his back. There wasn't much left of their original stores, but it was certainly added weight.  He thought a minute, and then found a long, thin vine.  He stripped all the leaves and shoots off.  He then cut off a small portion and tied his bundle to the end of the large vine hanging from the tree.  He tied the remainder of the thin vine to the knot around the bundle.  Summer furrowed her brow, but kept silent.

"Look," he said, motioning to the knot holding the bundle to the large vine.  "This is a slip knot.  I'll swing the supplies over first and, at the last minute, give a yank on this thinner vine.  That will undo the slipknot and the bundle will drop safely to the ground.  Trust me."

He pulled the bundle as far back as the vine would reach and found the nearest tree at that distance.  He climbed up with the bundle in one arm.

"I'll toss it from here," he shouted back to Summer.  "That way it will have some momentum going over the gorge.  I can jump down in time to pull on the slip knot."

He sounded more confident than he felt. Here goes nothing, he said to himself as he gave the bundle a push. It dropped in a downward arc as Sean jumped down from the tree. It cleared the ground by inches as it reached the lowest point of the arc and began to climb upward towards the other side of the gorge. Sean grabbed the thin vine and ran to the edge of the cliff watching the trajectory closely. As soon as the bundle reached its highest point and hovered a second or two before dropping back, Sean jerked the vine, releasing the slipknot.

The knot untied perfectly, and the bundle was set free. It hung in the air for a second or two and then began to drop. Summer and Sean had their eyes glued on it as it plummeted to the opposite side – nearly four feet short of the target. It crashed into the side of the cliff nearly ten feet below the edge. The wrapping tore loose and all their remaining food and the material for their shelter scattered as it tumbled to the bottom of the ravine.

They were both staring over the edge watching everything disappear when Summer turned her head towards Sean, saying nothing.

"OK," he said, "that was a good practice shot."

"Practice shot?" she shouted in disbelief. "You can't be serious. You still think you can make it across? After that?" She was pointing down at the supplies, some of which were still floating downward.

"We don't have much of a choice," he argued. "Besides, I can get up more speed and give a little kick."

"NO," Summer exclaimed. "You can't do this. If something happens to you, I can't go on by myself."

"You won't have to," he said. "Trust me. I know this can work."

She struggled to find an argument to dissuade him, but in the end had to give in and trust him. She hovered over his head and flapped her wings and waved her arms, sprinkling him with faerie dust.

"It's not much," she said, "but it may help."

"You're not jinxing me or putting a hex on me, are you?" he joked nervously.

"Shut up and get this over with," she answered, her voice cracking.

He wrapped the vine loosely around his wrist and walked as far back as he could and then started running with all his might. Just as his foot hit the edge of the gorge he dove downward to the full length of the vine. With a jerk of his arm, he reached the length of the vine. He kicked his feet up over the top of his head and began swinging upward towards the other side of the gorge. Summer was flying right behind him. She could see that he was going to come up short and would have to swing back to where he started. Before that happened, she heard the old tree crack. It was being uprooted and falling over the edge of the gorge. The added length of the tree gave Sean a little boost and put him closer to the other edge. He was high in the air, several feet above the ground, but the old tree was starting to fall into the gorge.

"Let go of the vine," Summer yelled. She flew up right behind him and began pushing at the same time. "Let go of the vine," she yelled again.

It had become tangled around his wrist. He kept his eyes focused on the approaching edge of the gorge while he freed his hand. He had reached the top of his arc and was heading down. His arms and legs were swinging wildly. He looked like he was trying to fly as he headed down towards the edge of the far side of the gorge. Summer kept pushing, flapping her arms wildly, sprinkling more faerie dust over his head, and hoping it was enough to lighten him and carry him to the other side. She was sure he was going to miss the edge, but as his body fell below the top of the edge, he lunged forward and grabbed the brambles and vines on the other side. Slowly he was able to pull himself up to safety on the other side.

"I sure hope we don't have to do that again," he gasped. He flopped on his back, spread eagled and closed his eyes, trying to control his breathing and the hammering in his heart. "That was too close. Thanks for the boost."

"You're welcome," Summer answered, breathlessly, "I hope we don't have to come back this way."

"If we do," Sean answered, still breathless, "you can leave me here. Once was enough."

They stayed there for a few minutes until they could find the strength to get up. Once they did, they looked at each other and decided they were too tired to go any further that day. They were both wrung out from the excitement, and it was getting close to dark. They decided to make camp right there and get an early start the next morning. Summer flew to the treetops to get one more look at the direction of the storm.

"It's moved a lot," she said when she returned. "It's far to the east, probably along the coast," she motioned to their right, "and slightly ahead of us, but not by much."

"We need a good night's rest, and we can try to get ahead of it tomorrow," answered Sean. "For now, let's make camp."

Summer scouted around for some twigs and fallen branches and Sean found some flint so they were able to make a fire. Sean found some nuts that were edible, and Summer found a bush covered with wild bauga berries. There was also a nearby pond that was fed from an underground spring. At least they would have something to eat and fresh water to drink. They had no shelter, but the night was clear and they didn't mind sleeping under the stars.

Even though they agreed to share the watch again, neither of them slept. The night was filled with the noise of something or some things creeping around in the brush. They heard growls and screeches, and were not so sure that they had made the right decision to cross the gorge. What was worse was that they knew there was no going back. They didn't have to worry about the growls and screeches, though. The noises they heard were not nocturnal predators searching for food.  They were the beasts of the jungle looking for an escape.  They were traveling to the south and west, avoiding the storm.  They were headed for the bridge that spanned the gorge, less than a mile from where Summer and Sean had crossed.

# Chapter three

In spite of the scary noises they heard periodically in the night, neither Sean nor Summer ever saw another creature in the forest. During the day, the absence of such noises was unnerving to them. They came across signs of large animals passing through the forest – tracks, broken branches, trampled bushes – but no other evidence as to where they were or what had happened to them. They stopped standing guard when they camped at night, almost welcoming the sight of something – anything – else.

After several days past the gorge, they noticed that the ground level had begun to rise. They were traveling uphill. And then it started raining. They weren't sure if this was separate from the ominous clouds, lightning, and thunder that seemed to be sweeping the land. Summer had tried on a number of occasions to fly above the treetops to locate that storm. She could still hear rumbles of thunder and see distant flashes of lightning, but they were masked by the overcast sky above them and the constant downpour of rain.

"I think this is just ordinary rain," she said to Sean. "I can't say why, but I don't have the same feeling of being threatened by this stuff."

"I think you're right," he replied. "Besides, there doesn't seem to be any thunder and lightning with this storm."

"Just rain," they both said together.

For almost six days they had to put up with rain and wind. It was relentless. The wind blew in their faces, making the ever-increasing climb more and more difficult. And the rain turned the ground to mud, which clung to Sean's feet like anchors. Sean didn't seem to be bothered too much by the rain, but Summer was soaked and miserable. She had to fly immediately behind Sean's body to have some shielding from the wind. At first, every few steps she flew into him and fell to the ground when he had to stop and kick the mud from his feet. Then she put a little more space between them and struggled against the wind.

When the rain finally stopped, and the sun came out, the heat turned the forest into a sauna. At the height of the day when the twin suns were hottest, the moisture from the days of rain turned into steam as the suns baked the earth. Sean and Summer had to stop nearly every hour to catch their breath.

They had been traveling for three weeks, debating about taking a different direction, when they first saw it. Ahead of them in the distance loomed a large mountain. It took another week before they arrived at its base. Even though the land had been inclining more and more as they went, the mountain appeared to jut out from the ground. It seemed like it rose straight up from the hills they had been climbing and nearly touched the clouds.

When they reached it, they discovered that it was an enormous wall of granite. There was no discussion about what to do next. To try to go around it was out of the question – it was far too wide. There was nothing to do but to go up. Sean started climbing. Summer couldn't see what he was able to grab on to, but somehow he managed to find small chinks in which to place his hands and feet, and he quickly scampered upwards. She flew alongside him offering encouragement and pointing out places he could use to pull himself up. Sometimes he had to literally jump from one footing to another. Even Summer was too nervous to look down.

They had started their climb at first light. Around noon they stopped, except there was really no place to stop. Summer was able to sit on a small branch that had grown out of the side of the sheer rock, but Sean just had to hang there. He had climbed on top and stretched out along the branch, wrapping his legs around it, but it drooped so low he was afraid he would uproot it, or just slide off. He then moved to straddle it like a horse, scooting back as close to the wall as possible. That was far from comfortable, but at least he was able to rest his arms.

As evening approached, they both became worried about what would happen when it got dark. There had been no openings so far that were large enough for Sean to crawl into to get some rest. In fact, the branches and shoots that Summer had sat on earlier had also disappeared.

"I'm going to fly a little higher to see if there's somewhere above that we can crawl into," she told him.

"OK. I'll just hang around here until you come back," he said, trying to lighten the tension.

The granite wall had started off rather rough and black. There had been plenty of places for Sean to get a footing and the climbing was relatively easy. There were also branches – stronger than the one they had found earlier – on which he could rest. However, as they inched their way towards the top, the granite had become smoother and smoother, almost to the point of being slippery. Footholds were farther apart, the cracks and chinks were smaller. Sometimes Sean had to twist his foot sideways and other times he only was able to get a toehold. It had also started to change color. Now it was a deep purple.

Above them it appeared as if the mountain was leaning outward. At first this change was barely noticeable. It wasn't until Summer paid a little closer attention as Sean jumped from one crag to another and nearly lost his grip. Then she could see the gradual outward sloping of the cliff. Summer flew up a little further to examine the higher levels. When she came back, she didn't look too happy about what she had to tell Sean.

"It looks like the mountain is flaring out instead of tapering in. In a little while, you won't be able to get the same kind of footholds because you'll be bent almost backwards."

"Is that the good news, or the bad news?" he asked between taking deep breaths. In addition to it feeling like his arms and legs were made of lead, he was finding it hard to breathe.

"That's the bad news," said Summer. "The good news is that there's a small alcove cut into the stone. I think there's enough room in there for you to fit and get some rest. It's about forty feet up. Can you make it that far?"

"I don't seem to have much of a choice now, do I? Look at the bright side though."

"There's a bright side?" Summer asked.

"Yeah. If we hadn't lost the pack of supplies, and I was still carrying that, I'd really be tired."

"You're really funny. You know that? Wait until morning and there's still nothing to eat and see how funny that is." She was a little sharper than she intended to be. The stress was wearing on her, but Sean just ignored her and kept climbing.

Reaching the alcove couldn't come soon enough. Sean didn't think he could hold on for much longer, and it was a very long way to the bottom.

He pulled himself along until he finally found the alcove Summer had mentioned.  It was more of a large crack in the stone, although centuries of rain, wind and snow had worn away the bottom of the crack so that it was somewhat flat.  As it turned out, he couldn't fit his whole body inside.  He had to sit all bent over with his feet dangling over the edge; but at least he could get some rest.  And the bottom of the opening wasn't exactly flat.  It slanted to one side, so it kept feeling to Sean like he was slipping.  There were also signs that some birds had made a nest in the opening at one time.

"Looks like Blue Falcons," said Sean.

"Wonderful," said Summer.  "Should we look for something else?"

"No.  We haven't seen any signs of animals or birds in weeks.  Whatever has chased them away probably scared off the Falcons.  I think we'll be safe."

They had made it to the alcove just before the darkness of night completely enveloped them.  Sean closed his eyes and seemed to fall asleep almost immediately.  Summer had to stay awake the whole night.  Well, she didn't exactly have to, but she just couldn't sleep.  She was afraid Sean would fall forward out of the alcove.  If that happened, there would be nothing to stop him until he hit the bottom and there would be no way she could catch him.  All the faerie dust in her village wouldn't keep him from crashing to the rocks below.  When morning came, they were still tired and very hungry.  They hadn't been able to eat at all the day before, and even though Sean had been able to sleep, his sleep had been fitful.  The night had been cold and his muscles were still screaming from yesterday's climb.

He didn't complain, though.  As soon as it was light, he began again to climb towards the top.  Summer flew above him, pointing out places where he could get handholds, or the locations of other large cracks where he could crawl in and get some rest. The day wore on and Sean seemed to have difficulty breathing.  He had to stop more frequently to catch his breath and to rest. Even Summer was having trouble breathing, and she was struggling more to keep flying. She had never flown this far or this long in her life. The air was getting thinner the higher they went, and it was getting colder, too. Every once in a while the wind would gust and Summer would be blown several feet in one direction or another.

Sean sometimes lost his footing and just swung back and forth until the wind settled and he found something on which he could regain his footing. When this happened, Summer could see the distance between his hanging body and the side of the mountain getting wider and wider. In some places he really was nearly climbing upside-down.

The mountain was now a very bright purple, and Summer noticed there were lines in the granite that seemed to shimmer. When she looked closer, she saw that they were veins of pink that seemed to sparkle. She had never seen stone like this before. Sean was now climbing almost upside down nearly all the time now. The stone was getting smoother and smoother, with fewer and fewer fissures large enough for Sean to climb into. And those that were large enough were often at such a steep angle that he would slide right out.

Just as Summer thought there was no way they could go any higher, they came upon what looked like carved designs and edges in the mountainside. Summer was stunned. Who could have come up this high on the mountain, let alone make these carvings and designs? She had been flying mere inches from the wall in her search for things Sean could cling to. She fluttered, backing away from the side to get a wider view of the mountain. Taking in a wider view, she saw the designs much more clearly. They looked like astrological signs. She also saw what looked like blocks.

"It's a castle," she said to herself. She couldn't believe her own eyes. "It's a castle," she shouted to Sean. She quickly flew back and was fluttering right in front of his face, shouting, "It's a castle. It's a castle."

"How much further?" he asked, panting as he spoke.

For the first time since they started up the mountainside, she got a really good look at his face. There were dark circles under his eyes, and his skin color was ashen. He was sweating with the exertion, but shivering because of the cold. Summer became very concerned that he might not make it much longer.

"I don't know," she said, "but there are carvings a little way above you. And blocks. You should be able to get a better hold, especially in the carvings. Some of them are pretty deep. Hang in there. I'm going up further to see what's above the engraving."

She quickly flew up towards the top hoping the end was near. Sooner than she had expected, she soared up over a rampart, and could see huge turrets along the wall of the mountainside. There were brightly colored pennants, all purple and pink, flapping in the breeze. The castle was so high up that she could see clouds floating by below the top of the castle wall. She reversed course and shot down towards Sean. The sight below her nearly took her breath away.

She hadn't really focused on how far they had come, before this. They had passed through a layer of clouds. The ground below appeared in patches through openings in the cloud cover. It made her dizzy just looking at it. She hoped Sean didn't take time to look down.

She was so excited about finding the castle and so nervous about how far up they were that she didn't think to find out if the occupants were friendly or not. She flew around looking for someone, anyone, to help. Finally she spotted a soldier walking guard along the battlements that surrounded the castle. She shot down to Sean to report.

"You're almost at the top. I just saw someone. I'm going to call for help."

She was off before he could warn her to be careful. He only hoped whoever was up there didn't decide they were being attacked and dropped a rock on his head.

"Help," Summer yelled as she flew up over the rampart and over to the soldier.  The guard had a purple vestment with a large, pink letter "S" edged in gold on the front. He didn't seem to be the least bit surprised or frightened by the unexpected appearance of a faerie.

"Well, now.  Who are you and why do you need help?" he asked.

"I'm Princess Summer of the faeries, and my friend Sean is climbing up the side of your castle.  He needs help before he falls off.  Please hurry."

"Why can't he just fly up here like you did?" the guard asked.

Summer told him that Sean was a forest creature and couldn't fly.  She pleaded with him.  Sean was exhausted and the air was so thin he could hardly breathe. The guard frowned.

"Forest creature?" he asked.  "And he's a friend of yours?  How can that be?  And how did you two find this castle?"  The guard seemed a little less friendly than he did at first, but in spite of this he followed Summer to where Sean was still struggling to reach the top.  As they were moving to the edge of the battlement, Summer noticed that the soldier was wearing chain mail and carrying a spear.  Who were they expecting this far up, she asked herself.

The guard called for help and two more soldiers appeared almost immediately.  They were all dressed the same with the purple vestments over chain mail.  The first guard took command, directing one of the others to bring a rope, while he and the second guard leaned precariously over the edge to look down on Sean.  Sean had stopped climbing and was clinging to the side with his head pressed against the stone.  He was clearly exhausted.

 The soldier arrived quickly with a rope, which they threw over the side.  Summer flew down and helped Sean tie it around his chest and let himself be pulled over the top of the castle wall.

The guards took Summer and Sean into the castle, through some hallways and into a small room. They were told to wait there. Someone brought in some food and something that looked like tea, but tasted very different. Then everybody left, and the guard shut the door, and then locked it. There were no windows or other doors. The room was lit by several candles on a table in the center of the room. Summer took a close look at the key hole in the door, but it was too small even for her to fit through.

"I wonder why they did that?" she asked.

"I think these are mountain people. I remember hearing stories about them in the lodge. They have magical powers and eat forest creatures. This was probably not a good idea," said Sean.

In spite of his comment, he stuffed food into his mouth and drank the beverage that had been provided.

Summer was a bit upset by his attitude. "Is there anybody the forest creatures didn't fight with?" she asked, as she helped herself to the food and drink.

"We didn't fight the mountain people. We ran away from them," he replied between mouthfuls of food. "Probably because they ate us. We're not too fond of being someone's dinner! I don't know what this stuff is, but it's really good."

Summer could only nod in agreement. She found that she, too, was stuffing her mouth. They were both tired and cranky, but there was nothing to do but relax until the mountain people decided what they were going to do with their new visitors. Once they had eaten their fill, Summer began to pace back and forth on the table, while Sean curled up on the floor and started to sleep.

"How can you sleep at a time like this?" she asked in amazement.

"Well," Sean answered, yawning widely, "they're either going to eat us or not. There's nothing I can do about it until they make up their minds.

Besides, I'm tired." With that he closed his eyes and in a few short minutes he was sleeping soundly.

As he drifted off to sleep, Summer studied him. His hands and feet were swollen and cut in several places. There was dried blood in several places. He had bruises on his arms and legs. She hadn't realized until now how much of a toll the climb had taken on him.

A few minutes later, the sounds of Sean's breathing had its effect on Summer and she sat down to rest, only to nod off almost immediately. Several hours later, the door was opened, and a woman in a flowing pink gown came in. She gently nudged Sean awake and cleared her throat, waking Summer. They both stared at her in silence. She had beautiful silver hair and a warm smile. When she walked it looked like she just floated across the floor. She was not much taller than Sean, but she was very elegant.

As they both rose to face the woman, Summer looked over to Sean. She was worried that he would not be able to stand with his injuries. He was on his feet in an instant, and she was startled to see that his hands and feet had been washed. The dried blood was gone and there was some kind of ointment on his cuts. They were closing and healing almost before her very eyes. What kind of place was this, she wondered.

"You will be seen now. Just come with me, if you please," she told them both, smiling broadly. "I hope the food and drink was to your satisfaction," she added, noticing that they had devoured everything.

"Yes, it was delicious. Thank you. Are you the princess of this castle?" Summer asked.

The woman smiled and laughed gently. "Oh no," she said. "But thank you for the compliment. I'm the Princess's Scribe."

"The Princess's Crime? What crime did she commit?" asked Sean.

The woman tilted her head, wondering if he was teasing her or not. She studied Sean closely and then deciding he was serious, smiled again and said, "Scribe. Not Crime. I keep the history and the records of this castle. There are six of us, although some are still in training. I've been doing it the longest. I've recorded meetings, debates, decisions, history - everything that's gone on in here for the last six hundred years."

Summer and Sean looked at each other speechless. Six hundred years. How old was this person they wondered.

As if she could read their thoughts, she said, "I'm seven hundred and twenty two years old." She looked over her shoulder with a grin, raising one eyebrow. "What's the matter?" she asked as they continued their silence. "Do I look older than that?" And then she gave a little laugh.

"Oh no," sputtered Sean, "of course not, although I really can't tell about how old people are. We don't keep track of that kind of thing where I come from. The faeries do, though, don't they Summer? I mean, Summer is a hundred..."

"She doesn't need to know that," Summer interrupted.

"A hundred and twelve," finished the woman. "I know. Oh, and by the way. We don't eat forest creatures. At least we haven't in the six hundred years I've served as Scribe."

Summer and Sean looked at each other. Summer mouthed the words, "How does she know this stuff?" And Sean shrugged his shoulders. The woman smiled to herself as she led them through several halls and up several flights of stairs, then across an open courtyard covered with lush grass and some large fruit trees.

Summer and Sean looked around them in awe. There were still thin clouds floating at eye level past the edge of the castle wall, but the sky above them was a brilliant blue. The air was cool, but comfortable. Where was this place, the both wondered. The woman continued to float along in front of them, pointing out the different kinds of trees and some of the other sights, as if she could read their thoughts. By now Summer was convinced that was exactly what she was doing.

Then they entered a large hall and walked through to the other side and into what looked like a small garden in a large atrium. In the middle of the garden was a beautiful young lady with flowing red hair. She was sitting at a small table that was set for tea.

"I'm Solveig, Princess of this castle," she told them. "How nice of you to visit. Please sit down. Would you like some tea?"

Sean and Summer approached the table. There was a small chair and stand on top of the table that was just the right size for Summer, and another chair across from the Princess that was set for Sean. They hesitated for a second, looked at each other and then back at the smiling Princess. Sean eyed the pastries on the table and had no second thoughts. He nearly pounced on the chair. Summer fluttered down to the table, looked everything over and then eventually seated herself. The princess poured them both tea, and then poured a cup for herself. Sean gulped his down, but Summer waited, watching the Princess.

The Princess raised her cup as in a toast and then took a sip. Summer figured that the tea was not drugged or poisoned, since the Princess was drinking it, and then took a sip herself. Her eyes widened at the taste. This stuff is fantastic, she thought. As they drank their tea, the cups seemed to magically refill, and the small cakes that had been set for each of them, and which Sean was wolfing down unceremoniously, magically replenished as they were eaten. As they all ate and drank, Princess Solveig asked them what brought them to her castle. Sean started the tale in the middle, and Summer had to back track and fill in the gaps. The Princess was amazed to hear of their adventure and especially how they had climbed up the cliff side to the castle walls.

She became somewhat concerned when they told her of the devastation caused by the passing storm. Summer watched her reaction closely, still not sure whether to trust her or not. As Summer described how everyone in her village and the lodge of the forest creatures had turned to stone, the Princess was visibly upset. Her people had not seen this storm, she told them both. She immediately summoned the Scribe to ask her about it. When the Scribe arrived, Princess Solveig invited her to sit and tell what she knew.

"Please, describe everything that you know. Our guests have shared some rather disturbing news," she said to the Scribe.

"Long before I became the castle Scribe, the creatures of the world lived together as one. During that time a sorcerer rose to power whose name was Ena Ray. The stories of his exploits are inconsistent. Some say he helped maintain peace and harmony in the land. Other accounts indicate that eventually he became too strong and powerful, and he began to abuse his position. It has been told that he persecuted any who disagreed with him. There are also stories about another like him; another sorcerer. Again, the chronicles are not clear and have never been confirmed. No one is sure if he really existed, and, if he did, what happened to him. There is evidence, though that Ena Ray had followers all over the land who became his secret army. Some legends tell that the other sorcerer also amassed an army and that the two did battle, but other legends tell a different story – one where a mighty enchantress battled them and destroyed them both.

"Whichever story is correct, the one thing that is agreed upon is that there was a great battle and the other creatures of the world united in opposition to him. In some way he was overthrown and banished to some unknown land. Before he vanished, he placed a curse on all those who opposed him. He declared that the creatures of the world would fight among themselves for a thousand years. Then he would return even stronger and more powerful than before. All those who opposed him would be helpless.

But as you know, my Princess, these stories themselves are well over a thousand years old. It is the inconsistencies such as this that makes each of the versions questionable. It is difficult to separate the myth from the facts."

"Thank you. That has been very informative," Princess Solveig told the Scribe. She then asked her to talk about how the mountain creatures came to live in this castle and to share with their guests some of their history.

"Of course, my Princess," she answered. "Long ago, even before Ena Ray, there had been conflicts between a faction of sorcerers known as Kelpies, and a number of enchantresses. Not much is known about these conflicts except that many villages, lodges and tribes were affected. The war between the Kelpies and the enchantresses affected all these civilizations, although little is known or has been recorded about this war. All that is known is that at the time of this war, the tensions between the different civilizations that lived near the mountain people had escalated. These were the forest creatures, the faeries, and the sea sprites. At that time the mountain people didn't live this high up on the mountain. Instead, they lived in the foothills that were bordered on one side by the Great Forest and the other side by the Cerulean Sea."

She turned to look at Sean and Summer and said, "The same forest and foothills you traveled through to get here."

"When the wars between the forest creatures and the faeries broke out and began to spread," she continued, "the mountain people were fearful of coming under attack. The sea sprites were closely allied with the faeries. Their early ancestors were related, so the sea sprites and the faeries share a heritage. They felt threatened by the forest creatures. They knew that the homes of the faeries had been destroyed and that their little ones had disappeared. The forest creatures were accused of these attacks, but denied them, and the truth of the accusations could never be proven. Even though the sprites were protected from the forest creatures by the sea, the sprites feared that the mountain people would join forces with the forest creatures.

"Like the sea sprites and the faeries, the forest creatures and the mountain people also shared common ancestors. Several incidents had occurred over the years that also led the sea sprites to the belief that they were vulnerable to attack from the mountain people. The sea sprites had discovered their island home had been burned, farms and gardens devastated and, like the faeries, some of their people had disappeared. All the signs pointed to the mountain people. But as with the forest creatures, the mountain people denied the charges and nothing was ever proven.

In their defense, the sea sprites began to attack the mountain people, who decided to move higher and higher up the mountain for their own protection and to avoid conflict of any kind. They moved further and further away from the forest and higher and higher up the mountain, but couldn't escape the assaults on their homes and people. Eventually, they began to carve the castle out of the purple granite that rose out of the mountain. As stone was mined from the center, it was used to make the blocks for towers and the walls. It was built specifically to be as smooth as possible and to curve out over the mountainside, making it a fortress that no one could penetrate. At least until now."

With that the Scribe and Princess Solveig looked at Sean who had managed to climb their castle wall. Sean and Summer immediately began talking at the same time.

"But we're not at war with anyone. In fact, we've been friends for months."

"We've never even met any sea sprites or mountain people before."

"Sure the faeries and the forest creatures don't get along too well, but that's because they don't really know each other."

"We don't mean you any harm. We've come for your help."

Princess Solveig sat back and thought for a minute. She was sure that Sean and Summer didn't pose a threat and that they were not a scouting party for an attack. The fact that they were a faerie and a forest creature – peoples who had been at war for centuries – seemed to support their story. Her guards just wanted to throw them over the side of the castle, but she had pointed out that, while that might dispose of the forest creature, the faerie could merely take flight.

She didn't ignore their warnings, though. She knew the history of her people and theirs was one of conflict; so just to make sure, she had put a potion in their tea that would make their skin turn blue if they told a lie. Their skin hadn't turned blue; not even a little bit, so they must have been telling the truth. But she was still not sure she could believe that a single forest creature could have climbed all the way to the top of her castle walls.

"I still can't believe or even understand how you were able to climb our mountain," she said to Sean.

Summer blurted out, "Oh, yes. He's an excellent climber. I've seen him climb like an arrow to the top of the highest trees in the forest."

She was clearly proud of Sean, and probably feeling a little guilty since she was able to fly to the top of the mountain while he had to struggle the entire way.

As an afterthought she added," And he's an excellent shot. I've seen him shoot the claws off a tree grub that was at least a hundred yards away."

With that Sean pulled out his slingshot to show Princess Solveig how he did it. He no sooner raised the slingshot when a guard standing nearby pounced on him and pinned him to the floor. Three others appeared as if from thin air, all aiming spears at him – spears with very sharp points.

"No one dares to bring a weapon in the presence of the Princess," the guard roared. He ripped the slingshot from Sean's hands and held a sword to Sean's throat, keeping him flattened to the floor, while the other guards kept their spears pointed at him. At the same time three more guards had appeared with spears – all of which were pointed at Summer.

51

The tips of each spear were longer than she was. If she hadn't been so intimidated, the sight would have been comical.

Even Princess Solveig had been startled by the reaction of the guards, although she also felt grateful that she was so well protected. She looked at Summer and Sean, neither of whom had moved an inch. The shock on Sean's face was enough for Princess Solveig to know that no harm had been intended. She ordered the guard to release Sean and to return his slingshot. The guard did so, although a bit reluctantly.

"I think it's time for us to visit my Sorcerer," she decided, and led her guests out of the room.

# Chapter four

Summer and Sean stared blankly after Solveig as she led them down the corridor and up a long winding staircase. After a few moments passed in silence, Sean asked, "What's a Sorcerer?" Solveig stopped short and quickly turned around. Sean nearly collided with her and Summer flew face first into the back of Sean's head.

"It's a wizard, a magician, a, a, a, fortuneteller, sort of," she answered. "Surely you must have someone like that where you come from."

Summer and Sean looked at each other and slowly shook their heads. "No," they both said, as they continued up the stairway.

"Does it live up here?" Sean asked.

"He," said Solveig. "Yes, he lives up here. He wanted to be as close to the stars as possible."

"I thought the sorcerers were the bad guys," said Summer. "Your Scribe just told us that there were ancient wars between the sorcerers and some other people."

"The enchantresses," answered Solveig. She stopped and faced them both. "Yes. That's true, but not all the sorcerers were evil, just the Kelpies. I know a bit more about this than my Scribe. And not because I'm older than she is," she said looking at Sean, who she was sure was about to make a comment along those lines.

"There was a bitter power struggle several centuries ago. The Kelpies were a group of sorcerers who were banding together for their own evil purposes. They were challenged and defeated by some very brave enchantresses and sorcerers. The sorcerer you are about to meet is directly descended from one of those who fought to vanquish the Kelpies."

"So, how much older than the Scribe are you?" asked Sean.

"Sean!" shouted Summer.

"What?" he asked. "I was just curious."

"I'm not older than she is," Solveig answered, trying hard not to laugh.

Shaking her head, Solveig turned back to the staircase and continued climbing. Up they went. The steps circled round and round up through the tallest tower in the castle, past the clouds. At various places in the tower there were long narrow windows carved into the stone. Summer flew up to one and looked out. All she could see was the sky. Below her, the entire courtyard and palace grounds were shrouded in a layer of clouds. Do birds even fly this high, she wondered.

Finally they arrived in a large circular room. There were no corners; it was a large round room with a domed ceiling. At one side there was a high window with a huge telescope peering through the opening at the skies. The walls were covered with maps and drawings of stars, planets, comets, asteroids and other heavenly bodies. Summer's eye was caught by one set of these drawings. They were the same as the ones she had seen on the side of the castle as she and Sean were climbing to the top. She wondered where the artist who drew the pictures had to stand to get a view of the carvings wide enough to see all of them.

Around the room were several tables with models of planets and moons, as well as more maps and drawings. Sitting at a desk next to the telescope was what Sean and Summer assumed was the Sorcerer. He was dressed in a long brown robe that was stained with what looked like peanut butter and jelly. The sleeves of the robe were wide and long, sweeping across the desktop as he wrote, often pushing some of his papers to the floor. He was apparently unaware of this, since there were several papers scattered at his feet. His hair was all mussed, he was barefoot and his head was bent over some papers on his desk. He was as tall as the Princess, which was slightly taller than Sean. His fingers were blotched with ink, as were the papers he was working on, and he was mumbling to himself. He hadn't noticed that anyone had come into the room.

Solveig stood there for a minute waiting for him to notice her arrival, and when he didn't respond, she cleared her throat. Sean stood patiently next to the Princess, while Summer flew over to the nearest table and sat atop one of the model planets. This one had some very colorful and interesting rings around it that seemed to be suspended in mid air. The Sorcerer still didn't notice their presence, so Solveig cleared her throat again, a little louder. When he still didn't look up, she stomped her foot on the floor and coughed loudly.

The Sorcerer looked up and began talking to her as if she had been in conversation with him all the while, completely oblivious to the presence of Sean and Summer.

"So you see, Princess Solveig, it's been here right before my eyes this whole time. I just needed to translate the ancient texts. It was only a matter of time. My calculations were right, as I had suspected. Of course, this only proves my point." He waved a finger in the air and took long strides to his desk as if to check his calculations and then back to the Princess to continue his discussion.

"And which point is that you may ask; well the point is that everything points in the direction I was trying to point out. That's the point." He suddenly stopped talking and noticed that he had guests.

He stared at both of them intently. He then walked up to Sean and examined him from head to toe. With his thumb he raised one of Sean's eyelids and looked closely into Sean's eye. He moved to the side and lifted Sean's hair from the side of his head, peering at Sean's pointed ear. He took one of Sean's hands and examined their roughness as well as the cuts and bruises that had already begun fading away. Then stepping back he proclaimed, "A forest creature. A skilled hunter and climber, and probably a Dozor in his lodge."

He then moved to Summer and examined her just as closely. He stood abruptly and returned to his desk. He rummaged around for a few seconds and found what he was looking for – a large piece of circular glass. He brought it back and held it over Summer. When she looked up through it back at him, she was startled to see a giant eye looking down at her. He ran the glass from the tips of her toes to the tops of her wings.

"A faerie! She looks to be just over one hundred years old. Probably a princess. How remarkable." He turned to Solveig and asked, "And they came here together? Up the side of the mountain? He climbed while she flew, I suppose."

Summer and Sean stared in amazement; Solveig just smiled.

"How did he know all that?" asked Sean.

"May I introduce my brother, Lochen, the Sorcerer of the mountain people?"

Before they could answer and without responding to Sean's question, Lochen turned back to his papers as if nothing had happened.

Solveig rolled her eyes. "Lochen! Our guests have some urgent news to share. I need you to stop what you're doing and listen to them."

"Certainly, certainly," he answered as he turned back. However, before they could start to tell him their news, he cut them off.

"Did you know this is a very unusual period, astrologically speaking? I've been studying the movements of the planets and their moons for several years, and I've never seen anything like this. Of course, I had predicted it would happen. It was simple mathematics – bound to happen sooner or later. I just didn't think it would happen in my lifetime. The last time it happened was just before I was born, so naturally, I assumed that any recurrence would not happen again so soon, although I suppose if I had bothered to attempt those calculations I would have discovered it on my own. Actually, I did discover it on my own, but through observation rather than…"

"LOCHEN!" interrupted Princess Solveig.

"Of course, of course. What did you have to tell me?"

He looked at Summer and Sean as if seeing them for the first time.

"And who are your guests?" he asked.

Summer and Sean looked at each other in silence. Who is this guy, they both wondered.

"You just identified them yourself," Solveig said in exasperation. "A faerie and a forest creature. You mean you already forgot?"

"No, of course not. I know <u>what</u> they are. My question was directed at <u>who</u> they are."

Solveig took a deep breath, clearly frustrated by the exchange with her brother. "Yes, you did indicate what they are, and yes, you did ask who they are." She silently counted to ten before continuing.

"This is Summer, a princess of the faeries, and this is her friend, Sean, a Dozor in a lodge of forest creatures."

"Just as I said," answered Lochen, still focused on his papers. "And what brings them here?"

Summer and Sean began to tell the Sorcerer of the storm that struck their village and lodge and how their family and friends had been turned to stone, but before they could get very far, the Sorcerer interrupted their story.

"Yes, yes, a storm of apocalyptic proportions, tornadic winds, resounding thunder, ferocious lightning, clouds that take the shape of ominous beings breathing curses that turn all living things to stone. I've been watching it for the last several weeks. It's headed this way, I'm quite sure. Some believe it to be the return of Ena Ray – back from exile and more powerful than before. What about it?"

Summer, Sean and Solveig stared at Lochen in stunned silence.

"You've known about this?" asked Solveig in disbelief. "And you didn't think it was important enough to mention to me?"

"But it appears you already know about it," Lochen responded.

"I know about it NOW," Solveig nearly shouted. "From strangers. Who scaled the side of our castle. NOT from my brother." She was clearly irritated.

Finally Summer found her voice. "How do we stop it?" she asked.

"I haven't really thought about that," the Sorcerer replied.

Princess Solveig stepped a little closer to the Sorcerer and, putting her hand on his elbow, moved him a few steps away from his desk and papers. She held his elbow as he craned his neck around and continued to read numbers from one of the sheets until she had pulled him too far away for him to see. When he finally turned to look her in the face, she said, "Perhaps it would be worth some of your time to think about this."

She led him back to his desk and turned him back to his papers. "It would not be acceptable for us to let this happen to our people. There must be some way to divert the storm or to protect us from its wrath."

"Of course, your highness," Lochen answered. "When this castle was built, I conjured up some spells to make sure there were sufficient protections for all of our subjects. Have no fear, none of us will come to harm."

He turned his attention back to his papers, and continued. "As for diverting the storm, I'm afraid that's not possible. However, I believe the storm is in some way connected to finding and releasing Ena Ray. If I'm correct, and I'm sure I am, I also believe there is a way to defeat any such effort. I'm just not sure I have all the facts, yet. As I said, this is a very unusual time astrologically speaking. The planets Hermes and Athena have already aligned, as have Terra Firma and Ares. Before Luna has passed twice more, Varuna, Capurnica and Poseidon will have aligned as well. When this happens the portal to the underworld may open unless the crystal key is discovered and the portal is locked."

"What is he talking about?" Summer whispered to Sean.

"I don't know," Sean whispered back, shrugging his shoulders. "Something about aspercology and some places called Herpes, and I seen her – which even I know is bad grammar – and some loony person getting poisoned, and some porridge and underwear and crystal trees. Whatever. What does all this have to do with that lousy storm?"

"Well," replied the Princess, ignoring the whispering behind her. "That seems simple enough. We just need to locate some crystal key and keep the underworld locked."

"It's not that simple; not at all," Lochen answered. "I don't have any guide to the crystal key and I don't know where the portal is."

Summer had become very impatient with all this talk of planets, portals, and keys. "I don't care about all that stuff. I just want my family back," she shouted. "You're a Sorcerer. You must be able to do something."

Just as Lochen was turning back to answer Summer, he took a step towards her. Sean mistook this, and stepped in front of him, placing himself between Lochen and Summer. He raised his hands in a motion for Lochen to stop. As he did this, Lochen's eye was caught by the armband Sean was wearing. He stepped closer to Sean, and pointing at the band asked, "Where did you get this?"

"I don't know," he said, placing his hand over the band protectively. "It's been passed from Dozor to Dozor for as long as anyone can remember."

"May I see it?" Lochen asked.

Sean waited for a second or two trying to gauge Lochen's intentions. Finally, he slipped the band off his arm and handed it to the Sorcerer. There were strange markings on the outside that had initially attracted Lochen's attention. He turned the band in several different angles. Upon closer examination, he discovered similar marking on the inside of the band. He compared the markings on both sides and then he discovered that there were actually two bands: one fitting tightly inside the other. In the center of the outer design was an odd shaped indentation. Lochen took the armband back to his desk and began rummaging through some old papers.

"I've seen this before," he exclaimed. He put the band on his table and seemed to lose himself in a pile of dusty old parchment. After a minute or two, he found what he was looking for.

"I thought so. It's a celestial map." When the others looked at him blankly, he went on, "I was looking over some ancient manuscripts about an Alchemist who had done some marvelous studies of the skies. He was quite an extraordinary astronomer, not to mention a very talented conjurer. The design on this armband is clearly his work. It's a map of the planets and stars. Well, it's actually more than that. It's a key of sorts."

"The kind of key to lock the portal?" Solveig asked.

"Not that kind of key. It's more like a legend. But there's a piece missing."

He turned the armband over in his hand. "These ancient notes tell of a map with a secret code that can be broken only once this missing piece is found and even then it can only be read by an enchantress."

"What kind of missing piece?" asked Sean.

"A stone, I believe," Lochen answered.

"What kind of stone?" asked Summer.

"I'm not sure exactly. The legend is that it's part of a pendant that was worn by an ancient Enchantress. The pendant was destroyed and the pieces of the stone were scattered. One piece of that pendant fits into this band."

"What does the missing piece look like?" Solveig asked.

"A simple triskelion," replied Lochen.

Summer, Sean and Solveig looked puzzled. "What's that?" they asked.

"Oh! It's a symbol with three curving lines radiating from the center."

Summer looked shocked. She reached to her neck and felt her locket. "Like this?" she asked and lifted the locket towards Lochen's eyes.

He picked up a magnifying glass and looked closely – first at the locket, and then at the indentation in the armband.

"That certainly looks like the right shape," he said. "May I try it?"

Summer untied the locket from her neck and handed it to Lochen. He carefully removed the symbol from the locket and placed it in the armband. The indentation in the armband was exactly the same shape, but not the same size. It was somewhat larger than the stone. As soon as

Lochen put the stone into place, however, it slowly expanded and fit perfectly. Then he was able to slide the inner ring to match to pattern on the outer ring.

"That's interesting," he cried. "I have to admit, I never expected that to happen."

"Nothing is happening," said Solveig, waiting for several seconds after the stone had filled the space.

"Of course not," answered Lochen. "We need an enchantress. I'm a Sorcerer. It's not the same thing. I know people often confuse us, but an Enchantress' powers are very different from…"

"Well, where can we find an enchantress?" interrupted Summer impatiently.

"Oh! Nowhere near here," answered Lochen. "The closest one is a long way from here, and well protected. As I last recall, the mountain people were not on the best of terms with the guardians of the enchantress." He looked up from the stone and armband and turned his head towards Sean.

"But then, we're not on such good terms with the forest creatures, either, since we left the alliance with them and moved to this mountaintop. And, yet, here one is. Right in our very castle. So far there's been no bloodshed, so I have to presume that our relationship might be on the mend. I'm not sure how things are with the faeries. On the other hand, even if I were sure before, seeing you two together would likely make me less sure. I never thought I would see the day…"

"Lochen!" interrupted Princess Solveig. "Can we get there from here?"

"How does she put up with him?" Summer whispered to Sean.

"I heard that," Lochen announced. And to Solveig, he responded, "Of course we can get there - with a little magic."

"Then let's get started.  What do you need?" the Princess asked him.

"Let's get started?" asked Sean.  "But we just got here.  Where are we going now?"

"I have all that I need, but we'll have to go down to the lower level of the castle," Lochen said, ignoring Sean's questions.

With that, he gathered up the hem of his robe and strode out of his room and down the stairs.  Solveig hesitated only a second and then began to follow him, leaving Summer and Sean behind staring at one another.  When they didn't move, Solveig stuck her head back through the doorway and called to them.

"You brought this problem to us.  If you want to find any answer, you'll have to come along.  I trusted you.  Now you have to trust us."  Without waiting for an answer she turned and left.  Summer and Sean didn't need a second invitation.  They were right behind her.

The foursome headed back down the long spiral staircase.  Lochen set a pace that was hard to keep up with, and soon became dizzying.  Once they arrived at the large courtyard, Summer and Sean thought it was nearly night time, the sky had gotten so dark.  They didn't think they had been in the tower that long.  Then they heard the winds and the thunder, followed by the earsplitting crashes of lightning.

"Oh no," they cried.  "The storm is on top of us."

"Not yet," replied Lochen much too calmly in their opinion.  He stopped in the center of the main courtyard and gestured to the side of the castle.

"It's at the base of the mountain and rising up the sides of the castle, very much as I had predicted it would."  He then continued on as if giving a lecture.  "Of course with storms of this or any other nature, precise calculations are next to impossible, given variations in temperature, the orbital location of Luna and the related gravitational effects."  He started pacing back and forth with his hands held behind his back.  "Then there are such factors as ambient air temperature, previous climatological events, existing precipitation…"

"Lochen," Princess Solveig interrupted. "Thank you for your discourse on the weather, but it might be more useful if you advise us of how to proceed."

Without waiting for an answer, she gently pushed him forward.

"Of course, your highness. I will need you to escort our traveling companions to the travel tube. Where we are going, however, we are much too big. The faerie princess is all right, but you, the forest creature and I must reduce our size."

Sean stopped walking and jerked his head up, "Reduce our size? How are you going to do that?"

Summer, who had been flying immediately behind once again nearly ran into his head.

"You have GOT to stop doing that!" she mumbled.

"Don't worry," said Solveig. "It's very simple. I promise it won't hurt, and it usually can easily be reversed. What will you be doing in the mean time, Lochen?"

"Usually?" whined Sean, as Solveig took hold of his wrist and pulled him along.

"I will be enveloping the castle in a protective shroud and ensuring the inhabitants are secured and unseen by the approaching storm. As soon as that's done, I'll join you. However, don't wait for me. It is more important that you escape. Promise me that you won't wait. No matter what; you must leave."

"Wait a minute," Summer said in a startled voice. "This was your idea. We can't leave without you. We don't know where we're going or what to do if we even get there."

"I agree," said Solveig. "Besides, you're my brother. I will not leave you behind. I am also your Princess, so I command you to not stay behind."

"I've already programmed the travel tube to our destination" Lochen said to Summer. You have the armband and the key. Once you arrive seek out the enchantress."

He turned his attention to Solveig. "I am well aware of our biological relationship – YOUR HIGHNESS. Command me all you like, and I'll obey you as I always have, but you must promise me that you won't wait. I promise you – I'll be all right."

"When did you program the travel tube?" Sean asked.

"Before we left my tower," the Sorcerer answered, and before he could be asked another question, he smiled and said, "Magic. Now get going before it's too late. We've already wasted precious time in this interesting, but rather pointless discussion."

Reluctantly Solveig acquiesced to his instructions. As she led Summer and Sean through a narrow doorway and into the depths of the castle keep, they all turned and got a final glimpse of Lochen as he swirled his arms in the air above him. A long, thick cloud of purple smoke began to emerge from his fingertip. Soon the courtyard was so full of the smoke that the sky could no longer be seen. Even the flashes of lightning were being blotted out. But nothing could blot out the horrendous crashing sound of the thunder.

As Summer, Sean and Solveig descended lower and lower into the castle, they could hear Lochen shouting from behind them, "to the burrows; to the burrows. Everyone move quickly to the burrows. You'll be safe there."

"What are the burrows?" Sean asked.

Solveig told him, "When this castle was constructed, Lochen built burrows, tunnels and hideaways for every inhabitant. That's where he's sending them.  There is space there for everyone to hide.  These are all protected by various magic spells to shield us from any force of evil.  He must make sure that all are hidden.  He won't join us until everyone is safe."

When they finally reached the lowest level of the castle, they came upon a long narrow cylinder on the edge of a hole carved into the floor below. The top half of the cylinder was open revealing four seats.  Summer was able to hop in and fit quite comfortably.  With a wave of her hand, Princess Solveig cast a quick spell on Sean and herself.  In the blink of an eye, they shrunk in size to less than half.

"Wow, neat," shouted Summer.

"Ohhhh," whined Sean.  "You better be able to reverse this.  I'll never be able to show my face in the lodge again if I'm this small."

"Hey," complained Summer.  "Didn't anyone ever tell you that good things some in small packages?"

"Only the ones who got the small packages," replied Sean.

By now the castle walls were shaking with the reverberations of the thunder from the storm and the bolts of lightning that were crashing all around.  In addition to these noises, a roaring sound could be heard.

"The force behind the storm is angry," said Solveig.  "It can't find anyone or anything to destroy."

"You make it sound like the storm is intelligent," said Summer.

"I'm sure it is," answered Solveig.  Seeing the doubt on Summer's face, she added, "Think about it.  You said yourself that the storm seemed to be moving from one side of the land to the other.  Those movements were systematic.  It's looking for something and destroying everyone as it moves."

The thought that the storm had intelligence worried Summer even more. She listened to the roaring and felt the vibrations as she thought about what Solveig said.

The storm raged even more fiercely, shaking the castle to its very foundations. The ceiling above them began to cave in as they sat in the cylinder waiting for Lochen. Bits of stone and dust dropped down on them. The cylinder shook violently.

"Is this place going to cave in?" Sean asked as he held tightly to his seat and looked at the ceiling.

"No," said Solveig confidently, even though she had an uneasy edge in her voice. "Lochen cast the spells himself. There's no place safer."

"And we're leaving here – why?" asked Sean.

Before Solveig could answer his question and before any of them could stop it, the glass top of the cylinder began to close.

"Wait," shouted Summer. "We have to wait for Lochen."

She banged her tiny hands on the glass as it sealed them in tightly. In spite of her efforts, the cylinder closed on its own. The hatch secured tightly with a hissing sound. There was a moment of silence, followed by a slight tremor and the cylinder shot through the hole, rocketing downward into the darkness.

# Chapter five

Own they went, deeper and deeper inside the mountain. Soon the sounds of the storm were far behind. The tunnel they traveled through was black as pitch; the only light came from a glow from within the cylinder itself. Sean was unusually quiet, sitting silently in a corner looking at the edges of the tunnel through the glass top of the cylinder as it continued to speed downward. Summer fluttered around, pushing on the glass top, still shouting for it to stop. Solveig sat across from Sean with her head down murmuring some kind of incantation that the other two couldn't distinguish.

"Hey," shouted Sean. "Can you stop banging on the glass? What would happen if it opened now?"

Summer sat down with a thump, folding her arms. She turned to Solveig, who appeared calm, still mumbling to herself.

"Aren't you worried?" Summer asked her.

"Of course I am," Solveig replied. "But my brother is very resourceful and clever, which is why he's a Sorcerer. He wouldn't have sent us off without some kind of plan. It's just that he doesn't always remember to tell the rest of us what he's doing." She looked as if she was going to say more, then, wringing her hands, bowed her head again and continued the incantation.

Before long, the travelers began to notice that the tunnel was becoming lighter. They could make out a bright blue cast in the path ahead. As they got closer to it, Sean began to become agitated.

"That's water ahead!" he said in a startled voice. "That's water. What water is that?"

Solveig raised her head and looked in the direction Sean was pointing.

"It appears that's the Cerulean Sea," she answered.

"We're headed to the Cerulean Sea?" he shouted. "The Cerulean Sea? We're headed to …wait! We're going under water!"

He tried to stand up, bumping his head on the top of the cylinder. He leaned as far forward as he could, and with his hands pressed against the glass like he was bracing himself for a sudden impact.

He shouted, "Oh, no! Water! We're going under the water. We'll drown. Make this thing stop." He started banging his hands against the glass frantically.

"Aren't you afraid you'll break the glass?" Summer asked sarcastically. "What do you think will happen then?

He had become very agitated and Summer's words only made it worse. He spun around towards Solveig, shouting, "Do something. You have to make this thing stop. Can't you see we're going under the water?"

Solveig quietly looked up into his face, and, passing her open hand in a gentle motion as if she was waving to a friend, she cast a spell over Sean, telling him to be calm. Sean's eyes glazed over slightly and he sat back in his seat with a "plop" and a silly grin on his face, as if this were nothing more than a ride in a park on a nice spring morning. Summer's eyes moved from the Princess to Sean and back without a word.

Solveig smiled and said, "Sometimes a little peace and quiet is best. Don't you think?"

Summer just nodded her head in agreement. Soon the cylinder crashed into the Sea and slowed down only slightly as it continued following an invisible path towards the bottom. The light from the sky above the Sea began to diminish slightly as they got closer and closer to the bottom; but before it became dark, they began to approach an eerie glow just ahead of them. As they descended, they passed a giant school of lancet fish. They were an iridescent yellow. There were thousands of them and they separated as the cylinder shot through the middle of them.

Summer stood on her seat and peered at the fish and then looked towards the source of the light.

"It looks like a giant bubble," she said. As it neared, she could see buildings inside the bubble. Off in the distance, she was sure she could see people. Then, as the cylinder dropped lower and lower, the buildings fell out of sight.

The cylinder slowed down gradually until it was only inching its way forward. The nose of the cylinder touched the edge of the bubble and gently pushed its way inside. It was like passing through a thick layer of gelatin. The bubble barely moved. Only the area immediately surrounding the cylinder as it was passing through displayed any movement. Once completely in, all motion stopped. The cylinder settled gently to the sandy floor, and the glass top slid open.

"I guess we should get out," said Solveig. She waved her hand across Sean's face and the silly grin disappeared. He opened his eyes widely and looked around. Seeing that he was on the sand, he appeared oblivious to the fact that the Sea was above and around him.

The three emerged from the tube and looked around. They were on the edge of a forest of what looked like seaweed. Summer went up to the edge of the bubble, and put her hand on the wall. She could barely feel anything at all.

"Don't do that," Sean shouted to her. "What if you put a hole in it?"

That was when he fully understood where they were. His eyes focused on the wall of water immediately in front of Summer and rose up the wall of the bubble until his head was looking straight up. He slumped down to the sand, still staring upward, and muttering, "Oh poop, it's a bunch of water – it's a bunch of water."

"He'll be fine in a minute," Solveig assured Summer as she gazed at him in disbelief.

Then she turned back to the wall in front of her. She pushed her hand against the bubble. Nothing stopped it. Her hand felt the cold water and she pulled it back into the bubble, raising it to her mouth. The water tasted salty, just like she had expected it would. On the other side of the bubble, she could see several different kinds of fish swimming back and forth, curious about the mysterious hand that had just appeared on their side of the bubble. Every once in a while one or two would approach the edge and look in, but then skitter away.

The ground was the same sand as the rest of the bottom of the sea, littered with sea shells and bits of rock and coral. Summer walked across the sand to where Sean was still sitting, staring at the Sea above him. The sand was warm. She looked towards the forest of seaweed. There were open spaces through the plants, but nothing that could be called a path.

"Which way should we go?" Summer asked.

Her question brought Sean out of his reverie. He shook his head and jumped up.

"This way, I think," answered Sean, and he led them off through the seaweed. Neither Summer nor Solveig thought to question him. They just followed. Solveig gave Summer a half smile as if to say, "What did I tell you?"

He had come out of his trance, apparently not remembering anything about how they had arrived. As they walked, they came across a number of beautiful and brightly colored sea flowers. The sand beneath their feet glittered with crushed shells and small stones. The glittering made Summer realize that it was light inside the bubble.

"Where's the light coming from?" she asked Solveig.

Solveig looked up. "It appears that the sunlight above the surface of the Sea is magnified by the bubble."

Who did all this, Summer wondered to herself.

After a while they saw off in the distance what looked like a building of some kind that appeared to be carved out of the rocks and coral. They could see spires poking out over the tops of the forest. When they got closer, it became clear that the building was a palace. It was bright white and sparkled as if it was covered with diamonds.

The palace had a huge entryway at one end that looked like an enormous conch shell. No one was standing guard, so they just walked in. Through the entry way they entered into a long, wide corridor, except that there was no roof to the corridor, other than the top of the bubble. It was like walking between very tall sides of a cliff under an open sky; except this sky had fish floating overhead, instead of birds. On each of the sides of the corridor were dozens of small and medium sized openings like windows or archways. In several of these openings plants and vines hung down.

"I wonder if people live in those holes in the sides of the wall," wondered Summer. "This almost looks like a village, except no one's home."

Eventually, the corridor wound around and opened to a large court. In the court the trio came upon dozens of people sitting on the ground. It was like a scene from a picnic. Many of them had blankets and large pillows scattered about. Several were eating and drinking, but no one was talking. Everyone seemed to have their attention focused on two people at the other end of the court atop a large rock.

One of them was a beautiful young woman with short dark hair and very bright blue eyes. She wore a flowing gown of blues and greens that looked like the sea itself. On her head was a tiara made from starfish and seashells, and glittering with diamonds. She sat on a throne carved from beautiful pink coral. She, like all the others, was focused intently on the other person who was speaking.

"Oh, yes, Your Highness, there are many, many other worlds. Most of them cannot be seen without the aid of a telescope. That's a long tube with several pieces of special glass inside. It makes everything much larger and much closer. Hermes is the one closest to our twin suns, but it is much too hot to sustain life. After that is Athena, but it is covered in poisonous gases, so, it too is not inhabitable. I myself have been to Ares, the red planet. Many think that Ares is a hot, volcanic planet because of the red color, but it is not. It is a cold, dead planet, although it may have once supported life."

Summer, Sean and Solveig stopped immediately in their tracks.

"No!" said Solveig. "It can't be."

"I don't believe it's possible," said Summer

"It's Lochen," all three of them said at that same time.

At that interruption Lochen stopped talking to the Princess and turned at the sound of his name.

"Aha," he announced. "You made it. I was certain you would. And it appears that you heeded my instructions to not wait for me. Excellent. I thought that you might disregard those instructions, so I put a spell on the traveling tube to close automatically and leave before it was too late. And I can see by the expressions on your face that this is exactly what happened. Well, I hope you weren't too startled and that your journey was uneventful."

Summer and Sean were still too surprised to speak, but Solveig was more familiar with her brother's antics. She was upset with him for not telling her about his plans. She marched right up to him with one hand on her hip and the other shaking a finger at him. Since she was still under her own spell, which had shrunk her down, she was shouting up at him, reaching up as far as she could.

"You have no idea how much we were worried about you! You could have at least had the decency to let me know what you were planning and where you were sending us. If I wasn't so happy to see you safe, I'd be really mad at you," she shouted.

"I see you cast a spell to help you fit in the tube," he said somewhat sheepishly. "Allow me."

He waved his hand, but nothing happened. Solveig snapped her fingers and the spell dissipated, returning them to their former size, but not diffusing her anger.

The Princess on the throne stood up and walked over to intercede on Lochen's behalf before things got out of hand.

"You must be Princess Solveig," she said, extending her hand. "Your Sorcerer has told me so much about you. Welcome to my palace. I am Princess Natalie of the Sea Sprites."

She then turned her attention to Summer and Sean. "And you must be Summer, the faerie princess, and you must be Sean, Dozor of the forest creatures. You, too, are welcome. Would you like some lemonade?

Please join us. The Sorcerer was just treating us to a discussion on the planets and stars that make up the heavens. It was very interesting. We have lived in this bubble for quite some time, and this far under the Sea, we don't get an opportunity to see the wonders of the night sky."

With a clap of her hand, Natalie made three more cushions appear as well as some lemonade and cookies. Summer, Sean and Solveig sat down and began assaulting Lochen with questions: what had happened, how did he get out, how did he get here, where was the storm now.

"Well," he explained, "I've never really been fond of traveling through that tube. It's convenient and all, but it was really just designed to do what it did – provide an escape in the event of an emergency."

"How did you get down here before us," asked Summer.

"I just happened to have this transporter stone, so I used it instead." He held out his hand and in the palm was a small oval translucent stone that gave off a milky glow. It had curious markings on it that looked a bit like hieroglyphics. "Princess Natalie was kind enough to give it to me on one of my first visits here. I find it much faster and certainly a much more comfortable mode of transportation. Of course it's not without its own hazards. If one is not careful, one could arrive in the center of a mountain or under water – and not in a protected bubble like this."

Solveig looked surprised. "You've been here before? When and how often?"

"Oh, yes. Didn't I mention it to you?"

"It must have escaped you," she answered, her voice heavy with sarcasm.

"I had been studying some ancient texts on star patterns and super novas when I came across an account of a battle between mountain people and the forest creatures that had become the basis for naming a series of constellations. It was really quite interesting. It seems that an astronomer had been mapping the celestial charts at the time at the request of the Queen of the Sea Sprites — a formidable leader named Else…"

"Lochen," interrupted Solveig. "You were about to explain your previous visits here."

"Yes, of course," he said. He scrunched up his face, trying to recall his original train of thought. When he remembered where he had left off, he raised his eyebrows, shot a finger in the air and continued.

"Ah, yes. Anyway, I learned about this hidden civilization not far from the shore but deep beneath the surface of the Sea, and decided to do some exploring. I had read about how they had gone into hiding to avoid being involved in the wars being waged on land. You recall them, don't you? The wars between the faeries and the forest creatures, which spilled over to the mountain people and the sea sprites?"

He was nodding at them waiting for some sign of recognition. When no one responded or gave an indication that more explanation was needed, he went on.

"Their enchantress created this bubble and over the centuries the city grew from there. The bubble is really quite amazing. I hope to have some time to study it further. But it was during one of my early visits that I met Princess Natalie. We have become good friends over the years. I have helped her with some of her maps and charts, and she, in turn, gave me the transport stone as a gift. I'm sure I must have mentioned this at some point in time."

Solveig just shook her head and responded, "I'm sure you think you're sure, but, no, you seem to have forgotten to share that bit of information."

Princess Natalie explained that the Sea Sprites had not wanted to take a side in the wars between the faeries, the forest creatures and the mountain people, so had gone into hiding. That was more than five hundred years ago, maybe even closer to a thousand. It was difficult for them to know, since the passage of time in their bubble was not measured the same way as it was on the surface.  Also, because they have had little or no contact with the people of the surface, their historical information was often incomplete.  For better or for worse, since that time they had lived beneath the surface of the Cerulean Sea.

"Our historians have told us of the rise and fall of Ena Ray, so we are well aware of at least some aspects of his tyranny.  We thought, though, that he had been permanently exiled and was locked away in the Crystal Citadel."

Summer said she had never heard of the Crystal Citadel.  Sean knew nothing about it, either.

Natalie explained, "Our legends tell us that as he was becoming a very powerful sorcerer, there was a great conflict between several sorcerers.  One group was comprised of about twelve who were known as Kelpies and the other group, a smaller number, were aided by an Enchantress.  It's not clear what happened to Ena Ray.  Our archives are incomplete.  Some lore describes a battle in which the creatures of the world united against him, and stripped him of all his powers.  Other myths talk of a second powerful sorcerer who was in league with Ena Ray, and that both of them were destroyed by the Enchantress.  The only part of the history where the different versions agree is that his army was banished to the underworld, and he was locked away in the Crystal Citadel, buried miles under the ice in the North Country."

"Yes, that's correct," interjected Lochen.  "Furthermore, I believe the spell that was used to overthrow him was predicted to last a thousand years.  If the story of the mighty Enchantress is true, and my calculations of the time line is accurate, which I believe it is, the power of the Enchantress was amplified because all the planets in our solar system were in perfect alignment.  If that was true, then I also believe that the banishment will be lifted only when the planets are aligned.  At that time, the locks to the Crystal Citadel will open and he will be free to reunite his army from their underworld confinement, unless the creatures of the world reestablish the barrier."

"What barrier? And who exactly has to reestablish it?" Solveig asked.

"I haven't quite figured that out," said Lochen. "Although, it seems that each of us holds a part to this puzzle. Sean and Summer brought us the map and key. The library that Solveig and I have gathered over time provides information that explains much of the myth. If we could locate an enchantress, we'd have someone who might be able to read the inscriptions on Sean's arm band."

"We have an enchantress here."

At that everyone turned to Princess Natalie.

"How is it that you didn't know this?" Solveig whispered to Lochen.

"She alone would have to make her presence known, as I was unable to detect it on my own. It appears that my powers are blocked inside this bubble."

Natalie turned to them both and explained, "The arrival of a sorcerer to our home was met with mixed reactions. Many of my people were suspicious. I was counseled to bar entry altogether, but I believed it was time to send envoys to the civilizations that live on the land. Lochen seemed like an opportunity to see if the time was right. Still, I couldn't risk sharing all of our secrets. Our Enchantress is critical to our survival. I could not place her in jeopardy. Please excuse my caution."

"Not at all," said Lochen. "That was a perfectly understandable safeguard. I hope your fears have been allayed."

"Yes, they have," Natalie smiled, relieved. "Please allow me to summon the Enchantress."

She clapped her hands once. There was a sudden flash of a bright yellow light, followed by a growing yellow and white mist. Out from the mist stepped a beautiful young lady with wild curly hair and piercing blue eyes. She was wearing a gown of yellow and gold and beams of soft white light circled her head. She seemed to float rather than walk as she approached the Princess.

"Yes, your Highness. How may I be of service?" she asked.

Natalie gestured to her new guests and said, "Enchantress, I would like you to meet my new friends: Princess Solveig of the mountain people and her Sorcerer, Lochen, Sean, a Dozor of the forest creatures, and Summer, a faerie princess. I am pleased for you all to meet Stella, the Enchantress of the Sea Sprites."

Natalie then explained to Stella the journey that the others had recently undertaken, while Lochen, Summer and Sean filled her in on the movement and devastation of the storm. Lochen explained his theories on the alignment of the planets and the legends of Ena Ray.

"What's not clear," said Solveig, "is whether there's any connection between the spell on Ena Ray, the alignment of the planets and the sudden appearance of this devastating storm."

"The people of our villages were turned to stone only after that storm passed over them," inserted Summer.

"And it was like those clouds were chasing us," said Sean.

"Of course, we are well protected from the storm here beneath the Sea," explained Natalie, but Stella cut her off.

"I'm sorry, Your Highness, but that's not true. I've had a vision of this storm. Even as we speak it has begun its search of the Sea. That storm is filled with much hatred and violence. It boils the water it touches. We are not safe here for long. I will be able to disguise our home and move it from the path of the storm, but those actions won't protect us forever. My visions also have shown me that the legends of Ena Ray are true. He was banished to the Crystal Citadel. His power is growing as the planets align. It is his power that the storm is drawing on. It is searching for something – what, though, I can't say for sure. I have visions of another powerful sorcerer, but those images are weak. I don't think that one is a threat. What our visitors have shared has made these visions much clearer. Your Highness, we must join forces with these adventurers and find a way to stop the return of Ena Ray."

Natalie was stunned at this news. She reacted quickly and decisively.

"If that's so, Enchantress, then I ask you to do what you can to protect our bubble, and then leave with our friends. I will stay here with my people and mount an army against the intruder. We'll do what we can to buy you enough time."

Stella responded, "No, Princess. Your staying behind won't help. I can't explain how I know this, but I do. You must join us in this quest. At some point in the journey, we will need you. Trust me in this."

"My powers are minimal," Natalie argued. "You and the Sorcerer have much more ability than I. You are kind to inflate my importance, but such flattery is hardly necessary, especially in this time."

"It is not flattery," Stella insisted. "You MUST be a part of this mission. I can't say why, but you must trust me."

"But how do we know where we're supposed to go?" asked Summer.

"The armband, of course," said Lochen. "We must go someplace secure. There is inexplicable magic in that band. I can sense it. I'm afraid that once the vision of the armband is activated, the power of the storm will be alerted. We'll have to act quickly, but if we can open its secrets in some place more sheltered than this court yard, that would be better."

"Come with me," said Natalie. Before she led them away, she turned to the commander of her guard and gave instructions to her to secure the realm. She then led her small party from the courtyard, through a series of halls into a room deep inside the coral palace. It was a large circular room with no doors or windows, and a domed roof, very much like Lochen's room in the tower of the mountain castle. It was dimly light by a glow that emanated up through the floor, which appeared to be made of the same milky glass as the transporter stone. "This should give us the needed privacy and protection," announced Natalie.

"Sean," said Lochen. "If you would be so kind as to hand me your armband"

He took the band and held it out before him pointing it towards the walls of the Sanctorum. Nothing happened. He then turned, aiming it in a wide circle around the room. Still nothing happened. Perplexed, he handed the band to Stella and asked her if she felt or sensed anything. She did not.

"I was so certain this was the key," he said dejectedly. "The key! That's it. The key. Summer, if you would give me your locket."

She did as he asked, and once he inserted the triskelion in the center of the band, he moved the inner band to align with the outer band, the two bands expanded in size, more than doubling. As the band expanded in size, the triskelion did as well. He again pointed the band to the walls, but once more nothing happened. Furrowing his brow, he looked down at the band and then to Stella. The band was now large enough for her to place it on her head like a crown, he thought to himself. He moved close to her and raised it over her head.

"Trust me," he said to her.

"I do," she answered.

He lowered it to her head. It fit snugly around the top, across her forehead, with the triskelion in the center just above her eyes. She took a deep breath, and then went rigid. Her eyes rolled back and it seemed like she had fallen into a trance. Lochen took a few steps back, ready to react if something unexpected happened. All at once a flash of light burst from the triskelion and the symbols on the band lit up as if on fire. Images then began to be projected on the walls of the Sanctorum.

The images flashed across the walls in no particular order as scenes from a nightmare. Some of them were just letters and numbers; others showed scenes of devastation and destruction. Planets raced across the universe, volcanoes erupted, tsunamis crashed along shorelines, and oceans sprayed boiling geysers miles into the air. Lights flashed from one side of the room to the other. Trees were torn apart by blasts of lightning. Billowing white clouds sprang across horizons of snow-white ice fields. Animals were stampeding, escaping some unseen terror.

A large shadow appeared and grew in size. The shadow seemed to have a shadow — as if it was a double of the image, but not separately distinct. Thousands of grotesque figures appeared. Their impressions were blurred, but from the shapes alone, their bizarre and misshapen forms were evident. Then a light began to emerge. It started off as a low radiating indigo color. Gradually it lightened until it flashed. Everyone but Stella covered their eyes.

As the visions raced across the walls a presence not visible in the images was felt inside the room. Something evil — something very powerful — seemed to be whirling silently around each of them. It was nothing any of them could see or touch, but it was enough to raise the hairs on the backs of their necks and to run shivers down their spines. They could all feel a myriad of emotions from exhilaration to betrayal to intense anger.

The violence of the images combined with the deafening silence unnerved each of them. They were unable to turn away from the sights. Throughout all of this the only sound that could be heard was that of Stella breathing. Everyone else had been holding their breath in shock and amazement. No one had noticed that as the visions increased in tempo and intensity, Stella had levitated off the floor. She was hovering with her arms spread slightly from her sides, her eyes closed and her hair fanned out behind her as if being lifted by a gentle breeze. In less than fifteen seconds it was over. Stella lowered herself to the floor, took off the band, which immediately shrunk back to its original sized, and she quickly fell asleep.

"Wow," said Summer.  The tips of her wings were flickering with sparks of static electricity.  She looked at each of the others.  They were all equally stunned.  Lochen seemed to have a slight glow that surrounded his entire body.  Slowly it faded away.  Solveig and Natalie looked as if a strong wind had blown through the room.   Their clothing and their hair were disheveled.  Sean had curled up in a ball and was hugging his knees.

"What did all that mean?" she asked.

"I have no idea," answered Lochen.

# Chapter six

"Give me some time to think about it," he said to everyone. He reached down, picked up the armband and removed the triskelion. He gave the stone back to Summer and handed the armband back to Sean.

"In the mean time," he said, "I suggest you all get some rest. I can sense that this experience has drained each of you and I think we'll have to get an early start tomorrow morning. Princess Natalie, if you would be so kind as to make sleeping arrangements, I would like to wait here for your Enchantress to wake up."

"Of course, Lochen," Natalie said, starring at her sleeping Enchantress. She collected herself and asked, "but where will we be going tomorrow?"

"I don't exactly know – at least not just yet," he answered.

"Will you be all right?" asked Summer. "Won't you need some rest?"

"No," he said, somewhat distracted. "It's not time for me to sleep, yet."

Summer looked at him oddly, not understanding his answer. She didn't pursue it, though. He was right. She was exhausted. She could barely keep her eyes open. It took all her strength to fly behind Natalie as the Princess led them to quiet rooms where they could sleep. By the time they got there, Summer thought it wouldn't matter if the storm struck right now with full fury. She would sleep right through it. The others had exactly the same thoughts.

Once he was alone with the Enchantress, Lochen took a small vial from a pocket inside his robes. He removed the cork and poured a few drops onto her lips, and then returned the potion to his pocket. Stella listlessly ran her tongue over her lips where the drops of liquid sat, and then took a sharp deep breath. Her eyes fluttered and she woke up almost instantly.

"How long was I asleep?" she asked.

"Not long," he told her. "Do you understand your visions?"

There was an urgency in his voice that she could feel, and which she suddenly shared.

"Yes, I think so. Do you?"

"Yes. They filled in some gaps for me and verified what I was able to discover in reading the ancient myths of my people. This may be worse than I had initially thought. We have a very difficult and dangerous journey ahead of us."

She reached up and put a finger to the side of his head, reading his thoughts. He waited patiently until she had finished.

"It's him, isn't it?" she asked.

"I believe so," Lochen answered.

"Do you think the others are ready for this undertaking?" Stella asked him.

"It doesn't really matter if they are ready or not. If we don't act, we'll perish. Having such few options makes the decision much easier. I've suggested that they get some rest so that we can start early in the morning. I would like to spend the rest of the time with you planning on the best approach and gathering needed supplies. Do you need to rest?"

"I have no need for sleep. We can begin immediately," she answered as he helped her to her feet. "How much do you plan on telling the others about what you know?"

"Not very much. At least not right away. I'll share with them enough to keep them going. Too much may discourage them. I know the courage of my Princess well enough, but the faerie and the forest creature are unknown to me. I'm sure their hearts are in the right place, but their resolve is as yet untested."

"I agree. So, where do we go first?"

Lochen thought a minute, and then replied, "We need to locate the Pathfinder."

"Can he be trusted?" she asked. "I know very little about him, other than that he lives as a recluse."

"His people have suffered more than each of ours. I have heard from my spies that he has refused to submit to the forces that we will likely face, and that in spite of all the dangers, he still resides in the Venomous Swamps."

"That means to reach him, we will have to cross the Devil's Desert to find him. You're right. Our journey is going to be very perilous. We'd better begin our preparations. Should we use transporter stones? If time is of the essence, they will shorten our travel."

"I think not.  That land is far too uncharted and unknown.  Control of the transporter stones is much too difficult to ensure safe arrivals.  As much as we need to hurry, it is more important that we all reach our destination together.  You were correct.  Not only is your Princess necessary for our success, so are the others.  I don't know how, at this point.  I just know that they are."

"Yes," Stella agreed.  "I sense that, too."

The Sorcerer and the Enchantress went off to gather what they needed for their journey.  Early the next morning, Natalie gathered everyone else.  She had looked for Lochen and Stella, but hadn't found them.  They would have to fend for themselves, she thought.  She led everyone to the kitchen and to pass the time until they had to leave, and to ease the tensions, she was telling them about the history of the coral castle and the bubble.

During the conversation, it was obvious to her that Summer was somewhat distracted.

"I can tell something is bothering you.  What is it?" she asked.

"I'm just thinking about my home and all those who had been turned to stone.  I hope what we're about to do will help bring them back."

Natalie thought a minute before she answered.  She lowered her head to look closely at Summer.

"I believe the Sorcerer and the Enchantress know more than they are telling us," she said.  "I think they're worried that we won't have the courage to face the dangers ahead, and I'm sure that there will be dangers.  However, I have complete trust in them to lead us in the right direction and find the means to set things right.  We have to trust and support them and each other."

Summer ran these thoughts over in her head as she recalled the images that filled her head the night before as she fell asleep.  In her dreams she saw a mixture of competing visions. She felt like she was running across a vast wasteland, all the time being chased by a beast she couldn't quite make out. At first she was so hot she felt like she was on fire, then she felt colder than she could ever remember. She saw Solveig get swept across a frozen lake, unable to stop until she disappeared over the horizon. The images were accompanied by a howling like a pack of wild, lost dogs. Finally, she heard the wind calling her name over and over again, until she realized it was Natalie, who had come to wake her up. Her reverie was broken by Solveig's voice.

"It's time," she said. "The others are waiting for us."

They hurried down to the courtyard where they found Lochen and Stella. They were each given dark clothing, and fully loaded packs to carry on their backs. Once they had changed and secured their back packs, Lochen led them over to what looked like a small boat, except that it wasn't sitting in water; it was leaning to one side right there on the sand of the court yard.

"What's that?" Summer asked.

"That's our transportation. At least for the first leg of our trip," Lochen answered.

"Why can't we use one of those transporting stone that brought you here?" asked Solveig.

"Because we don't have enough for everyone, and besides, without knowing exactly where we're going, we could end up on the edge of a cliff, or in the middle of a lake, or surrounded by wild animals," Lochen explained.

"OK," Summer replied. "But how are we going to get that boat back to the top of the water?"

"Leave that to me," answered Stella. "Just get on board and make yourselves comfortable."

"Water?" groused Sean. "Again? Who can get comfortable with that thought?"

Summer and Natalie climbed in on one side, and Solveig and Sean sat along the other side of the boat, holding on tightly to their seats. Lochen sat in the bow and Stella was in the stern. When everyone was situated, Stella spun her hand around in a circle above her head and a large bubble formed around the boat. As the bubble began to rise, the boat gently straightened and the passengers spread themselves out, peering over the side. The bubble climbed higher and higher inside the larger bubble that enclosed the sprites' village and buildings. It then eased through the larger bubble and floated upward, surrounded completely by the Sea. When this happened, Sean began a long low moan, and closed his eyes, murmuring about all that water.

"Please don't break. Please don't break," he muttered as the small bubble climbed higher and higher.

The bubble rose faster and faster and finally broke the surface. As soon as the boat emerged from the water, the bubble disappeared and the boat bobbed up and down like a cork, eventually settling down. They were surrounded by water. Sean reached out both arms and hugged the mast in the center of the boat. He lifted his head up far enough to look around in all directions. With no land in sight, he again moaned slightly, dropped down to the floor of the boat, crawled slowly to the center of the boat and hunkered down.

"Is something wrong?" Lochen asked him.

"I don't like water," Sean answered abruptly. "I'm all right with streams and brooks, and rain's all right, but if I can't touch the bottom, I try to stay away from it."

Lochen just nodded. He then stepped over Sean, reached in between Sean's arms and raised a sail. He looked at the sky, and announced that they would sail towards the west. He asked Sean if he would be able to steer the boat.

"Me?" he asked. "Do I have to move?"

"Just a little," answered Lochen. "And you won't have to look at the water. I just need you to keep your eyes on the sail and make sure it stays filled with the wind."

Sean crab-walked to the back of the boat, nudged Stella out of the way, took hold of the tiller, sat on the floor and kept his eyes fixed on the sail. This seemed to calm him somewhat. The rest of the day passed uneventfully. Every once in a while a fish broke the surface of the water startling Sean, but other than that, they saw no other signs of life. At nightfall Lochen announced a schedule for everyone to sleep while someone continued to steer and keep watch. Sean declared that he was not tired and would keep steering, but he didn't object to someone keeping him company on watch.

At first the night sea was not much different than it had been all day long. But a few hours after midnight, the waves began to swell, and the wind became much stronger. Even in the darkness they could tell a storm was moving in. Solveig was keeping the watch with Sean and commented on the sudden shift in the weather.

"Do you think this is normal, or has Ena Ray found us?"

"Well," he answered, "I don't know what's normal and what's not, but this looks more like an ordinary storm. I don't see the same flashes of lightning or hear that roaring thunder like before. But maybe you better wake the others, just in case."

By now the boat was riding the waves like a roller coaster. It almost seemed to leave the water when it reached the top of one wave and then sank like a stone as it dropped to the bottom. Sean struggled to keep the tiller from swinging wildly. Solveig stood up to move towards the front of the boat just as it caught an upward wave. She reached for the mast to steady herself, but was thrown to the back and lost her balance. As she was falling backward, Sean let go of the tiller to reach out for her. Without his hand steadying the tiller, the boat took a sharp turn throwing Solveig in a different direction.

As fast as he was, he wasn't quite fast enough. A large wave swept her over the side, crashing down on the deck of the boat, soaking Sean. He shouted her name again, and then, without a second thought, he tied off the tiller and jumped overboard after her. He wasn't sure where she had fallen and just jumped where he had last seen her. The water was black as ink, and so was the night.

Summer had been nestled in a lamp house at the top of the mast. The radical swaying back and forth had shaken her awake, bouncing her from one side of the lamp house to the other. She became fully alert when she heard Sean shout. She leaned against the glass of the lamp and looked out at the menacing sea, and then down at Sean. She could barely make him out in the darkness, but she saw enough to see him jump into the sea.

Just as she was climbing down the mast line, she noticed that Lochen, Natalie and Stella had awoken. They were holding onto the sides of the boat as Lochen made his way back towards the tiller.

"What happened," shouted Lochen. "Where's Sean?"

"He jumped in," Summer shouted back.

"Are you sure he wasn't washed over?" Natalie asked.

Yes, I'm sure," Summer answered. "He jumped."

"I thought he was afraid of water," shouted Natalie.

"He is," Summer said. "I don't know what got into him. He was there, and then he just jumped."

The rocking had settled down somewhat, now that Lochen had secured the tiller, but she was holding tightly to Natalie's sleeve. She looked at the worried expression on Natalie's face and then turned back to look at Stella and Solveig.

"Where's Solveig?" she shouted. The ship was tiny and there was no place for her to be out of sight. "Solveig's gone."

"She must have fallen overboard," said Stella. "He went in after her."

Lochen made a throwing motion with his right arm and shouted the word "shine." Off in the distance and behind them a glowing light appeared several feet below the surface of the water. Lochen turned the ship to pull alongside of the glow. By the radiance cast off by the light, they were able to see Sean swimming. He turned and headed towards the light. As he got closer to its source, he dove under the water. He seemed to be gone far too long, but eventually he burst through the surface, coughing and gasping for breath. In his arms he had brought the light with him. The light, as it turned out, was an aura that surrounded Solveig's body. The spell Lochen had cast turned the aura into a beacon for Sean to follow. He had Solveig in one of his arms, but she wasn't moving. He was kicking and pulling with his free arm to keep his head above the waves.

Stella quickly grabbed a piece of rope from the deck of the boat and shouted an incantation. The rope began to move out over the water straight towards Sean and Solveig. Once it reached them it wrapped itself around their waists and began to pull them back to the boat. As they got within reach, the others pulled them into the boat. Natalie waved her hands in a circular motion. Warm blankets appeared and were wrapped around the swimmers.

Stella and Lochen took Solveig from Sean's arms and stretched her out on the deck of the boat. Lochen felt her neck for a pulse and then slowly waved his hand along a line from her waist to her head. Solveig gasped and, spitting out a mouthful of water, took a deep breath.

"What happened," she sputtered.

"It appears you decided to go for a swim," answered Lochen. He turned to Sean and added, "and this forest creature thought it would be a good idea to join you."

"I thought you didn't like water," Summer said to Sean.

"I hate it, but it didn't look like the Princess was having fun. I thought I had better help her out," Sean replied, shivering and a bit breathless.

Solveig sat up and Natalie moved next to her, putting her arms around to help dry and warm her. Summer staggered over to Sean and started to chastise him for being so foolhardy.

"Are you crazy?" she asked. "You both could have been lost."

In spite of her words, the concern in her voice was evident.

As the others were preoccupied, Stella leaned over to Lochen and whispered, "I guess his resolve has been tested. I don't think his courage will fail when faced with danger."

Lochen nodded but kept silent. Stella moved over to join Natalie and Solveig. Lochen, still holding the tiller told Sean that what he did was very brave.

"I'm not sure about brave," Sean replied. "In fact, I was scared to death. Please don't tell the others. I couldn't even look at what I was doing. I just jumped."

"It's easy to be brave when one's not afraid. Real bravery occurs when we face our most dreaded fears," Lochen said. "Don't treat your actions lightly. Your lodge would be proud of you. We are all proud of you – and grateful."

After a second or two, Lochen added, "I am especially grateful to you."

Lochen reached over and put his arm on Sean's shoulder and told him to stay warm and to get some rest. As the night turned into day, the storm blew itself out and the Sea returned to the calm of the day before. Lochen was still at the tiller as the others awoke, one by one. By midday the first sight of land rose on the horizon. Shortly before the trail, or second, sun set, the small group arrived at the mouth of a river. They steered the boat into the delta and made for land. The shore was muddy and covered with tall grass and cattails. They were able to wedge the boat into the mud. Lochen extended his arm and several rocks rose to the surface of the mud, creating a walkway for them to cross to drier land.

Summer flew ahead a few yards and found a clearing that would make a suitable place for camp. Stella pointed to the ground and a campfire sprung up. She waved her arm in a circle around the fire, and one of the backpacks flipped open and began to unfold. Two large tents popped out and arranged themselves around the fire. One of the tents was large enough for Lochen and Sean, and the other big enough for Summer, Solveig, Stella and Natalie.

Stella spun her finger in a circle and another backpack flipped open and began to unfold. Sleeping bags sprung out and slid into the tents. She looked at the others who were watching, and then back at the sleeping bags.

"No," she said, "That just won't do."

She snapped her fingers and the sleeping bags turned into thick, down filled mattresses and large cots.

"That's better," she said, smiling.

In the meantime, Lochen had conjured up a large pot that hung over the fire. The aroma from the pot had everyone's mouth watering.

"That smells great," said Summer. "What is it?"

"Conch chowder," said Lochen.

"Chowder? Really?" asked Solveig. "Don't you think we could use something more substantial?"

Lochen thought a minute and said, "Yes. I suppose you're right."

He waved a hand and asked, "Beef stew? Would that be better?"

"Yes," they all agreed.

They ate dinner and talked a while about Solveig's experience and Sean's bravery in jumping in after her. Before long, they were all quite sleepy. No one had noticed any signs of wildlife in the area, but Lochen thought it wise to cast a protective spell around the camp and told them all to get some sleep. In spite of the protective spell, he remained awake on guard. As the night settled in, he gazed at the stars and those planets he could see with the naked eye.

Even without being able to see the others, he knew exactly where they were positioned. He calculated how much time was left before they all would be in alignment. He hoped they would be able to learn their final destination and reach it in time. He still wasn't sure exactly where they were going, or what was supposed to happen when they arrived, but he sensed they were headed in the right direction. He made a mental note to confer with Stella. He had known much about Enchantresses, but had never met one with her power. He was certain that even she was unaware of the extent of it.

Shortly after the lead sun rose, Lochen conjured up what he thought would make an appropriate breakfast. Personally, he seldom ate at regular intervals, and sometimes not at all for long periods of time. He was aware, however, that others could not survive such eating habits. At dawn, when the trail sun emerged over the horizon, the smell of bacon and eggs woke everyone up and brought them out of their tents to the camp fire.

They all had slept soundly. Lochen had ensured that with a potion he had placed in the stew. He normally didn't like doing such things, especially not to his friends, but the previous day had been harrowing and their immediate future would be no less stressful. They needed to rest as much as they could – whenever they could. When they had finished eating, Lochen explained where they would be going on the next leg of their journey.

"We are in search of a person called The Pathfinder."

"Who's he?" asked Sean.

"He's reputed to be able to find anything just about anywhere. If we're to find this Crystal Citadel, he just may be the one to lead us there. That is our ultimate destination. I am certain that the storm that has left a trail of destruction is connected in some way to Ena Ray. The key to defeating the power of this storm is inextricably tied to defeating Ena Ray, and ensuring he remains imprisoned within the Citadel – the exact place to which he has been banished. The way there, however, is likely to be hidden by false leads and mazes. We could easily get lost and die or go mad."

"You said he's reputed to be able to find anything just about anywhere" asked Summer. "You mean you don't know this person?"

"Oh, no," said Lochen. "I've never met him."

"Then how do you know you can trust him?" Summer persisted.

Lochen thought a minute before answering.

"The Pathfinder is the last of his kind. From what I've been able to discover, around the time it is assumed that Ena Ray was banished, it is possible that his followers were exiled to the underworld. If so, it is also probable that they entered through a portal hidden in the Swamp. At that time the Swamp was the home to hundreds of different kinds of animals and some of the most beautiful plants and flowers in the world. The Pathfinder's people took care of the plants and animals and lived in harmony with them. Something caused life in the Swamp to change.

"Over time, the Swamp became poisoned and a home to some of the most dangerous and violent creatures known. The legends indicate that these creatures were guardians to the portal through which these banished followers were driven. However, these same creatures that were created to guard the portal also destroyed the home of the Pathfinder's people, and over time, destroyed the people themselves, except for the Pathfinder, who managed to escape. Obtaining his help will not be difficult. Locating him will."

"Wait a minute," interjected Summer. "You keep referring to legends and what you've discovered. We only met you a few days ago and you didn't seem to know about all of this then. When did you have the time to refer to these so called legends and do this so called discovering?"

Lochen looked a bit puzzled.

"Mostly while you were sleeping, I suppose."

Summer put her hands on her hips, flew up and fluttered directly in front of him.

"I'm small," she said. "Not stupid. We left your mountain in the blink of an eye and then we were on that boat. How did you do all this research while we were supposedly asleep? Did you fly back to your library?"

"No," Lochen laughed. "That would be ridiculous. I brought much of my research with me."

Summer just stared at him waiting for him to explain.

Seeing that this explanation was not sufficient, Lochen reached into a pocket in his sleeve and pulled out a narrow roll of paper about six inches long and a inch in diameter.

"That's your library?" Summer asked dubiously.

Seeing that she was still not satisfied he said to her, "You may want to move."

"I'm not going anywhere," she answered defiantly.

"Have it your way," he said.

He placed the scroll on the palm of his left hand and pointed his right index finger at it and said, "Unroll."

The scroll rose slightly off his palm and widened to double in size and began to spew one long roll of paper out. After a few seconds, hundreds of yards of parchment had flown off the scroll, burying Summer, who had declined to get out of the way.

"Oh," she said, muffled under the pile of paper.

"So where do we have to go to find him?" asked Sean to break the tension, as Lochen ordered the scroll to reroll.

"My last reports indicate that he was in the area of the Venomous Swamp."

"Aren't we in the Swamp now?" asked Solveig.

"No. We're a long way from the Swamp. We will have to cross the Devil's Desert to get there. And to anticipate your next questions, no, we can't use magic to cross the desert. I'm afraid that once we begin our journey, our magical powers will be greatly diminished. We are entering areas that are protected or guarded by various spells, or have spells cast to detect the use of magic. Enjoy this repast. Once we break this camp that will be the last time we use any magic. From this point on we will have to be on our guard all the time. As we travel through the jungle and across the Desert, any use of what little magic power we have is likely to alert our enemies to our location. After today, we must be very judicious in its use. Once we enter the Swamp, other enchantments that have been placed on the Swamp will make the use of magic almost impossible."

They all sat in silence as they thought about Lochen's words. Finally he announced that it was time to go. With a clap of a hand and a wave of an arm, the camp was cleared up as if no one had ever been there. He asked Summer to fly ahead to see which path led to the stream that created the mouth of the river along which they had camped. Then he led the rest of them into the jungle.

# Chapter seven

Summer had managed to find a path towards a clearing, but before long the path disappeared and they were back in the thick of the jungle, crawling under giant leaves and over vines. The temperature had risen considerably even before midday, and continued to climb. Soon it was very hot, even though they were under the shade of the surrounding trees. Sometimes the ground was solid - hard, cracked dirt - but then for no particular reason, it would get soft and muddy. Sean said he had seen this happen in his own forest. Water from the streams seeped into underground channels and springs.

His explanation didn't make the traveling any easier. They would sink in the mud up to their knees, making walking harder and harder. Every time they pulled a foot out of the mud, it was caked and heavy. The air that was trapped in among the vegetation was hot and humid. Their clothes were soaked through with sweat and clung uncomfortably to their bodies. It didn't take long before they were exhausted. Even Summer was quickly tiring. She had been flying ahead and returning to report. The repeated trips back and forth were taking their toll on her. Soon her wings were drooping and the humidity was hanging on her like a heavy wet cloak. They needed to stop frequently to clean the mud from themselves, to rest, and to drink some water.

As it got hotter, gnats and mosquitoes began buzzing around their heads. For the others this was an irritating nuisance. For Summer, they were the size of birds that would peck at her and chase her. Her left wing had taken the brunt of an attack by one of the more aggressive mosquitoes. It had a large tear in it that would take a few days to repair itself. It would go a lot faster if she could have used faerie dust. As it was, though, she had to put more strain on the good wing, and she flew a bit off kilter.

More than once a number of the pesky insects ganged up on her and chased her through the jungle. The dodging in and around the vegetation had little success and quickly had her gasping for breath. She was finally able to escape by blending into her surroundings and disappearing from sight. It took all her effort to control her breathing and to maintain the camouflage until her attackers got bored and left.

As she was hiding, she remembered what Lochen said about using any magical powers. She panicked for a second, but then rationalized that making herself change colors and blend in with the jungle didn't use much in the way of magical power. It wasn't like casting a spell or conjuring up fire. Besides, she couldn't keep running and hiding from the insects that were after her, especially with a damaged wing.

Once the attackers had gone off to find other prey, she continued her reconnaissance. However, a few miles away a giant, black beast that was asleep in its lair, subconsciously picked up a tingling in its sensors. It was a ferocious black panther taking a midday nap. Even asleep, it was sensitive to its surroundings. Suddenly it could feel the presence of an intruder. Without moving any other part of his body, his eyelids popped open revealing a pair of deep yellow eyes rimmed in blood red. Slowly he raised his head and sniffed the air. His giant head swung one way and then back the other as he picked up the direction of the scent. His whiskers twitched as he sensed the distant use of magic – Summer's magic. In absolute silence, he sprang to his feet and began to move in the direction of the scent. His head hung low and the muscles in his legs and along his shoulders rippled as he picked up speed.

Not far away, the travelers had been climbing a long hill that ran parallel to a stream. An opening in the foliage began to take them higher, but away from the water. They had opted for following the slightest of paths instead of struggling with the undergrowth that hugged the stream. The grade had become quite steep and the heat was quickly wringing the energy out of their bodies. Lochen had pushed them on telling them that as soon as they reached the top of the hill they could rest. Summer had scouted ahead and assured them that they didn't have too much further to go.

The narrow path curved to the right into a small clearing just as it crested the hill. Their respite was visible to those in the front of the line. Before any of them could stop and sit down they discovered they had come face to face with an enormous black panther. It had come up from behind them and then swung around to position itself in front of them. It had been waiting for them, hidden under some low branches.

Surprised at seeing so many intruders, the cat hesitated after it jumped from behind the branches and growled at them. It stood there ominously, waiting to see which one would run first. It was crouched low in position to spring at a moment's notice, but no one moved.

"Everyone be still. This might be a time to use magic, but let's wait and see if he just goes away," Lochen advised. He didn't really think the panther was going to leave, but he didn't want everyone with magical powers to each be casting different spells. It would be nothing but chaos.

As they all stood there frozen and staring, Sean slowly pulled his sling shot from his belt and loaded it with a stone from a pouch he carried. His gaze was fixed on his target and his movements were imperceptible. And then with one quick, fluid motion he pulled back and let the stone sail. It shot straight as an arrow, and made a dull thudding sound as it struck the panther in its left eye. The cat let out a horrendous roar, dropped its head down and covered the eye with its paw. While it was caught off guard, Sean yelled for everyone to run.

"Run to the left," shouted Lochen. "Head for the river."

They turned to the left and scrambled behind the cover of the bushes, running towards the water. They soon found themselves at edge of the river, but at the top of a deep water fall, instead of near an embankment as Lochen had hoped. The current of the river at the top of the falls was too strong for them to cross. Lochen looked furtively for an escape route, while Summer flew down the edge of the water fall and discovered some stones that ran behind the falls.

"Come this way," she called to them. "Be careful. There's not much room, but you may be able to squeeze behind the falls and cross over to the other side. Step carefully, though. The stones are covered with moss and are probably slippery."

She showed them the way, and once the last one had started to cross, she flew back to look for the panther. She didn't have to go far. He was right behind Stella who was at the end of the line, as she stepped behind the falls. Summer dove down and picked up some sand from the shore near the riverbed and flew as close as possible to the panther's face. She buzzed around much like the gnats and mosquitoes that had plagued her. The panther followed her movement closely, and then, in the blink of an eye, she blew the sand into his face.

Some of it went up his nose, and the rest of it flew into his one good eye. He sneezed and roared, and then sneezed and roared again, swiping one of his massive paws blindly at Summer. The razor sharp claw sliced through the air, narrowly missing her, but snagging on the edge of her clothes. The panther flicked his paw and Summer was thrown several feet until she crashed against the side of a tree.

She slid semi-conscious to the jungle floor. The panther, growling in a low voice crept towards Summer, his fangs glistening. His one good eye was watering extensively, and his vision was blurred, but clear enough to see where Summer had fallen. Just as he was inches away from her he felt a sharp sting in his ear canal. Sean had struck again. This time the small stone was lodged in the panther's ear.  He shook his head, but the stone didn't budge.  He clawed at the blockage and shook his head some more, but was unable to loosen the stone.  While he was rolling around and bellowing, trying to get it out, Summer regained her senses, sprung up and flew across the river to join the others.

Sean stood there triumphantly, almost taunting the panther that just glared at him from across the river, still trying to clear its eye and dislodge the stone.

"You bought us some time," said Lochen, "but not much.  He won't give up that easily and all you've done is made him madder.  We need to keep moving."

The stone finally fell from the panther's ear and the sand had cleared from its eye.  He quickly spotted the fleeing prey and had already started moving upstream looking for a place to cross.  The travelers moved deeper into the jungle, away from the river, but still climbing upward. Once they felt it was safe, they stopped to rest.

"I wonder how that panther found us," Solveig wondered aloud.  "I thought we were pretty quiet and I don't think any of us was using magic."

Summer had been unusually quiet.  She realized that she was probably the reason the panther was able to locate them.  Finally she said, "It may have been me." She looked up guiltily and quickly added, "I was changing my colors to blend in with the background to get away from the insects."

Lochen became enraged and shouted at her, "I told you not to use magic."

He looked around at the ground and then reached down and wiped some mud from his feet.  He took three quick long strides over to where she was sitting on a stump and smeared it all over her.

"That would have kept the insects away from you," he said angrily.

"But I can't fly with all this mud on me," Summer protested, sputtering through the mud that dripped from her head and covered her body.

Lochen picked her up and stuffed her in the backpack that Natalie was carrying, so that only her head stuck up.

"There," he announced. "That takes care of your need to fly."

"How dare you grab me like that," she shouted – more embarrassed than insulted. "I am a Princess of the Faeries. You have no right to treat me this way."

"You were almost a dead Princess of the Faeries," Lochen shouted back. "And you almost got the rest of us killed right along with you. And don't think that panther is done with us yet."

He stomped off while everyone else stared in shock, not knowing what to say. Their initial reaction was that Lochen had been too hard on Summer. Then the adrenalin wore off and the close brush with death finally sank in. Then they weren't so sure anymore.

Summer was deeply ashamed to be stuffed into a backpack and carried like a lump of cheese. She was equally ashamed to have done something that put everyone in such danger. What made matters worse was that deep inside, she knew Lochen was right, and the silence that greeted her from everyone else told her that they thought so, too. She felt like crying, but she was so mad that she just turned away and pulled the flap of the backpack over her head.

As the travelers continued their hike, they would rotate, taking turns being in the front of the line. Consequently, much of the time, Summer was facing whoever was behind Natalie in line. Watching them struggle along the path while she rode in a back pack made her feel even worse. At first she thought that couldn't be possible, but as the day wore on and each hiker she faced looked more worn out than the one before her just made her feel more and more depressed with each step.

The fact that there was no one to scout ahead to find the easiest path also meant that the group often had to double back over ground they had already covered, because they had run into a dead end or a passage too dangerous to attempt.  Her anger and misery, combined with the stagnant air inside the backpack sapped her strength.  Eventually, that and the rocking motion in Natalie's stride made Summer drowsy, and she fell asleep.

From the depths of her sleep, something startled her awake.  It was nothing specific that she actually heard, but more something she sensed. The hairs on the back of her neck were standing on end.  Danger was near, something was shouting to her.  She struggled to lift the flap of the back pack off her head, but Natalie's must have shifted something while Summer was asleep, and she was too off-balance to lift it completely. Natalie's gait was also jostling her around.  Just when she got her footing, Natalie would adjust the straps on the backpack, jerking it one way or another and covering Summer in whatever it was Natalie had stuffed in the bag.

She struggled to the top of the pile and gave the cover another shove.  It flew up and she was able to create a fold in the material just enough to peek out.  No one was behind Natalie.  They were at the end of the line, with everybody else in front of them.  In the corner of her eye, she saw a flicker of movement through the bushes for just a second.

In a panic, she tried to get her feet under her and to lift the flap completely off her head, but the angle that Natalie was climbing up the hill kept pushing the other contents of the back pack on top of Summer. She pushed with all her might and got another quick glimpse from under the flap.  What she saw made her blood freeze.  Her vision zoomed in like a telescope on a pair of eyes moving directly towards her.  One eye was deep yellow rimmed in red, and the other was the milky white of the stone Sean had shot into it.  The panther was right behind them and coming quickly.

Summer shouted, but her shouts were muffled. She fought to move the contents blocking her from the opening of the pack. She pulled herself up to the edge and pushed the flap back again to see that the panther had started its attack run and was bounding through the bushes. It was now close enough that Summer knew it wouldn't make any difference if Natalie heard it, she would never be able to outrun him.

With one more herculean effort, Summer gave it everything she had and finally pushed the flap up enough to squeeze out. She shot free and almost flew into the snapping jaws of the panther, bouncing off its nose and up into the air. It was enough to distract him from Natalie. Summer quickly reached into the pouch on her belt and grabbed a handful of faerie dust. She didn't care if this was magic or not, she had no choice. She threw the dust into the panther's face, just as it was about to pounce on Natalie's back.

The panther froze in mid air and dropped like a rock. The sound of the cat landing in the brush was enough for Natalie to realize what was happening. She spun around long enough to see the threat, and then turned back to run for her life. The panther turned its head to see Natalie escaping. Summer took advantage of this shift in its attention, and flew into the panther's face again. This time stuck her fist into its one good eye. The panther howled and swiped a paw, narrowly missing Summer. She ducked and spun, flying under its snapping jaw and back into his face to poke its other eye.

The panther flashed its razor sharp claws, scratching its own face as it missed Summer. She dodged the heavy paw and reached into her pouch again. She blew more faerie dust into his nose. He roared and sneezed and swiped at her. She flew backwards a little bit and then shot forward, taunting him. He snapped his huge jaws and one of his whiskers struck her wings, spinning her to the ground. She landed with a thud and quickly skittered backwards away from him.

He pounced, slamming his paw down, but not quite fast enough. She shot out from under him, soared into the air and then dive-bombed him once again. By now he was in a rage, roaring at her, snapping his jaws and swinging his claws at her. She moved in and backed away in rapid succession, each time changing the direction of her attack and retreat, infuriating him. Every time he jumped she dodged – barely staying out of his reach. One time his claw cut into her already damaged wing, throwing her off balance. With one wing shredded even more than before, she was not as fast in moving away from him. He was getting closer each time he lunged for her.

She continued to fly backwards through the jungle, daring him to attack, drawing him further and further away from her friends. She only hoped they had made it to safety. She was getting tired, and wasn't sure how much longer she could sustain this diversion. The heat of the jungle, the fear that ate at her, and her damaged wing were all taking their toll. She knew she wouldn't be able to keep this up, and she was backing herself into undergrowth that further confined her movements.

She was now in a dense thicket. She took furtive looks around her, keeping a close eye on the panther. She knew where she was. She recalled the others had to turn back from this area not too long ago. She fluttered backwards away from the latest swipe of the panther's paw and felt a wall of vegetation behind her. Just then the panther knew he had her trapped. She was backed up against a tangle of vines. He crouched, focused his one good eye on her, watching her struggle to find an escape and then lunged.

At the last possible second, Summer dropped to the ground like a rock, instead of flying to the right, or left or up, as she had previously. The panther hadn't expected that and he jumped just over her head, snapping and swiping at her as he sailed over her, crashing through the vines. He kept his eye fixed and glaring at the escaping prey and didn't see what was on the other side of the tangle he had just jumped through.

Summer had backed her way to the edge of a deep gorge. The panther's lunge carried him through the vines at the edge of a steep cliff. As he flew out over the gorge, he realized he had been tricked and scrambled to turn himself around. But he had been too powerful and too heavy to stop himself and the gorge was too wide for him to reach the other side. His massive paws flailed in the air as he dropped several hundred feet to the rocks below. Summer sat sprawled on the jungle floor, exhausted.

The others rushed up to her, looking over the edge at the vanquished panther. Lochen saw the remains of the attacker, the gaping hole in the vines and the limp, wrung out form of the bedraggled Faerie Princess. He bent down and gently picked her up. With a flourish of his hand and a mumbled incantation, he repaired her damaged wing, and wrapped her in a cocoon of cool, breezy air.

"If I may be permitted, Princess," he said to her in a gentle voice. "I ask you to do me the honor of allowing me to carry you so that you can rest."

Without waiting for her answer, he placed her in the folds of his hood. It was like riding in a hammock. The spell in which she was wrapped made it feel like the breezes on the shores of her home. In a few minutes, she was sound asleep and only woke long after the group had stopped to make camp for the evening.

When she finally opened her eyes, she found it was night and she was nestled comfortably next to the campfire. There was a bowl with something that smelled wonderful in it right next to her. She assumed it was meant for her and she ate heartily. When she was done, she noticed that the others had all gone to bed, except for Lochen and her.

"I want to apologize to you for getting angry earlier," he said. "My reaction was completely uncalled for."

"There's no need to apologize. You were right. In fact, I owe you the apology. I didn't think about your warning against using magic. Well, maybe I did think about it, but I didn't take it seriously."

She smiled at him and then, looking guilty, added, "I'm afraid I ignored your instructions again when the panther attacked."

"Under the circumstances that's quite understandable," he laughed. "It seems I, too, ignored my own instructions. I suppose it's our nature to use the gifts we've been given, and it's hard to go against our very nature."

She agreed, but then said, "Somehow I don't think that panther will be the most fearsome thing we'll be seeing. Is it?"

He thought a while before answering. "You acted quite bravely. I'm sorry I ever had any doubts about you. And, yes, to answer your question, we will be facing some similar, and most likely, more sinister dangers as we continue on our journey; some of which I can't even imagine. Each of us will be put to the test. I know I can count on you no matter what we come up against. I hope you have the same trust in me."

"I never doubted you for a second," Summer answered.

Lochen smiled at her response. "Thank you, Your Highness. I'm not sure I deserve that level of faith, but I certainly treasure it, and will do all in my power to live up to it."

They sat and talked for several hours. He told her about life in the granite palace and she told him about her family and friends along the shore of the Cerulean Sea. He pointed out various constellations and planets that were visible through the forest cover, and she regaled him with life in her village. Before they knew it the first morning sun was rising and the others were waking up. One by one, they emerged from their tents and joined them.

They all asked each other if they slept well and acknowledged that the exertion of the previous day's trek and the excitement of the panther had been very effective sedatives. All had slept soundly, and thanked Lochen for taking the watch. Summer wondered when the last time was that Lochen had slept and asked him that very question.

"Oh, I think it was on Middleweek."

"That was four days ago," she said. She was shocked. She thought it been only been a day or a day and a half at most that he had been without sleep. She had no idea it had been four days.

"Four days?" he said questioningly. "No. That doesn't sound right."

She didn't think so, either. She thought back to four days ago and couldn't recall him sleeping then, either. She pointed this out to him.

"Yes, I think you're right" he said. "It couldn't have been Middleweek four days ago. I believe it was Middleweek three weeks past."

"Aren't you tired?" she asked, not sure she believed him.

"Not yet. Sorcerers are able to go for long periods of time without sleep – weeks; even months on rare occasions. But when we finally do close our eyes, almost nothing will awaken us. We have to be very careful. Because we sleep so deeply, we are vulnerable to attack from our enemies. Often times we must find secret places to sleep, just to be safe. You can't imagine some of the places we go. Fortunately, we only need an hour or so of rest and then we're good as new."

Stella came up to them both and asked to join them.

"By all means," said Lochen.

She sat down and turned to Summer.

"I haven't thanked you yet for saving the life of my Princess – for saving all our lives."

Summer tried to deflect the compliment, "No, don't thank me. I almost got you all killed."

She looked at Lochen and then back to Stella, and added, "Lochen was right to be angry – well, maybe not to stuff me in a backpack." She stole a quick glance at the Sorcerer and quickly continued, "No – even that was the right thing to do. I wasn't being responsible."

"Don't be modest," Stella contradicted her. "I am glad to be traveling with friends such as you and Sean. Your bravery will make us all strong. We will need all of our courage in the days ahead. Especially since where we're going, our magical powers will be limited and we'll be facing a foe like none we've ever encountered."

Summer turned to Lochen and gave him an inquisitive look.

"You two have already discussed this, haven't you?" she asked.

He exchanged looks with Stella and then said to Summer, "I think we should bring everyone together to explain our plans. As you have so correctly stated, we will need to trust each other with our lives. It is important that we all know the risks ahead and what's at stake."

With everyone gathered, Lochen began by apologizing for not sharing everything at the onset.

"We really don't know each other – some of us not at all. It is difficult to establish a high level of trust in one another without having a history with each other. That's not an excuse for being secretive, though. It's an explanation; so let's just leave it at that. I have had some strong premonitions long before we had the pleasure of the arrival of Summer and Sean. Those premonitions were confirmed with Stella's visions in the Sanctorum."

Stella reminded them of what they all had seen when Sean's armband was placed on her head. She then explained what she and Lochen had understood from those visions. With that as the background, Lochen explained the journey ahead, as far as he knew it.

"There are still large gaps in all this. I think it's clear we need to get to the Crystal Citadel. It is my hope that we are able to locate the Pathfinder and that he will lead us the rest of the way. We will soon be out of the jungle and faced with crossing the Devil's Desert."

"How long will we be in the Desert?" asked Solveig.

"No reliable maps exist to be able to answer that question. Most travelers and explorers have opted by going around the Desert – either far to the east, sailing the Cerulean Sea, or far to the west crossing the forests, jungles and mountains in that direction. Unfortunately, either of those courses would take us far too long."

"Do you know where to find the Pathfinder?" asked Sean.

"No," replied Lochen. "But we will be venturing into his domain. I expect he will quickly become aware of our presence and will seek us out; even if he only views us as trespassers."

"Oh, great," moaned Sean. "So the guy we're looking for may think we're a threat?"

"I don't think so," said Stella. "I don't have that sense."

"But you don't know for sure," countered Sean.

"No," said Lochen. "We don't know for sure. In fact, the further we go, the less and less we know for sure. What we do know for sure is that there is an evil force that has emerged and needs to be stopped. With what we know, this seems to be the best plan forward."

"So what happens if we find the Pathfinder, and if he agrees to lead us to the Crystal Citadel?" pressed Sean.

"We will have to decide that as it presents itself," answered Lochen. "If you're looking for clear cut answers, I don't have any. None of us do. Nor do any of us have a better suggestion for returning the faeries and the forest creatures of your homes to you."

Summer and Sean looked at each other as the silence in the group lingered.

"OK," Sean said with finality. "I just wanted to know where we were going. I'm in."

"Me, too," announced Summer.

Solveig and Natalie nodded agreement and it was decided. Shortly before midday the group resumed its trek. Summer resumed her duties and flew ahead as scout while the others rotated the lead as they had the day before. They were all a little more alert and a lot more aware of the risks of using any of their magical powers. In spite of the uncertainty of their plan and the threats that awaited them, there was a confidence and determination in their steps. About an hour before dusk Summer returned from her most recent foray.

"The jungle ends not far from here. I've never seen anything like it," she reported. "It just ends. It doesn't thin out or taper off. It comes to a complete stop. After that it's just desert. There are a few odd looking trees, but they don't have leaves. I didn't see any water or signs of life. Just dunes of sand and patches of dried, cracked ground in no particular pattern."

"How much further to the end of the jungle?" asked Solveig.

"We should be able to make it by nightfall," Summer told them all.

"That might be the best place for us to make camp for the night," Lochen suggested. "From there we can get an early start the next morning before the twin suns make it too hot to travel."

With an end to the jungle in sight, their spirits rose and they were almost excited about the change of scenery. Lochen let them enjoy the anticipation. He didn't say anything to them, but he was concerned about what they might come across in the desert. He wasn't sure why, though, and couldn't identify anything specific that troubled him. It must have been something he read in one of the old manuscripts he had come across in the library in the sea sprites' palace. It would come to him sooner or later. For the time being, though, he thought it best to be vigilant and wait until he had a better idea of what was bothering him before he shared his concerns with his companions.

# Chapter eight

Natalie woke everyone just before dawn. She had taken the last watch and had made all the preparations for an early departure. Lochen had kept her company on her watch, while studying the stars during the night. In pointing out the planets that were visible in the predawn, he had located a landmark barely visible on the horizon line. As before, Summer would fly ahead to scout, but Natalie would be taking the lead on the first leg of the journey this morning. As the lead sun rose, the flat unbroken horizon was displayed before them. Natalie fixed her gaze on an imaginary target and the image was imprinted on her mind. Now she would be able to travel in that direction regardless of whether there was any visible landmark or if such a landmark was later obstructed from view.

They began walking shortly after the lead sun began to rise. It wouldn't be long before the trail sun would appear in the sky. There were no clouds to be seen from one end of the horizon to the other. Natalie had not paid much attention to the suns before today. None of them had. When they were traveling in the jungle, the trees protected them from the direct light and the extreme heat. Now there was nothing. The ground was coated with a layer of hard, sharp sand that gave way with each of their footsteps.

The bleakness of the surroundings made Natalie even more aware of the heat. She began chanting to herself, willing her body to cool down. She was careful not to use any incantations that were related to spells. There had been enough problems with magic already. The mantra she repeated was designed to take her mind off the heat. She created mental images of some dark, secluded spots she used to visit under the Sea.

In a few minutes she was beginning to feel a difference. She had reduced her body temperature and was actually feeling quite comfortable. She looked at the others and realized that only Stella had the same ability to control her internal thermostat. She could see Stella's closed eyes as she concentrated on managing her thoughts. She looked at Solveig and Lochen, who lived in the cool air of the mountain castle. They both seemed to be suffering most from the heat. Sean was bouncing along, apparently oblivious to the suns.

At half morning she stopped the group to rest.

"We have stopped too early," Lochen said to her, panting for breath. "I had hoped to keep going until midday."

Natalie looked closely at him. His hair was matted with sweat and his robes clung to his body like a soaked blanket. In spite of his desire, she could tell he would not be able to go much further without a rest.

Once they all stopped, Lochen dropped to the ground and hung his head down, gasping. The sweat was pouring out of him. At this rate, Natalie thought, he'll be quickly dehydrated.

"You should wear some lighter clothes," she said to him. "Your robes are much too hot for this climate."

He could barely raise his head to look at her, but nodded in agreement.

She then went over to Solveig and told her the same thing. Solveig, too had sunk to her knees, drenched.

"But I don't have any lighter clothes," she said, struggling to lift her arms and display her soggy sleeves. "These heavy wools have served us well in the mountains, but you're right. Here they are draining us of all our energy."

With that she pulled a dagger from her belt and with one quick slice, she cut the bottom of the robe just above her knees. She then cut the arms away, as well as the midriff, leaving her with a short skirt and a vest. She took a deep breath and, in spite of the beating suns, felt cooler almost immediately. She passed the knife to Lochen who did the same thing.

"Should we bury the parts we've cut off?" she asked Lochen.

"No," he answered. "Put them in your pack. When we get closer to the Crystal Citadel, we may need them."

By midday, the temperature had soared and the air was so dry it was pulling what little moisture remained in them from their bodies. Even with their ability to cool themselves, Natalie and Stella were having a hard time walking. Natalie spotted Summer returning from her most recent scouting.

"Is there any relief ahead," she asked.

"I found a small cluster of some dead looking trees up ahead. It's not much but they're all bunched together and I think they can provide a little bit of shade. We might be able to stretch some cloth from one to another for some shade. That should be a good place to stop for a rest."

Natalie signaled for Lochen, who was almost in a trance-like state. He staggered up with Solveig and Sean close behind him.

"Summer found a small cluster of trees up ahead. If we can go a little further, I think we should stop up there and rest until mid-afternoon. Maybe even later. It might be better to travel at dusk and dawn instead of during the heat of the day," she told him.

"I agree. Besides, I will need to take a short nap. The heat is wearing me down much faster than I had anticipated."

By the time the group reached the outcropping of trees, they were all stumbling.  Summer, who had lived all her life in a warm climate on the shore of the Cerulean Sea had never been this hot before.  Her wings were drooping and she was exhausted.  Sean fell face forward in the sand next to one of the tree trunks.  Solveig lowered herself to the ground with a groan, as Natalie and Stella found a place in the almost non-existent shade.

Natalie and Stella pulled tent material from one of the backpacks and threw it over some of the less brittle branches, providing some protection from the suns.  Solveig took the remnants of her robe from her backpack and picked up a branch from the debris among the trees and fashioned a small tent to crawl under.  Even though it protected her from the suns, there was no breeze and soon the air inside her makeshift shelter was sweltering.  She was too tired and too drained to move, and decided to just stay where she was.

Lochen leaned his back against one of the larger tree trunks and immediately fell asleep.  The rest of the group watched him for a few seconds, and then, one by one, dozed off, too.  But their sleep was light and not very restful.  It was too hot for them to fall into the deep sleep that Lochen seemed to be enjoying.  Only Natalie remained alert.  She had been in the lead since they started, and had managed to conserve her strength with her meditation.  Besides, she had an uneasy sense about the Desert.  Although they hadn't seen any signs of life along their journey, she had a feeling that they were not alone.  Eventually the heat became too much, and her eyes, too, became heavy, and she drifted off.

In her sleep Natalie began almost immediately to dream.  The sky was clear and the day was not nearly so hot.  She was sitting on a tiny island watching the tide flow gently back and forth.  Wonderful, cool, bright blue water was all around.  There was a light breeze blowing her hair.  Somewhere in the distance she thought she heard someone rowing a boat. She could hear the creaking of the oars against the oarlocks in a slow, but regular rhythm. But no matter in what direction she looked, she couldn't see the boat. The sound was nearby, but never seemed to be getting closer.

Was someone rowing around the island? She tried to stand up to move to the hilltop and get a better look, but she was stuck. She looked down at her feet and found them buried in the sand. When did this happen, she wondered. Then the breeze from across the water started to spray her. She leaned her head back to feel the cool mist on her skin. At first it was pleasant, but then it began to sting. She needed to move away from the spray.

She tried to dig her feet out of the sand, but it kept filling in as she pushed it out away from her legs. It seemed to be drawing her into the ground. The more she struggled, the deeper she sank. She opened her mouth to call for help, but the sea spray hit her full in the face. It was no longer a mild cool mist. She got a mouthful of water before she could call out. But the water wasn't wet; it was dry – dry as cotton. She tried to spit it out but it stuck to the inside of her mouth. She began to suffocate.

Suddenly her eyes sprung open and she was wide-awake. She looked around and recalled where she was, not sure if she was glad to be there or not. She attempted to stand and felt her legs were stuck. She looked down and saw they were covered in sand. The sand was washing over her like water. She looked around and saw that the surrounding desert was moving like the sea. It was moving in low waves and was covering all of them.

She heard the creaking of the oars from her dream. She turned towards Lochen and found the source of the sound that she dreamt was the boat being rowed around the island. The tree he was leaning against was folding itself around him. He was being slowly sucked into the trunk as the trunk expanded and wrapped itself around his arms.

She called out to Stella, who was curled up not far from where Natalie was sitting. By now Natalie was almost completely covered in sand. She tried to stand, but it was like trying to stand in water. The sand literally splashed up when she moved against it.

Stella wasn't responding to her calls. Natalie called again and again until she was screaming her name. Finally the Enchantress raised her head. She moved sluggishly, but was able to pull herself up to her knees by pulling against the trunk of the tree on which they had hung the tent. Stella pulled herself up. Each time she stepped away from the tree, she sunk into the sand. She turned to Natalie and instantly saw what had been happening. She turned back to the tree trunk and pulled herself up to the nearest branch. Climbing out the limb she reached down to pull her Princess free.

"Solveig has a knife in her belt. See if you can awaken her, but in any case get her knife and get it to me," she directed Stella.

Stella shinnied out to the end of the branch. When she was as far as she could go, she dropped down. She sank to her knees, but was able to make her way over to Solveig. Natalie leaned over as far as she could and wrapped her fingers around Lochen's wrist and pulled to free him from the tree. It was almost as if his body had started to become part of the trunk. He couldn't be moved, and he was sleeping so deeply, he was unable to awaken. She was able, though to pull herself free from the sand. Stella called to Natalie and then tossed her the knife.

"I'm going to see if I can cut him away from the bark. Tend to the others. As they are able to pull themselves free of the sand, have them come and help."

Stella saw that Solveig had fallen back asleep. She shook her back to consciousness. Stepping nimbly, she was able to stay atop of the surface of the sand. It was difficult, but not impossible, to get a footing. Once Solveig was fully alert, she moved the scrap of robe underneath her to make the ground a little bit firmer.

"Find Summer," she directed Solveig. "I think she was somewhere near you. I'll get Sean."

Solveig fished around in the shifting sand. There was no sight of Summer. After a minute or two, she sat back and took in the whole clearing looking for some indication of where the faerie princess was. She spotted a small mound of sand to her left and, looking closely, noticed the faint edge of something that looked like a peacock feather. It was Summer. She leaned over and dug Summer out from beneath the sand, then they both went to help Stella with Sean. As each one of them cleared their heads and became fully awake, the shifting of the sand abated and the ground became somewhat firmer. Finally, it returned to the hard, sharp sandy surface of the desert. As it did, they all joined Natalie to help pull Lochen free.

Natalie cut carefully at the bark, trying to drive the knife into the wood and avoid cutting Lochen. Each time she dug the knife in, the tree seemed to groan in pain and the color from Lochen's cheeks began to fade.

"Stop," shouted Solveig. "You're hurting Lochen."

"I'm cutting at the tree," answered Natalie, watching as more and more of the tree crept around Lochen. "If we don't free him, we'll lose him."

With each cut of the tree, though, Lochen reacted as if the cuts had been made into him. Although he made no sound, his face looked pained and he lost more color. In desperation Solveig placed her hand on his head and began an incantation.

"No magic," shouted Summer. "Please. Remember what happened with me."

"If we don't, we won't be able to free him," Solveig shouted back, and then she repeated her incantation.

As she chanted, the sound of the wood moaning became louder. The other trees in the clearing were creaking as their limbs bent to a wind that seemed to come from nowhere. The sand began to swirl around the entire clearing. It was beating down on the small group like a very localized sand storm. Instead of being pelted with drops of water, though, they were slashed at by waves of hard, sharp sand. It began to cut into their skin; it blew into their mouths and noses; it blinded their eyes. The other trees began to lean into those attempting to rescue Lochen. Their branches poked and pulled at them as if they were arms on a giant. Limbs struck their heads and shoulders, beating them. They were being pushed and beaten back from the tree that had a grip on Lochen.

This isn't working, Stella thought to herself. She backed away from the group and raised her arms. With a rapid circular motion, she conjured up a protective bubble. She had tried to create one large enough to cover them all, but could only generate one big enough to cover herself.

Lochen was right, she thought. Our powers are diminished in some way. She swung her arm and shot the bubble covering her over to Natalie. Then she conjured another one and propelled to at Lochen. One by one, she covered each of them. Then she pushed forward and her bubble merged with Natalie's and both their bubbles then merged with Lochen's. Sean, Solveig and Summer leaned in close and combined their bubbles as well. Natalie continued to cut and dig at the trunk of the tree and was finally able to cut Lochen free.

They pulled him away from the clearing into the open and the wind suddenly stopped. The sand that had been swirling hung in the air for a second and then dropped to the ground. And the trees resumed their frozen stance. Through it all Lochen had slept as if he was in a coma. When he finally awoke, he was instantly alert. He looked up to see everyone hovering over him.

"I needed that respite, but I have to admit that I had the strangest dream," he announced.. "I was sinking into a soft feather bed and all of you were trying to pull me out. I wanted to sleep and you just wouldn't leave me alone. Very unusual. I trust you are all rested. We must move on."

He stood up and brushed himself off.

"Oh, and by the way," he continued. "We need to avoid having contact with those trees. I believe they are Muscipula Carnivoraes. Man eating plants. They must be dormant now, but we can't be too careful."

The others just stared at him in silence.

They traveled on without further mishap as dusk turned into night. At the darkest part of the night, they stopped and made camp. Lochen studied the stars and planets, making sure they were headed in the right direction, even though he commented on the fact that he didn't think they were progressing as much as they should. They had to stop too often to rest. He noted that as they traveled further north, they were coming closer to the apex of the orbits of the twin suns. In a few days, there would only be about two hours of a combined dusk and dawn, with no real night at all. By then the days would be very long and very hot. The worst of the heat was yet to come. They needed to get out of this Desert as fast as they could, and should make fewer stops if possible.

They reached this point three days later, but they hadn't been able to make fewer stops, as Lochen had hoped. They had been crossing the desert for almost a week now, and, aside from the incident with the man eating trees, they had seen no plants, no springs of water, no birds, insects or animals. In spite of this, each of them had the uneasy feeling that they were being watched, if not followed. In addition, as the intensity of the heat continued to rise, whether they traveled in the daylight or at night, none of them felt like they had gotten used to it. Instead, it was getting increasingly difficult to keep walking each day.

Their supply of water had run out the day before. Summer was making longer and longer scouting runs, not only keeping a watch on any potential danger, but also searching for water. They had discussed using magic, pointing out that nothing had happened after the incident with the trees, and that they had used a lot of magic then. Stella agreed with Lochen, though, that they should refrain if at all possible. The danger was just too great.

The sand they had been walking across had long turned into hard cracked clay. With every step a fine powdery dust rose into the air. It filled their mouths and noses, making it hard to breathe and swallow. Even the breeze from Summer's wings as she flew raised the dust. It caked on her wings and hung in everyone's clothes. Nothing they did could keep the dust from finding its way into their hair, their eyes, and inside their clothes. It began to rub against their skin, creating rashes, which blistered and turned into open cuts. The dust found its way into these as well.

They finally got to a point where they felt they could go no further. The heat, the sand, the dust, their inability to sleep well when they were able to sleep at all, had made them irritable and confrontational. They had started snapping at each other. Summer had straggled back to report no change in the land ahead, and she collapsed before she could finish her sentence. Natalie could stand it no more. She clapped her hands once and pressed her finger to the ground.

Lochen shouted, "No. Not water; not here!"

But it was too late. A small spring gushed up from the ground like a fountain. Soon a small pool of bright clear water formed around the spring. All the others ran forward. Natalie tentatively stuck her hand in and felt the coolness. She cupped some in her hand and took a sip.

"It's wonderful," she announced,

The others joined in and began to drink from the spring and splash water over themselves. Lochen looked on in panic. When nothing seemed to happen, he slowly moved to the spring and took a drink. The water seemed to be all right. He then splashed it over his head and face, enjoying the relief.

When they had all cleaned themselves off and filled their water containers, Natalie asked Lochen why he had reacted the way he did.

"I know you're concerned about us using magic," she said. "But we had to use magic back at that clearing to free you from the trees, and there don't seem to have been any consequences from that."

"Yes, you're right," he said. "It's just that I believe there are dangerous creatures that inhabit the Desert. We haven't seen any, but it's likely that the live beneath the sand and clay. If so, they may be trapped there unless an opening is created, such as a well or a spring. I think water releases them."

As he said this, Sean noticed a small black object poked its way through the dampened ground.

"You mean like one of these?" he called to Lochen.

Everyone crowded around, but at a safe distance, as an ugly scorpion-like object wriggled up from beneath the ground. It had crab-like pincers, a spider-like body, and a tail like a scorpion. Once it came up out of the ground it looked around, but made no movement towards the group. It was about half the size of Summer, but seemed more frightened of her than she was of it. It moved slightly in a circular motion near the edge of the pool of water. It seemed to give no indication of straying too far.

Everyone was about to dismiss it and return to the spring. Natalie bent down to fill one more canteen with water, when the small creature suddenly jumped into the air and made a striking motion at her. It moved much more quickly than she could react and it would have stung her with its tail if Sean hadn't armed his slingshot and fired first, hitting it in mid air.

"Thank you, Sean," Natalie gasped in shock. "I didn't think that thing was dangerous. I guess I was wrong."

"It doesn't seem too dangerous to me," he announced as he stepped closer to look at the carcass.

It had been split in two by his shot. He was just about to walk away when he heard a scratching sound. When he looked back, he saw the two parts of the creature start to move. Each half was regenerating the missing part. In a few seconds, there were now two complete scorpion beetles. At the same time, two more had made their way through the ground and were moving forward.

"Whoa," said Sean. "That's not good."

And he quickly fired four stones in rapid succession before Lochen could stop him. Each of the four shots found their target, splitting each of the creatures in half. As quickly as before, the halves each regenerated another full scorpion beetle and now there were eight. This time eight more came up from beneath the ground.

"I think it's time for us to leave," announced Lochen.

As they turned to go they heard the same scratching sound that was made when the first pair were regenerated. Each of them slowly looked back and watched as the pack of scorpion beetles divided themselves and regenerated new whole parts.

"I didn't do that," protested Sean. He looked to the others. "It wasn't me. Honestly. I didn't do that."

"I know," answered Lochen. "They're doing it themselves, and each time they split themselves, they bring forward an equal number from underground. We need to leave here immediately."

They picked up their things and all began to run away from the spring. Within a few steps, though, the ground behind them had turned black. There were dozens of the creatures poking their way through the ground. Not only were there more of them, they were now getting bigger. Each successive wave of emerging scorpion beetles was larger than the one before. And they were becoming more aggressive.

One large one jumped at Solveig. In a flash, she drew her knife from her belt and in one motion she sliced in it half and then stomped on each of the halves, squashing them into the ground. She looked down at the spattered pieces. Nothing happened. That seemed to keep them from regenerating, but in the time it took her to do this, a dozen more had popped up from underground.

Now there were hundreds of them and they began to move towards the group as if in an attack mode. As if communicating with each other in some kind of silent code, they began to spread out and surround the travelers. As Lochen turned around he saw that the scorpion beetles were acting as a unified pack and cutting off their escape. While one section of the swarm was heading directly towards them, two other sections had flanked them and joined behind them, completely cutting off any escape. There was nowhere to run.

"OK," shouted Lochen. "Now, I think, would be a good time to use magic."

Solveig didn't need any more of an invitation. She pointed her finger at the swarm and quick little flashes of lightning shot from her fingertip blasting the beasts. She mentally noted that the flashes were not as powerful as normal. She started shooting blasts from both hands.

Lochen produced a cloud of purple smoke off to his right, which enveloped the attackers from that side. The cloud caused them to quickly shrivel up and turn to black dust. He had opened a narrow escape route that was quickly closing, and hurried the others through it. He produced several more clouds of the smoke to keep the route opened until everyone was through.

Stella produced another protective bubble around each of them. As they fought back the attack they continued to run away from the spring, further into the desert. The swarm continued to chase them, repeatedly trying to outflank them. At one point Natalie let the others get ahead of her. She stopped running and turned back towards the attack. She stood alone facing the main swarm of advancing beetles and ran her finger in a long line across the clay.

"What are you doing," shouted Solveig, who stopped and ran back. "Don't stop." And she ran up to pull Natalie back with the rest of the group.

"Go," she told Solveig. "I know what I'm doing."

Solveig took a few steps back, but would not leave her friend. As soon as the others realized Natalie and Solveig had stopped, they, too stopped running.

"I'm not sure this is the best strategy," said Lochen. "A wiser course of action might be to at least try to escape." In spite of his caution, he stopped running and turned back to the others.

When the attacking monsters got closer to the line she had drawn, Natalie clapped her hands and the ground split open along the line she had drawn. A wide chasm gaped just before her feet. The sand was sucked down into the opening as it widened away from her and towards the assault. The front lines of the advancing creatures fell into the crevasse and were quickly followed by those behind them. As soon as the creatures realized what was happening, they slowed their attack. Natalie clapped again and the earth closed, trapping those that had fallen deep underground.

The numbers of attackers had greatly diminished. The rest were stunned and confused. They stopped their advance and before they could regroup they were covered with another blanket of purple smoke and fried with a few more of Solveig's lightning bolts. When the group thought it was finally safe, they stopped to make sure everyone was accounted for and all right.

"I'm sorry," started Natalie, but before she could go any further, the others cut her off.

"I'm not," said Sean. "It was getting boring, anyway."

"You have nothing to be sorry about, Lochen told her. "Without the water you provided, we would not have made it. There was no way of knowing what the consequences would be."

"That's right," said Solveig. "Getting cleaned up was worth a little excitement."

"But Lochen knew there was some danger present," she continued.

"I only suspected, but that's the way I am," he replied. "I worry about everything. Right now, though, I think we have other things to worry about."

He had been looking past her and as he spoke, he pointed off in the direction they had come. The distant sky was turning black. As they stood their looking at the approaching storm, they began to hear a faint rumbling of thunder. Every once in a while, through the black clouds, they could see intermittent flashes of lightning. The Fury was on its way.

"It looks like our use of magic has been discovered," said Stella.

Without a word, they all turned back the way they had been headed. After only a few steps Natalie stopped. There was something on the opposite horizon.

"Is that more of the storm?" asked Sean.

"I didn't think it could divide itself," said Summer.

"I don't think that's part of the storm," said Lochen as he raised his hand to shield his eyes from the sun. He watched the formation and the direction of a distant cloud of dust on the horizon.

"Someone or something is coming from the other direction as well, and is much closer, he said. "I think it's safe to say that we've been discovered."

# Chapter nine

They all looked in the direction of the dust cloud that was headed towards them. A sense of confusion and frustration settled over them, and was eventually followed by a feeling of defeat. The storm and the scorpion beetles were behind them, and who knew what was in front of them. There was nothing but desert to the right and to the left of them. Each of them struggled to consider the best next steps, but was at a loss for any ideas. There didn't seem much point in walking on. Even though the scorpion beetles had given up their attack; the storm was slowly moving towards them, and the cloud of dust that was approaching from the other direction would greet them soon enough.

"We might as well conserve our strength," suggested Lochen, somewhat exasperated, as they all prepared to meet whoever or whatever was rushing towards them.

He smoothed out an area of the sand and sat down. No one objected, and following his lead, they looked at one another. Realizing there were no viable alternatives, one by one they settled in to wait. Sean was the only one who declined to sit. He paced back and forth mumbling. Finally, he stopped and turned to his comrades.

"How can you just sit there? Aren't you going to fight? I can't believe you're all just giving up."

"It's not so much giving up," said Lochen, searching for the right phrase, "as it is taking a strategic break."

"What's that supposed to mean?" demanded Sean.

"What would you have us do?" asked Lochen, avoiding Sean's question. "Run to meet who or whatever is coming towards us? Gather arms? Find allies? We could run away, but in what direction? None of us has magical powers strong enough to ward off the storm or to reach the object headed our way – whatever it is, and assuming it means us harm, which we don't know at this time. For all we know, we could be attacking a potential collaborator. All things considered, it seems most prudent to wait and see what develops."

Sean thought about the question for a while. He had to admit, he didn't have a very good answer.

"Well," he started to say, "I just don't want to sit here and wait for something to happen."

"You're not," said Lochen. "You're pacing. And you're doing an excellent job, if I may say so. I have to admit, I have seldom seen more effective pacing."

Sean turned and glared at Lochen. He wasn't sure if he was being mocked or if Lochen was being his usual oblivious self.

"Chill out, Sean," said Summer, not sure herself where this was headed. "Lochen's right. There's no sense in getting all wound up before we know what we're facing."

Sean looked at the both of them and then back at the approaching cloud of dust. He knew they were right, but he had difficulty just waiting for something to happen. Begrudgingly, he plopped down on the sand, but he pulled his slingshot out and had several stones ready to be loaded and fired. He kept his eyes on the approaching sand storm, waiting for whatever it was to get close enough to attack.

They didn't have to wait much longer. The cloud of swirling dust had been coming faster and faster, seeming to gain more speed the closer it got. The source had been obscured by the dust that was being raised, but soon they were able to see what had been creating it. The suns rays managed to penetrate some of the dust and glimmer off the side of what looked like a long, narrow tube or boat with a single tall sail. Once it got closer, they could see that the craft was not "sailing" on the desert sand, but was on large, thin wheels. Since there was little breeze, the sail just flapped limply against the mast.

Whatever was propelling the wheels was moving the vessel at an incredible speed; however, no one could see what was making the craft move at all, let alone so fast. It was coming towards them at somewhat of an angle and as the sunlight glanced off the side of the hull they could see that the ship was not made of wood, or anything like it. It seemed to be covered in some kind of flexible armor plating. There was no evident opening at the top, like most sailing vessels they had seen before. Rather, the entire tube seemed to be covered.

Sean jumped up, slingshot pulled, ready to fire.

"I don't believe your weapon will pierce the surface of that vehicle," said Lochen. "You might just be wasting your ammunition." As an afterthought, he added, "and you may be only irritating a possible rescuer. Where are your manners?"

"Someone or something is driving that...that...whatever it is. I'm just going to be ready," he answered defiantly, dividing his attention between the approaching object and being somewhat annoyed at Lochen's sarcasm.

Lochen was able to see that the shielding was a patchwork of hundreds of pieces of an unusual material that was covered with large translucent scales. The covering was stretched over some kind of framework, the shape of which could be seen under the fabric. The color of the material shifted for no apparent reason or in any obvious pattern. It was sometimes a murky brown, and then would turn to a grayish-green. It looked like the surface of a stagnant pond when sunlight reflected off of it. The scales that covered and apparently further protected the fabric at times seemed clear, but at other times took on the color of the material beneath them.

The ship took a wide turn and then was headed straight for them. Just as it seemed like it was going to run them over, it made a sharp turn and pulled to a stop right in front of them. As it skidded to a stop, a large cloud of dust rose up, nearly engulfing the craft. There was no sound or movement until the dust settled and the air was clear. Only Sean had risen to meet the visitor. The others remained sitting in the sand, staring expectantly at the strange arrival.

A large canopy separated itself from the top section of the pod and then slid open. A rope ladder was lowered over the side, and a thin young man stepped over the side and onto the ladder, and climbed down to the ground. He was about as tall as Lochen, and his appearance matched the desert surroundings. He had a fair complexion and light colored hair and eyes. His clothing matched the look of his ship, but without the scaly covering. In spite of the heat, he had long sleeves and long pants, made of a very light weight, but seemingly strong fabric that had the same appearance and properties as the material that covered his ship.

He wore a floppy wide brimmed hat made of the same material. His shirt and pants were covered with several pockets. There were pockets on the front and back and sides of his pants and on the front and sleeves of his shirt. He had a long narrow knife strapped to each leg, three more in his belt, one strapped to his back between his shoulders, and what looked like two more short ones hidden up his sleeves and strapped around his ankles under his pant legs.

It seemed as if he had as many knives as he had pockets. He had sandy colored boots on that looked hard as steel. Lochen and Sean had both taken note of the weapons and both believed that the boots he wore probably also contained weapons of some kind. Whoever he was, he was clearly ready for battle. Lochen wondered to himself how he was able to move with so many armaments attached to him.

"My name is Liam," he announced. He looked towards Lochen and, smiling, said, "Some people call me The Pathfinder."

He didn't wait for a reaction or response from Lochen. Turning toward the others, he quickly added, "You all look like you could use a ride. If you want to avoid the storm that's headed this way, I suggest you climb aboard and come with me."

He turned his glance at Sean who still had his slingshot in firing position.

"Or you could stay here and shoot stones at that storm. Your choice."

Sean looked a little flustered at the rebuke, but didn't lower his slingshot. The others were all too stunned to speak until Solveig found her voice.

"How did you know we needed help and how did you know where to find us?" she asked.

"Well," he said, "first of all, not too many people vacation in the Devil's Desert, so I didn't really know you needed help. It was an educated guess. But, with all the magic you were using, it was like you had a big sign in the sky shouting, 'Here we are. Come find us.' So it didn't take a genius to guess you needed help and it wasn't too hard to know where you were. By the looks of that approaching storm," he added, motioning to the ever-blackening sky, "I'm not the only one who knows where you are. From what I've seen so far, that's not a gentle summer rain approaching. It think it means to do some harm."

"Actually, we were coming to find you," said Lochen.

"Yeah, I know," Liam replied.

"But how?" asked Stella.

"You'll see soon enough."

He looked past them at the sudden shift in the direction of the storm clouds, and said to them rather insistently, "I think you need to get on board. We need to get to some place safe. I wouldn't recommend being in this much open space too much longer. The sooner we get going the sooner we'll be safe."

He turned to go back up the rope ladder and glanced back at Sean who was still holding his slingshot in the firing position.

"You, too, sharpshooter" Liam added, smiling, "and you can bring your little toy."

Sean slowly relaxed his grip on the slingshot and watched suspiciously as the others all climbed up the rope ladder and onto the odd looking ship. The comment about his slingshot being a little toy rankled him, but he was beginning to realize the options were limited. Reluctantly he followed.

There were several seats in two rows down the center and they all sat down. At the stern of the interior of the ship was a large seat with a steering wheel and foot pedals attached to a series of chains, ropes and gears. Once everyone was seated Liam took his place behind the steering wheel and pulled a lever that shut the canopy. It, too, was covered with the same kind of scales as the rest of the ship. These seemed to be a little clearer than the others - just enough to see through them to the sky above.

Sean had tensed up when the canopy closed, but hadn't moved from his seat. He glanced furtively to the others. Seeing that they didn't appear frightened, he relaxed a bit.

"Is everybody ready?" he asked, not really waiting for or expecting an answer, but looking at Sean as he said the words. Sean stared back at him wordlessly. He still wasn't sure if this guy was a friend or an enemy.

Liam began pedaling and shifting. The ship gained speed as he made a wide turn and headed back the way he had come. The others sat in silence, for the time being just grateful to be riding instead of walking. He seemed to be pedaling effortlessly as the craft continued to gain speed. There were several levers on either side of him that he moved and shifted, further increasing speed. Before long, they were racing across the desert sand.

Lochen was studying the construction of the ship and in particular its armaments. He noticed that the floor was constructed of a latticework. It was very strong, but open enough to see into the compartment below. There he saw another system of levers and pulleys, attached to which were several long sharp blades. He surmised that these could be made to protrude through movable ports on either side of the ship. He had glanced at these ports as he was climbing on board. They must be able to open in conjunction with the extension of the blades, he thought.

Looking towards the bow of the ship he saw a similar weapon. It appeared to be controlled by odd-looking cables that reached back to a position next to Liam's seat. Lochen leaned down to feel the cables.

"I would strongly recommend that you not touch those," Liam warned.

"I was just curious to see what they were made of," Lochen responded amiably.

"Helix vines," Liam told him.

Lochen turned back with a look of surprise on his face. "Really? Those are extremely rare and nearly impervious to destruction. I've only heard about them. I've never seen any before. I see that your craft is ready for close-quarters combat."

"Where I live close-quarters combat is the only kind there is, and if you're not ready, you're dead," he answered bluntly.

"It sound like you live in a rather inhospitable neighborhood," said Solveig.

"You could say that," he answered without further comment.

"Then why don't you move?" asked Summer.

"It's my home," he answered, again without further comment.

"What is the material that covers the frame of your ship?" Lochen asked.

"Gargoyle skin," he answered. "It's the only thing that protects against their arrows and darts, and against snakes, bats, scorpions, harpies, poison plants or any of the other lovely inhabitants of the swamps."

Solveig and Summer exchanged stunned looks.

"And your clothes are made of this, too?"

"Yes," Liam answered again as he studied Lochen.

"And the scales?" Lochen asked.

"From their armor plating," he said.

"If these materials are so protective, how were you able to take them from the gargoyles? I'm assuming they didn't provide it to you voluntarily."

The faintest glimmer of a smile shown on Liam's face, as he said, "No, you're right about that. They didn't give it up freely."

With one hand still on the steering wheel, he flicked his other hand and the knife up that sleeve shot out. "These blades are forged from wizard's steel. They have special powers and can cut through the hardest surfaces, like the scales that cover a gargoyle's skin. But they're useless on anything that doesn't carry the curse of Ena Ray." He then reached out and sliced it across Lochen's bare arm.

Lochen pulled back in shock. Everyone else stood, ready to defend Lochen or attack his attacker. He looked down at his arm, expecting that the razor sharp knife had cut through to the bone, or worse. Instead, there was no mark whatsoever. Liam just smiled at him.

"Relax," he said to them all. "If I had thought for a minute that you were in the army of Ena Ray, I'd have left you in the desert."

"I see," said Lochen. "Very interesting." He made a mental note of the reference to Ena Ray, but returned his attention to the Pathfinder's weapons. "The only place I am aware that one can find wizard's steel is from the core of a meteorite that has been treated in the acid secreted by fire lizards. And fire lizards are very rare."

"In my world fire lizards are the pets of the gargoyles that guard the portal to the underworld. They're not as rare as you might think."

Stella's interest was piqued. She was not completely sure she trusted this stranger. There was too much at risk to be so easily taken in. She recalled Lochen's discussion about the Pathfinder. How long ago had that been, she wondered. It seemed like ages. Lochen had said that the Pathfinder's people had suffered much. She decided to ask some questions to which she already knew most of the answers, to see if she could catch him in a lie.

"Do your people live in harmony with the gargoyles?"

He turned to look at her and didn't answer immediately.

"No one lives in harmony with the gargoyles. They are the minions of Ena Ray. Over the centuries they have destroyed my land, destroyed my home and destroyed my people. I am all that's left.

"Why do you stay there, then? Why not seek out allies?"

"It is the home of my ancestors. I won't be driven from it. Besides, the best way to defeat your enemies is to learn as much as you can about them. There's an ancient saying – hold your friends close, but hold your enemies closer. I have survived because I have lived like the gargoyles – enough to know how to defeat them, even if it is one by one."

Before anyone could ask another question, he continued, "You had asked before how I knew you were looking for me. Your journey and the quest you have undertaken are not a secret. Ena Ray knows about it and is waiting for you."

"How can this be so?" asked Natalie. "We ourselves didn't know who or what we were looking for, and even now are not completely sure."

Liam looked at her intently. "He's a powerful sorcerer. Even in his banishment, he has been able to extend his control over the slow-witted gargoyles, who were once his army. His followers have been preparing for their escape from exile in the underground and for their siege of the prison that holds Ena Ray. Their portal is hidden in my swamp and I've noticed several recent scouting forays by their guardians. The gargoyles are vicious creatures, but they are very stupid. They've been openly amassing weapons and have made several attacks against my sanctuary. All they've managed to do is to show me what weapons they are using and how to defeat them. What I still don't know, though, is where, exactly, Ena Ray is being held."

"Are we near your sanctuary?" asked Stella.

"It's not far – only about three days."

Stella was stunned. She had expected him to say it was only an hour or so away.

"How could you have known we were coming and where we would be if you were that far away?" she asked.

"Someone used faerie dust about a week ago. Then someone used an incantation to ward off the desert heat. I could feel the magic on both those occasions. And then there was a whole bunch of stuff that seemed to happen at once. Besides, I also sensed a change in the storm. From the looks of the direction of that storm, I wasn't the only one who felt the magic"

Summer, Stella, Solveig and Natalie looked at each other, and then looked away a bit guiltily.

"I started out then," Liam continued. "I was able to locate your exact position when you all sent out that beacon by creating the spring and awaking the stingers. Using magic to fight them off was like setting off fireworks. Not too smart for a bunch of smart people."

They rode in silence for a while. Finally, he asked them, "I've told you about me. Now it's your turn. Who exactly are you? I know that you're not followers of Ena Ray, and it's obvious at least some of you have magical powers, but you don't look much like each other." He glanced at Summer and then towards Sean.

Summer started with her part of the chronology. Sean chimed in every once in a while to fill in whatever gaps he thought there were. He was beginning to change his opinion of the Pathfinder. Lochen and Solveig continued the saga, which was added to by Natalie and Stella. All the while Liam just listened, only occasionally asking a question. Lochen and Stella discussed the visions and their related exchange of information, all of which led them to their current situation and location.

"Does all this make any sense to you?" asked Solveig.

"Well, it fills in some blanks," answered Liam. "As I said, I've seen a lot of activity recently, so I knew something was happening. I just wasn't sure what. From what you've told me, it seems like that storm is Ena Ray's work, one way or another, and that he or it is searching for something – either something he needs to be able to escape, or something he needs to be able to destroy whatever – or whoever – will try to stop his escape."

"So does that mean you'll help us?" asked Sean.

"Help you?" Liam asked back. "Seriously? There's no way you can keep me out of this fight."

Lochen and Stella exchanged glances that told each other they had found the real Pathfinder and not some imposter.

 As nightfall approached Summer asked if they would be stopping someplace to make camp. Liam told her they would not. By now an evening breeze had picked up and the sail had filled. He no longer had to pedal to keep the craft moving forward.

"Nothing around here is safe," he told them. "Just because you can't see the danger, that doesn't mean it's not out there watching you. It's best if we keep going until we reach territory I'm more comfortable with. It may not be less dangerous, but at least I'll be on my own turf."

"How can you be comfortable with all the deadly things around you?" Summer asked.

"I don't know," he answered. "Maybe because it's what I grew up with."

Solveig asked him how he became a Pathfinder, and did he enjoy all the traveling he did.

"I seldom leave my swamp," he told them.

Everyone was speechless and just looked at each other. How could this person be a Pathfinder if he never left his home, they all asked themselves.

"They why are you called the Pathfinder, if you don't ever go anyplace?" asked Sean.

"My people don't have...didn't have powers like the sorcerers or enchantresses. Our only ability is that we just know where things are," he said. "I don't have to have been to a place before, and I don't have to look at a map, but I know how to get there and I know where things are once I've arrived.  It's like I've got a compass and a map inside my head.  I can find things in the dead of night or even blindfolded."

He could see the looks on their faces.  They were staring at him in undisguised disbelief.

"How do you think I'm navigating this ship in the dark?" he continued.  "The canopy blurs the night sky, so I'm not following the stars.  I know where danger is and where the safe places are.  I know where to find food and water, and I know when it's time to run away and when it's time to hide – or to stand and fight.  And I know that right now it's time for you all to get some rest.  Me, too.  I've had a long day.  Don't worry.  This ship knows the way home, too."  And with that he pulled his hat down over his eyes.

The rest looked at one another, wondering what to do next.

"I suggest you do as he recommends," said Lochen.  "We've had a long day and a difficult journey thus far.  We would be wise to rest when we can."

He turned to Liam, and hesitated before he asked, "Is it safe...and...I guess permissible, to open the canopy?"

Without raising his hat from his eyes, Liam waived his hand in approval and merely said, "Sure.  Just don't fall over, because we aren't turning around," and in a few short seconds he was fast asleep.

Lochen turned to Sean, knowing he was still a bit on edge, and asked, "Would you like to come?"

Sean thought about it for a few seconds, and then seemed to visibly relax.

"No," he said, taking a deep breath.  "I guess it's safe to get some rest.  Besides, it won't make me more comfortable to just see darkness whizzing by."

Lochen nodded and chuckled. He watched as the others settled in to get as comfortable as they could. Since he wouldn't need sleep again for several days, he carefully open the canopy and stepped up on the top deck. The odd ship had picked up an incredible amount of speed and was whipping across the desert. All he could hear was the wind as it pulled on the large sail. He held on tightly to a kind of railing that ran along the length of the main pod. The wind flew through his hair, and was still quite hot, but refreshing. He looked up to his beloved heavens.

The night was so dark that he could barely make out the line that separated the ground from the sky. The only distinction that broke up the inky night was the glittering stars, planets, and the moon, Luna, above the invisible horizon line. It was a trisect moon this evening, lit from one side by the lead sun and from the bottom by the trail sun. The result was a pie shaped triangle of darkness in the top left quadrant of the moon's surface. By this Lochen knew that the planetary alignment was much closer; now less than a month away.

"There is still so much to do," he said aloud, speaking to himself.

A voice behind him responded, "Yes, but we have already come so far." It was Stella. She had seen him go up on deck and followed silently behind him.

"I'm not so sure," he said, turning to help her up and over to the railing.

"I know there is still much ahead of us, but think about it," she continued, "We have found The Pathfinder even before entering the Venomous Swamp. He knows much of Ena Ray, and he knows of the portal. Admittedly, he doesn't know exactly where it is, but at least he knows of it. I'm sure he can lead us to the Crystal Citadel."

"Yes," said Lochen, "I have no doubt he can. But what do we do when we get there, and how is that related to the portal?"

He was starting to wave his arms as he spoke, and struggling not to raise his voice and wake the others.

"And even if we learn what we're supposed to do at the Citadel," he continued, "can we get back to the portal in time to do whatever it is we're supposed to do there? Assuming that we're supposed to get back to the portal in the first place. Look how long it's taking us to get to the Swamp. Who knows how long it will take us to get to the Citadel, and are we even supposed to go to the Citadel? There are so many unknowns. I haven't a clue as to where or what we're to do next. There are…"

"Lochen," Stella interrupted, whispering his name.

She had learned from Solveig that Lochen often got wrapped up in whatever he was thinking about and would begin to ramble. He had to be forcefully interrupted to be brought back to reality. She also knew that when someone was highly stressed out, being forceful could have the opposite effect, and that whispering would more likely get their attention.

"We'll figure it all out in due course," she whispered again, when he jerked his head in her direction.

"But what if we don't," he said, clearly still agitated.

"We have no choice," she answered calmly. She reached up and held his arms to further reduce his agitated state. "Once you reconcile that, you will be able to see more clearly how much we have accomplished and that the next steps will make themselves known to us when needed."

He relaxed his shoulders and took a deep breath. "Yes, of course. One step at a time. And you're right. We've found The Pathfinder. He will take us to the Citadel, even if we don't know for sure right now why we're going there or where it is. I'm sure it will become clear to us when it needs to."

"Yes, it will," Stella said assuringly.

He returned his gaze to the night sky and the glittering lights.

"I miss traveling to the planets," he said. "It was so peaceful up there."

# Chapter ten

Three days later, the terrain began to change, and so did the heat. Just when everyone thought it couldn't get worse, it did. In the desert, it had been like an oven. As they entered the swamp, it became more like a sauna. There was no relief from the temperature. At best it didn't rise; but it never abated. Even at night the air felt like fire. What made things worse was the humidity. The humidity was so thick it felt like breathing cotton. The weight of the air itself was oppressive. When the twin suns were at their apex, it felt like the travelers were moving through hot water instead of air.

The sand of the desert slowly began to be replaced with tall grass and marshes. The ship transitioned from gliding on wheels to skimming across mud and grass. Trees began to appear. At first they were inviting: tall, lush trees with low hanging branches covered in moss. Everyone but Liam had been looking forward to reaching the trees when they were first spotted on the horizon. He hadn't bothered to spoil their anticipation. That had turned sour when it became apparent that the moss was infested with huge spiders, and large, poisonous snakes hung from almost every branch. Soon everyone felt like they were back in the jungle, the vegetation had become so thick. This jungle, though, was far more treacherous than the other one they had traversed.

Liam made sure the canopy was sealed tight as he maneuvered the ship through the trees and brush. Initial complaints that he was cutting off any breeze quickly stopped when the local inhabitants made their presence known. As spiders, snakes and other creatures dropped from above onto the craft, Sean readied his slingshot and the others ineffectively raised their arms to protect themselves. Liam looked at them in mild amusement as he pulled one of the many cords hanging near him.

The plates of scales that covered the ship quickly heated up and the intruders would sizzle and pop. If they didn't escape on their own by skittering off the shell, they quickly became fried to ashes. Soon their unwelcome visits stopped. Somehow the message had been transmitted throughout the swamp that The Pathfinder's defenses could not be penetrated, and those that tried failed with their lives.

Their progress had slowed considerably once they were deep into the Swamp. When the waterways were stronger and wider, they were able to sail fairly easily and quickly. However, these times were infrequent. More often they were winding in and out of narrow streams or through reeds and rushes so thick that the water in which they were standing was barely visible. The suns crept across the sky baking the air around them.

It was hard to tell when nightfall arrived, since very little sunlight was able to make its way through the foliage, but Liam knew it had come and that they had to get to shelter soon. Finally, he maneuvered the ship into a narrow channel that ended in an enclosed pier. He slid the canopy back and told everyone to quickly climb out. As they did so, he secured the ship and sealed it tightly when everyone was off.

He then led them down a dark boardwalk and into a large cave. Along the way they all focused their attention on the branches and foliage above them, expecting unwanted objects to drop on their heads. Liam was more focused on what may reach up from the marsh over which the boardwalk extended. Once inside the cave, he found a torch and lit it from some burning embers in a fireplace. He then blocked the entryway with large rocks, until it was sealed completely. Leading them a little further into another large room, he lit other torches placed in sconces hung around the room. Soon the room was ablaze with light.

Everyone wandered around the cavern looking at the furnishings and the various charts and maps that covered the walls. Finally, Lochen commented.

"These are maps of the rivers and estuaries that feed this swamp. Where did they come from?"

"I made them," answered Liam.

"Have you traveled all of them," questioned Lochen.

"Most of them. Others I've just guessed at based on the direction of some of the tributaries, the strength of the flow, the depth and things like that."

"But how can you know the course of the water without actually seeing it?" Lochen asked in amazement.

"I don't know," answered Liam. "I just do. And I've never been wrong."

He then provided his guests with food and drink while Lochen continued to study the maps. There were several locked containers around the cavern from which he took food items and liquids. It was apparent that the retreat was well stocked. Once everyone had eaten they all began to talk about what they should be doing next. They discussed what they knew about the Crystal Citadel, Ena Ray, and the encroaching storm. Liam filled in some blanks with his experiences with the gargoyles, and the legends of his own people. They concluded that that they needed to make their way to the Crystal Citadel, but had no real idea where it was, just the general direction they had to go to get there. They asked if he could lead them there.

"Of course," he told them.

Lochen turned towards him, a bit surprised that Liam would know the way. "You know where it is, then?" he asked.

"No, not exactly," answered Liam. "Actually, not at all. But I know I can take you there." Before Lochen could ask, he added, "I don't know how I can do it. I just know that I can. I've already told you that. You'll just have to trust me. I can get you there."

For reasons he couldn't explain, Lochen believed him and trusted that Liam would not only get them there, but would find the safest route to travel. The rest felt the same way. Even Sean had to admit he agreed, even though he couldn't explain why. It made him wonder if Liam had put some kind of hex on them.

"We can take my ship part of the way," Liam explained, "but not very far. After that, we'll have to walk. I'll see that you have protective clothing and some weapons."

"I've never really liked the idea of weapons," said Lochen. "And since our use of magic has already alerted – well, everyone, I guess – to our position, I don't see why we can't rely on that."

"Your magic won't work very well in the Swamp," Liam explained. "There are too many spells that Ena Ray's followers placed on it to protect the portal to the underworld."

"I wasn't aware that gargoyles had any magical powers," said Natalie.

"Not the gargoyles," said Liam.

"Then who?" asked Solveig.

Liam hesitated a few seconds before continuing. "I don't know for sure. From the myths that each of you said were a part of your peoples' histories, and with what I know from the legends of my people, it seems like there are several possibilities – none of them very appealing. It might have been the Kelpies, or maybe the enchantresses, or some other sorcerers. Maybe even Ena Ray or that other really powerful sorcerer who was around about the same time. Who knows? I just know the spells are there."

The complexities of the history that they all knew so little about slowly descended upon them – as did the enormity of their undertaking.

The next morning Liam had set out clothing for everyone, even Summer.

"It was difficult to make things small enough to fit you," he told her. "In fact, I couldn't make anything to cover your feet, but since you can fly, maybe that won't be a problem."

She smiled broadly as she looked at the strange, tiny wardrobe. "Thanks," she told him.

Lochen immediately interjected, "Should we encounter areas where the Princess can't fly, I would be honored to transport her myself."

Summer smiled and answered, "The honor would be mine, Sorcerer."

One by one, they exchanged their robes and veils for the protective clothing Liam had provided. Lochen had some difficulty with the shirt, never having worn such a garment before. Liam had to help them all with the belts, cinches and clasps, especially for the weapons. When they were all prepared, they went back through the various rooms and hallways. They helped Liam remove the barriers that he had used to seal the entryway, and then moved quickly down the pier and boarded the ship. Liam untied the ship, jumped aboard, sealed the canopy and then backed the craft away from the pier and into the channel. There was no wind, so he had to pedal as he carefully steered his boat through the water.

He informed his passengers that the marsh was filled with sandbars that shifted as the rivers and streams worked their ways towards the sea. A ship that got caught on one of these sandbars could be stuck there for days at which time it would be extremely vulnerable to attack by the night creatures. Gargoyles were not the only guardians to the portal. He had included some innovations when he designed the present transport that would help them out should they get stuck. The wheels were just one of those innovations.

Everyone wondered what other ships were around that could get stuck. Sean was about to ask that very question, but Lochen, who sensed what was coming, motioned to him. Pulling him aside he pointed out that whatever ships may have run aground had probably held people close to Liam: people who fell victims to the gargoyles. Having him explain this would likely cause him pain. Sean quickly understood and let the matter drop.

For several hours Liam steered the ship through the winding channels, making turns for reasons that were not apparent to the others. As the day wore on, everyone knew they were making progress, but it was almost impossible to tell how much, and at times it was excruciatingly slow. The suns were often hidden from view, so Lochen was unable to get any readings from their positions. From one side of the ship to the other, and from front to back, everything around them looked the same. Solveig was sure they had passed the same gnarled tree at least twice before. She even mentioned this to Liam.

"You're probably right. They move," he said as if moving trees were something everyone encountered.

"They move?" asked Solveig in astonishment.

"Yeah," said Liam, "But they can't move very fast, and if you know what to look for, you can tell which ones have moved and which ones are still in the same place. Some of them can move on their own and can stalk their prey."

He anticipated their questions. "Yes, there are man-eating trees and plants in this place. Some of the other trees can move, but just their limbs. They can't change their location on their own. The gargoyles make them move, just to trap anyone who travels through the Swamp. One minute you think you're going in the right direction, and then the next minute you see a tree you're sure you've seen before – because you have – and you think you took a wrong turn and go back the way you just came – right into a gargoyle trap. That's why we don't get too many visitors here."

He looked up to see the shocked looks on their faces. "What?" he asked.

As the infrequent and faint glimmers of sunlight that were able to break through the moss and vines began to diminish, Liam drove the ship onto what looked like the smallest edge of a shoreline. He beached the boat, quickly opened the canopy and told everyone to stay close behind him. Once they were out, he secured the boat and sealed the hatch. He then drew a machete from his belt and began to hack at some of the bushes that had grown over the path. As he did so, the others could hear a faint whimpering sound. At first it was like a whisper, and no one was really sure what it was; but as Liam cut more of the plants, the sound got more distinctive.

"What is that sound," asked Natalie.

"Weeping willows," answered Liam. When he saw them staring at him, he added, "Just kidding. They're not willows. They're whimpering malachite vines."

They all still just stared. As he continued to cut away, the noise got louder and louder until it was more like screaming.

He then reached up and pulled some moss from an overhanging tree and handed it out.

"Roll this in your hands to make it a small ball and put the ball in your ears. You have to twist it tightly and push it as far down into your ear as possible. It will block out the sounds, but only for a short while. It will dissolve once its power is gone. I had to wait as long as possible to give this to you, because we still have a little way to go. If you used the moss

152

too soon, it would dissolve when the screams will be the most dangerous. Summer, you'll need to break up the smallest sprigs and then twist them back together. It's the twisting that then makes them expand to fill the ear canal. Make sure you twist them tight."

They all did as he instructed and the sounds were muffled, but not entirely gone. Even covering their ears with their hands couldn't completely block the sound. Just as he said, the power of the moss began to wear off and the wailing increased. He continued to cut at the foliage as quickly as he could, as he moved his team forward. Sean moved to help, but Liam stopped him.

"Thanks, but you have to be very careful. If you don't cut far enough, the screams will only echo and get worse. If you cut too much...well, you just can't do that, trust me."

Sean backed away and let Liam continue on his own. Eventually he led them to a small opening in the side of a large mound. By now the moss had almost completely lost its power and the screams were becoming painful. As soon as they were all inside, he rolled a large rock into the opening, sealing it tightly in place with moss and dirt that was piled next to the opening. He struck his machete across the rock and a spark appeared. It fell from the rock and ignited a small pile of dried moss that had been previously gathered at the base of the rock. Soon the full interior of a small cave was awash in light.

As Lochen looked around he noted that the cave was completely enclosed. He looked back at the fire that Liam was building with more dried moss.

"Won't the smoke from your fire need a place to go?" he asked.

"Fires that are made from this particular moss don't generate smoke. Actually, they release fresh air, so we'll have plenty to breathe during the night."

"During the night?" asked Natalie. "We're spending the night here? I thought this was where you lived."

"Yes," said Liam, "and no. Yes, we'll be spending the night here. Even in my boat, we're far too vulnerable in the Swamp at night. We'd need to be much better armed. And no, this is not where I live."

"It releases oxygen when it burns?" asked Lochen, returning the discussion to the moss that Liam had ignited. In all his travels and in all his reading had never heard of such a thing.

"This must have taken many generations to learn," he commented.

"To learn what?" Liam asked.

"All of this," answered Lochen in clear amazement. "To discover this cave, to find a rock that would fit exactly in the entrance, to learn that this particular moss would not produce smoke, but fresh air instead. Did you learn this from the others of your people?"

"There are no others," Liam told him. "I am the last of my people. It has been that way since I was a small child."

"Surely there must have been stories written down someplace for you to read, or handed down from generation to generation," said Lochen. "Otherwise, how would you know all this?"

"We have no written stories. I have no written stories," he corrected himself. "There is nothing to write on or with."

He looked around and then added, "The only writings I know of are some drawings on the insides of caves like this one. Those writings were made with stone by people who have been gone a very long time. I can't explain how I know these things, like the moss and the whimpering malachite vines. Some of these things I have learned by myself – making mistakes – trust me; I've made many, but not so many as to become someone or something's final meal. Maybe the spirits of those who came before me live inside me and share their wisdom. I have never questioned it. The only stories that have been handed down, as you say, have been the myths and legends about Ena Ray and the gargoyles. Those were told to me when I was very young, and I have forgotten most of it."

The gravity of his life weighed heavily on all of them. None of them had spent much if any time by themselves or on their own. To live a life of such solitude was incomprehensible to them.

The fire didn't need any more moss the entire night, but it burned brightly as long as it was needed. And as Liam had told them, the air inside the small cave was fresh and plentiful. In any other location their stay would have been enjoyable and peaceful. The night, however, was not peaceful, and the travelers got little sleep. Someone or something knew where they were and wanted desperately to get at them.

Pounding and scratching could be heard on the other side of the rock that blocked the entrance. At times it seemed as if it would be shaken loose. They also could hear the roaring and screaming of dozens of voices. The screams were not screams of pain, but more like screams of intense anger. Liam seemed to be able to pay no attention whatsoever to the noises of the night. When he saw the reactions of the others, he assured them that they were safe, and that the noises would stop before long, and any night creatures would be gone in the morning.

"But there is so little light from the suns, what makes them go away?" asked Natalie.

"I don't know for sure. It's just that I seldom see them in daylight – such as it is – and when I do, they are more easily defeated. I think that the power of their master – whoever that may be - is weakened by the daylight," Liam explained. "From what we've shared with one another, it seems that it might be that their master is Ena Ray. That seems to make sense. As long as Ena Ray is in exile, his powers are limited which would also limit their strength; although they seem to be getting stronger. I've seen that in the number and the strength of the attacks by the night creatures. And by the presence of that storm that seemed to be chasing you in the desert."

Lochen explained the approaching alignment of the planets and how he believed this was connected to the imprisonment of Ena Ray.

"That last happened about a thousand years ago, just at the time he was overthrown and banished, and his followers were cast into the underworld. I believe that this banishment won't last forever, and that it will be lifted once the planets again are in alignment. The presence and the strength of this storm, as well as what you've told us of the escalated attacks and strength of the gargoyles all seem to parallel the further alignment of the planet."

"If he was as powerful as the legends indicate," said Stella, "and as you believe he was, Lochen, then it makes sense that any spell cast by an enchantress, no matter how powerful, would be aided or boosted by an alignment of the planets. That spell would also last only until that alignment again occurred."

"That must be why we have to get to the Crystal Citadel," said Solveig.

"But why do you have to get to the same place that Ena Ray has been banished?" asked Liam. "Assuming that's where he's confined."

Lochen smiled at him and answered, "I don't know. I just know that the answer lies there, and that all of us who have traveled on this journey must be present. And on that you just have to trust me."

"Is our group now complete since we have found The Pathfinder?" asked Stella. "It's not, is it? You sense it too."

"You're right. I don't think we're complete," answered Lochen; "but I can't say for sure who else is to join us or where we might find that person. I expect that will be revealed to us when the time comes."

The next morning Liam slid the rock away from the opening. There was evidence that it had been battered and beaten in the night. The chips and scratches in the surface were minimal, but Lochen could see that the rock was so hard that it would take a tremendous force just to make the marks it now bore.  They moved away from their haven and Liam led the party along a different path than the one that had led them here.  When asked about this he explained that they had reached the point where they would have to walk.  The ship would be safe where it was, but he doubted he would be using it again.

Lochen looked at the ship and noted that there were no marks or any other indication that it had been attacked as the rock had been.  He wondered if the attackers recognized former friends or relatives in the skins that covered the craft and elected not to deface their memory.  He doubted it.

By midday they had not encountered any signs of other life in the Swamp. The absence of any sound whatsoever was eerie.  There were no birds, no insects, nothing.  Even the occasional snake or spider had not been noticed.  Sean mentioned this to Liam who told him that they were there; they just couldn't be seen.  They would come out when least expected. Sean was skeptical.  He had lived all his life in a forest and was a very capable hunter.  He found it hard to believe the predators of the Swamp could escape his detection.  He kept a watchful eye on every tree they passed under, but even with his keen eyesight, he was unable to see anything.  His natural suspicion flared and he wondered if Liam was playing pranks on him.

In the afternoon, they came upon a large open expanse.  The trees had thinned out quite a bit and the sunlight finally began to fill the sky.  Stella studied the trees and other foliage, as well as the landscape itself and their location compared to the path of the suns.  She noticed that Liam seemed to be leading them in a wide circle.  She could see off in the distance to the right what looked like an ancient fortress.  It appeared that Liam was taking them around this fortress, keeping it at a significant distance.

"You seem to be avoiding that fortress," she said to him. "Wouldn't we save some time by going towards it, or at least closer to it? Is it a stronghold of the gargoyles?"

"No," he said. "The gargoyles live deep underground. As far as I know, no one lives in that place. It was an ancient fortress of a people known as the Thumpers."

He turned to Lochen and added, "This is one of those legends I was told as a child. I have no idea if it's true or not. I remember other children saying things like, 'Don't do that or the Thumpers will get you,' or the village leaders saying, 'If you're not good, the Thumpers will steal you in the night.' I think sometimes that it was just a way to make sure the children obeyed the rules."

"So why are we avoiding the fortress," asked Solveig.

"Just in case those old threats were real," Liam answered with a wary smile.

"Well, who exactly were the Thumpers," asked Sean.

"They were the watchmen. They were responsible for making sure everyone in their community followed the rules. They weren't always called Thumpers. They were given this name because they all carried a small board on which was inscribed the basic rules of their community. At first, these boards were small, but over time, they grew larger and thicker to hold all the rules the Thumpers added. To demonstrate their commitment to those rules, they would thump the board against their foreheads. As time went by these boards were given to everyone and everyone was expected to thump them against their foreheads. This not only gave them their name, but it produced a mark by which they could identify those who followed their rules and those who didn't. If you followed the rules, you were allowed to stay. If not, you were banished to the Swamp. It wasn't as dangerous then as it is now, but it was still not exactly safe, especially at night."

"I've never heard of these people," said Lochen.

"Why would you?" asked Liam. "This area of the world is pretty far from your home. What interest could you have in them?"

"I've read traveled extensively," he answered, "I have a considerable library, as well. As a sorcerer, it is my responsibility to be knowledgeable. The more time I spend with you, though, the more I think I have to learn. Please continue."

"As far as I can tell, they were around about the time that Ena Ray was rising in power. It's likely that the Thumpers joined his followers and built the giant fortress. I went in there once and no, I'm not going in again," he said, anticipating the question.

"There are markings in there that are similar to those I've seen in the caves of the gargoyles. So some way or another, the people who lived there were connected to the gargoyles, who are in some way connected to Ena Ray."

"So what happened to them?" asked Sean.

"Like I said. At first the fortress was a shelter to all who lived in the area, even if they didn't follow the rules of the Thumpers. However, as their numbers and their power grew, they grew less tolerant of anyone who didn't follow their rules. They became more malicious and vindictive towards those who didn't join them or follow them. In the beginning, it made sense that anyone who stole or purposely hurt someone would be banished, but over time, they were banishing people who didn't speak the way they demanded, or people who didn't share the same beliefs they did, or people who didn't whack themselves on the head hard enough. Before long, there were more people banished to the land outside the fortress than were living inside.

"The people who lived outside the fortress were in huts and tents. They had built up an entire city around the fortress for protection against the animals of the night. Most of them were poor. Many of them had little food and water.

"And then one day the area was struck by a terrible plague. It had been brought in by some strangers from a distant land. It struck quickly and spread very fast. It struck the people who lived outside the fortress. Many people died. But there was an Alchemist – a healer, who just seemed to appear one day. He was from a distant land, and had overcome the plague. He constructed a large tent and was taking care of those who were suffering.

"He went to the Thumpers for help, but they locked the gates of the fortress. Every day he went to the gate and asked for help and every day he was turned away. As the plague got worse, the Thumpers built a cover over the top to keep the disease out. The Alchemist wasn't deterred by this. He continued to care for the sick. But they continued to die. Their bodies had to be burned to make sure the plague didn't spread any further. The Thumpers complained that the people were too close to the fortress; that the plague was coming through the walls. They instructed guards with spears to force the people further into the Swamp – away from the fortress. But they kept returning

"To stop them from doing this, the Thumpers planted poisonous bushes all around the outside of the fortress. These bushes were vile things. Many who planted them were infected with their poison and died. These bushes grew quickly, and their leaves and thorns were deadly. Soon they were thick around the fortress and had begun to climb the walls. Before long the entire fortress was covered with them. No one was able even to approach the fortress. The people were forced away from the only place of safety. Pleas from the Alchemist were not only rejected, but before long the Thumpers wouldn't even talk to him. They refused to open the gate, but by then, their refusal was only an idle gesture. The bushes were so thick that not only could no one enter the fortress; no one could leave.

"It took two years for the plague to end. All that time the Alchemist worked day and night to care for the sick. The death toll in the first year had been devastating. During the second year, just as many people contracted the disease, but not as many were dying. As a result of the Alchemist's efforts, especially in the second year, very few people died, although almost everyone had been afflicted. As the people regained their strength, they moved away. The fortress was no longer their home. Their land was gone; their homes were gone; their farms were gone. There was no place here for them to live any more.

"When the plague was finally over, and almost all the villagers had left, the Alchemist returned to the fortress. He noticed that the poisonous bush, which had grown quickly at first, hadn't changed much at all in the last two years. It was still thick and foreboding, The leaves looked old and withered, but still treacherous, and the thorns were more ominous than before. The leaves had turned black and the thorns were much longer and needle sharp. He called repeatedly into the fortress, but received no answer. He was infuriated with the Thumpers for having turned their backs on their own people, and for forcing them to leave their homes. He was determined that the plants that had grown around the fortress to keep the people out would no longer bar anyone's entry.

"This Alchemist carried no weapons, but had long ago discovered the power of blades forged from wizard's steel. Using his magical powers, he conjured an enormous ax crafted from the finest wizard's steal. With ax in hand, he chopped through the poisonous bush that blocked the gates of the fortress, carefully avoiding contact with the leaves, the limbs, and especially the thorns. Once the way was clear, he found the gates locked tightly shut. He waved his hand and cast a spell throwing the doors open.

He went in to confront the Thumpers and to shame them for their selfish behavior during the plague, but he was too late. He took only a few steps into the entryway and stopped. Even he was stunned by what he discovered. The interior of the fortress was thick with the poisonous bush the Thumpers had planted to keep everyone out. The bush had poisoned everything in and around the fortress. It had not survived well in the light of day on the outside, but had flourished in the darkness under the domed ceiling that had been built to hide them from the plague.

"It had taken root in the ground outside the fortress, but the roots had dug their way towards water – the water that filled the wells inside the fortress.  Those roots extended into the gardens inside the fortress, poisoning the plants that grew there.  The water had been poisoned; the ground had been poisoned; the food had been poisoned, and the air had been poisoned.  All the Thumpers were dead, and the air, still laden with the poison from the bush, was rank with the stench of decay.

"After that the Alchemist vanished.  No one knew his name, where he came from or where he went.  And since his departure, the gates of the fortress had remained open, but no one had ever entered it again.  The poisonous bush that surrounded and filled the fortress had long since died, but the poison it planted in the ground was still present.  It had done much damage that would last for a long time to come."

When Liam finished telling them all of the history behind the fortress, they continued along in silence.  As they followed the path around it, they all looked at the ruins.  There was no sign of the poisoned plant.  In fact, on closer examination, they all noted that there were no plants of any kind at least thirty feet around the building.  The walls were cracked and pitted – probably from the branches and thorns that had driven themselves into the block.  What once looked like it might have been a strong and imposing structure, now looked decrepit and dead.

The gate was open, but one door had fallen from its hinges and was leaning at an odd angle.  As they peered from their safe distance, they could see in past the gateway, but not very far.  The inside was dark as a tomb.  They all agreed that giving it a wide berth was the right decision.

# Chapter eleven

Once they had crossed the open expanse and were well clear of the ancient fortress, they were back in the heat and humidity of the swamp. For some of the time they seemed to be following an established path, but at other times they seemed to be just wandering through tall grass dodging overhanging trees. Their progress was slow, as Liam usually had to hack through thick vines and other vegetation with his machete. Most of the time, the ground beneath them was soft and wet. Often they would sink up to their ankles or knees in muck.

Not long after having passed the fortress, they began to hear things in the trees and vines that surrounded them. These were the first indications they had that there were other life forms in the swamp. Although Liam had assured them that they were far from alone, none of them had heard or seen any signs of other life. At first it was a light rustling noise. Then they could hear whispers and the movement of larger bodies – usually at dusk and dawn, and sometimes during the night, but never during the full part of the day. Stella, who had been at the end of the line on the most recent leg of the trip, spoke to Liam when they stopped for a break. She told him what she heard, but said that she hadn't seen anything, so she couldn't be sure how many there were or what they were.

"They're gargoyles," he told her.

When he didn't explain any further, she prodded him for additional information.

"There are four of them," he continued, "and they've been following us for two days. There are seven of us, so they won't attack until there are at least eight of them. I figure some time tomorrow."

Stella was initially surprised by this revelation. None of them had any sense or awareness of being followed. She told herself she should have known Liam would already have detected that they were being followed and would be prepared. This was, after all, the environment in which he lived, and had managed to survive pretty much on his own. In spite of this, she was still surprised he didn't tell the others.

That night when they had made camp in a cave similar to the other ones Liam had managed to locate along the way, he shared Stella's conversation and his own observations with everyone. He didn't reveal this earlier because he didn't want the gargoyles alerted to the fact that they had been discovered. He planned to use this against them. He told the others that there was a canyon coming up that they would reach by early afternoon the next day. This would be the best place for an ambush.

Stella was confused. "I assumed they avoided the sun light. That's the only time of day we haven't heard them. Why do you think they'll make their move in daytime?"

"They'll attack whenever they think they have the advantage. You haven't noticed them in the daytime because they've fallen back, far out of sight and sound. They don't need to see us to follow us. They can smell us."

"Are you saying we stink?" asked Sean.

"Well," Liam answered, half jokingly, "some of you are a bit ripe, but no, that's not what I meant. The gargoyles have a very keen sense of smell. Our scent is greater during the day while we're exerting ourselves. During that time they don't need to follow as closely – until they're ready to strike."

"What makes this location ahead a good place for an ambush?" asked Lochen.

"The gargoyles don't fight unless they outnumber their opponents and they usually like to pick spots where they have a clear advantage" Liam went on to explain. "I've been through this canyon before and have seen signs of how they have attacked their prey. There's an outcropping on the side of the canyon wall that overlooks the main path. It's apparent that the gargoyles don't know that in the middle of this canyon just before that outcrop, there is a break on one side. It's a very narrow passageway that is almost impossible to see from the outcrop above, and it circles around and behind the outcrop, ending just above it. That outcrop is where I expect them to be waiting for us to pass."

"We'll need more than just the knives you have if we're to attack a greater number of gargoyles," Solveig said. "Most of us are not skilled at close combat and would be no match for these gargoyles if they are as strong and vicious as you say they are."

"Wait a minute," objected Sean. "I'm not afraid of anyone or anything."

"Yes, I know," answered Liam. "It's not a question of bravery. It's a matter of making sure the odds are more in our favor."

He turned behind him and started digging in the dirt at the back of the cave. He quickly uncovered a large piece of gargoyle skin wrapped around several unusual looking weapons and a cache of small arrows.

"These are crossbows," he told them. "You load an arrow in the front, pull the bow back to arm it, and then hold it up to your shoulder to aim and fire. The arrow heads are made from wizard's steel, and will penetrate their scales."

"Couldn't we just use magical powers to drive them away?" asked Lochen.

"You could try, but your magic may not work. They may be protected by other more powerful spells. Maybe not, but I don't want to take that chance. And if your magic doesn't work, we'll easily be captured."

"But they wouldn't harm us, would they?" asked Natalie. "I mean, they could ransom us, or something."

"No," said Liam. "They don't care about that. They'd eat us – and not quickly. They'd start with our hands and feet, taking their time, keeping us alive as long as possible. Except for you, perhaps," he said to Summer. "You'd just be a snack they'd gobble whole."

Sean pulled out his trusty slingshot and announced, "This is all the weapon I need."

"Your stones won't get past their scales," Liam told him. "You'll have to aim for their eyes, and those eyes are small and beady."

"He can do that," everyone announced all together, having seen him shoot the panther in the jungle.

"We may have need of your skill, then," said Liam as he passed around the crossbows.

Summer was much too small to handle such a large weapon.

"What am I supposed to do?" she asked.

"Perhaps you could serve as a distraction," Lochen suggested. "Regardless of the level of their skills, I think you'll be too small a target for their arrows."

"I can make myself almost invisible, then fly behind their ears and make enough noise to draw their attention," she smiled.

"That might work," said Liam. "You'd have to get really close, and it might be really dangerous. They can be quick.

"I can do it," she said more bravely than she felt.

They got an early start the next morning and by midday were winding their way through the canyon Liam had described the night before. The path was a bog that wound between several soaring boulders that jutted from the ground. The foliage around them was far too thick to cut through, making the marshy passageway the only option forward. By now they were almost knee deep in mud, making them move even more slowly than before.

Solveig leaned over to whisper to Lochen, "I can see why they would chose to attack here. Not only do they have the advantage of the higher ground, but this mud makes escape nearly impossible."

Lochen looked around and nodded in agreement with her. He trusted Liam's plan, but he couldn't help but feel extremely vulnerable. If Liam was wrong and the attack came sooner, they would be easily trapped. He thought back to what seemed like another lifetime when they were living peacefully in their mountain palace. Solveig was the warrior between the two of them. She had studied the tactics of war and fighting, and made him take part. He never understood why she would want to study such a thing as war, and especially why she made him participate. Now, reflecting on that, he was glad she did, and wished he had paid more attention. He trusted her knowledge and understanding of military tactics. Between her and Liam, Lochen felt confident that they would prevail – if they made it to the breach Liam had described.

Suddenly Liam turned right, and everyone behind him hesitated. It looked like he was walking into the side of the canyon itself. The opening he had discovered could not be seen from the direction they had all been traveling. It was just as Liam had described – very narrow and serpentine.

They had to turn sideways and squeeze through – except for Summer who hovered in the air right behind Liam.

The path wove back and forth, but all the time led them upward. Parts of the opening were so narrow that Lochen could barely fit through. This would not be a good place to get stuck, he told himself as he scraped his chest and back against the stone walls. In a few minutes Liam slowed down and raised his hand for silence. They had reached an outcropping. They all crept forward as silently as possible. When they all reached the ledge, Liam motioned immediately below them.

About twenty feet in front of them were not the four gargoyles that Liam had said were following them, nor the eight he expected would be assembled to give them the numerical advantage, but twelve. They held bows and arrows as well as spears and knives. They were huddled close together and peeking over the edge of the overlook down on the marshy path below.

Their appearance was shocking. Summer gazed in near horror at the thought of getting close to them. Their bodies were gnarled and misshapen. Their skin was a grayish green and the color seemed to swirl and move beneath their scales. There were spikes of bristling hair in small patches on the tops of their heads and down their backs. A few of them could be seen in profile and their faces were scarred and ugly; their mouths were filled with long, sharp, crooked teeth. Their noses were large with flared nostrils. Their hands and feet were very large and had claws instead of nails.

Liam whispered to Summer, "Are you sure you can do this?"

She steeled her nerves and nodded yes.

Liam looked at her closely and then said in a voice as low as he could, "All right, then. Drop down off to the left, towards the direction they expect us to come. Get behind the one that's farthest to the left and buzz in his right ear. It doesn't matter what you say or if you say anything at all; then as quickly as you can, fly over to the one that's farthest on the right and yell in his left ear. I want them to start looking at each other instead of where they expect us to come. See what I need?"

Summer nodded that she understood. She took a deep breath and concentrated on changing her appearance to blend in with the rocks and plants that surrounded them. Soon she was barely visible. Even Liam who had been watching her transform and knew where she was could barely see her. She had been hovering right before him. If he didn't know she was there, he'd miss her completely. It was like looking through rippling water.

As Summer slowly and quietly flew towards the first gargoyle, she thought this had all sounded much easier to do when they were talking about it earlier. Now she wasn't so sure. She thought for a minute of the stone images of her family and friends, and her courage welled up. As she got closer she was repulsed by a terrible smell that the gargoyles gave off. In spite of her fear, she hovered closer and closer, careful not to make a sound or to create a breeze. She floated like a feather dropping from the sky, making subtle shifts in her wings as she moved closer to her target. Finally she was right behind the first gargoyle.

She leaned as close as she dared, but she couldn't think of anything to say. This is not a time for brain freeze, she told herself. She said the first thing that came into her mind and whispered, "You're ugly and your mother dresses you funny."

She almost laughed nervously as she said it. She didn't know what else to say, so she quickly flew up and over towards the second gargoyle, nearly getting struck by the nose of the gargoyle as he turned his head sharply in the direction of her voice. He had turned immediately to the gargoyle right next to him and slammed his fist into the other's nose, almost shouting, "Who are you calling ugly?"

The biggest gargoyle, the one in the middle, who seemed to be the leader, struck the first one on the head with his spear and growled at him to keep quiet. Just as he did this, Summer had arrived at the ear of her second target, and shouted, "Look out, the sky is falling."

This gargoyle ducked his head down and fell to the ground, knocking two of the ones standing closest to him into each other. The leader started clubbing all three of them. The two who had been knocked over, shouted objections. The leader beat them harder to quiet them. The one who had been struck in the nose took advantage of the leader's distraction to wreak vengeance on the one who had struck him. Soon there was chaos among them and Summer fluttered up and out of the way.

Liam let loose the first shot and the others immediately followed. Several of their arrows missed, since none of them had ever fired a crossbow before. Liam's and Solveig's found their targets. They had dispatched the two on the far left in the midst of their fight with one another. There were now only ten gargoyles, and they had yet to discover where the attack was coming from or even that the attack on them had commenced.

Summer swooped across in front of them. Lowering her voice as much as she could, making it sound gravelly, she shouted, "Look, down there in the swamp," and then flew up and out of the way again.

The gargoyles who had not been embroiled in the chaos leaned over the edge and looked down where they had expected the travelers to be, but could see nothing. Another volley of arrows was let loose, more of which found targets this time. Three of the gargoyles fell forward over the edge of the canyon and the fourth one fell next to the first two who had fallen.

Now there were only six left, but they knew they were being attacked. One of them shouted to the leader, who broke off fighting with the victims of Summer's second diversionary effort. He turned to see where the attack was coming from and directed the others to fire back. As they did so, Sean fired two quick shots and hit each of the two eyes of the leader. Gesturing blindly and in a rage, he turned the wrong way, collided with one of his own and fell over the side of the cliff.

Outnumbered and with their leader disabled, the remaining gargoyles fled, leaving their dead and wounded behind. Although he couldn't see and had fallen to the marsh below, the leader had survived the fall and heard his comrades deserting him. He could hear the arrows shot by the attackers whizzing by his head. He grabbed his spear and, roaring with frustration, threw with all his strength towards the sound of the firing crossbows, and fumbled to escape himself without knowing if he struck a target or not.

The spear sailed upward, narrowly whizzing past Summer. Natalie was looking down at her crossbow as she reloaded it. She didn't see the missile heading directly towards her, but her Enchantress did. Stella dove at the Princess, pushing her to the ground and out of the path of the spear, but she wasn't able to save herself. The razor sharp point struck her solidly in the center of her back, throwing her forward and slamming her into the side of the rocks. The breath shot out of her lungs with a loud groan and she slid to the ground.

Summer had spun to avoid the spear as it shot past her and saw it strike Stella. "No!" she yelled.

The others ceased firing on the retreating gargoyles and their leader, and rushed to Stella. Lochen shouted for them to not touch her. He knelt down, removed the spear from her back and gently turned her over. Her eyes were shut and there was a peaceful look on her face. Tears immediately formed in Natalie's eyes, and the others were too shocked to speak.

"Is there anything you can do?" pleaded Natalie.

Lochen only held her as Liam reached into a pouch inside his shirt and pulled a small leafy looking item that was mottled in orange and yellow. He moved Lochen aside and squeezed Stella's cheeks to open her mouth, and then pushed the leaf under her tongue. He worked her jaw up and down a number of times and then closed her mouth. In a few seconds her eyelids fluttered and then opened. She took in a deep breath and started to cough. Lochen sat her up while Liam gave her a canteen with some water.

"She's just had the wind knocked out of her," said Liam. He turned her around gently and examined the small hole in the material she was wearing.

"See?" he asked. "No blood. The armor I gave you all will protect you from being pierced, but it won't deflect spears and arrows. You're lucky that shot didn't break you in half."

"What was that leaf you gave her?" asked Lochen.

"One of the few plants in the swamp that's not poisonous," he answered.

"What does it do, exactly?"

"It provides medicinal remedies to several ailments – in fact to just about any ailment I've ever seen. It just seems to know what the patient needs and supplies it. In this case, she just needed air. If she can stand we need to get going."

"Why?" asked Sean. "Those gargoyles are on the run. You said they wouldn't attack if they were outnumbered. By my count there are more of us than there are of them."

"That won't last long," answered Liam. "They'll get reinforcements very quickly and they don't take kindly to defeat. They'll bring about twenty of their friends, but this time they won't try to kill us, they'll want to take some captives."

"Captives?" asked Solveig, gulping as she recalled what he had said about the gargoyles taking captives.

Liam looked at her, and for the first time she thought she saw a glimmer of fear in his eyes. "We've shamed them. They'll want to make an example of us – one by one."

He led them forward on the path and soon came to an open area from which several paths diverged in several different directions. It was like approaching multiple accesses to a maze. Without stopping Liam turned off onto one of them and then picked up the pace to a trot. The others followed silently; trusting him to lead them to safety, running after him down hill and back into the thick, overgrown vegetation. Soon they were back in the mud filled marsh, and had to slow down. When the muck was up to their knees, Liam quickly changed direction and created his own path through the grass and vines, hacking at them as he went.

The overhanging trees and moss eventually made their travel even more difficult. It was nearly impossible to see more than just a few feet. The darkness was broken up sporadically with nearly blinding flashes of sunlight as it burst through openings in the plant life.

"Stay close and keep alert," Liam warned. "This is a short cut, but it's filled with snakes and alligators. Try not to make any sounds and listen for any unusual noises."

"Unusual noises?" asked Sean. "It's all unusual. What's more unusual than unusual?"

Summer was flying slightly above and behind the group, thinking the same thing as Sean: Everything sounds unusual; how can we tell the difference? She looked up just in time to see a large snake hanging down from a tangle of moss directly in front of her. It was waiting for her with its mouth wide open. She stopped abruptly and dodged as it snapped at her, barely missing. She swooped down and flew a little closer to the ground. In her nervousness she shouted back to the snake, "No thanks. I prefer to dine with friends."

She was looking back toward the snake when she found herself entangled in a giant spider's web. She turned forward and only entangled herself more, bouncing back and forth in the silken web. Solveig jumped up as she ran beneath the trap and snatched Summer free without breaking her stride.

"Not a good time for a visit," she said breathing heavily as she released Summer from her grip.

"You're probably right," said Summer, as she resumed her flight as close to Solveig's shoulder as she could get.

In time the soggy ground became a bit drier and firmer. It was still muddy, but at least they were able to begin a slow run again. Summer had resumed flying at different heights and back and forth among the others. On more than one occasion in her flitting, she thought she heard something rustling in the undergrowth off to her left. She dropped back in the formation and hovered near Lochen's ear. He had rotated to the end of the line not too long before.

"I think there's something moving very quickly just the other side of these vines and shrubs," she whispered. "I keep hearing a rustling of the leaves."

"Yes, I agree," he whispered back. "I've heard it, too. It sounds like more than one of whatever it is. Or it's much larger than I care to consider."

"At the next break in the foliage, I'm going to fly over to see if I can get a glimpse of whatever's following us."

"All right," said Lochen, "but be careful. I'll be right behind you."

A few yards ahead Summer saw what she was looking for. There was an opening in the vegetation that led to another path. The encounter with the snake was fresh in her mind, so she thought she might be better off if she flew closer to the ground as she veered off through the vines and onto the branching trail. She and Lochen slowed their pace. The others moved on ahead, unaware that the two had separated themselves from the group. Lochen looked at them as they disappeared into the brush.

"We had better make a quick reconnaissance," he whispered to Summer.

She nodded agreement, and then fluttered slowly through the break in the wall of leaves, inching her way forward along the line of tall grass, peeking her head forward as she did so. She looked over her shoulder back towards Lochen to make sure he was close behind as she continued forward. Just as she was checking on Lochen's location and had turned her attention away from where she was going, the line of grass ended and she was fully exposed.

She heard a swishing sound slightly louder than before and uncomfortably close. She jerked her head back towards the noise and found herself along side of, and eye to eye with the largest alligator she could ever imagine. The reptile was almost as startled as she was, but its reactions were a split second quicker. As soon as the beast saw the fluttering motion of Summer's wings in the corner of it eye, it swung its massive head in her direction and snapped its giant jaws as it lunged towards her.

She was just quick enough to narrowly avoid the rows of knifelike teeth as they chomped down with a crash. The air that whooshed from the motion of its closing jaws pushed Summer backwards, knocking her down to the ground. Not knowing or caring if it had caught her or not, it snapped its jaws again and again, all the while moving forward.

She jumped up and was again blown back by the force of air bursting from the snapping jaws, and landed with a splat in a puddle of mud and ooze. Her body was half-buried in the mire; her wings were coated with mud, and she found herself stuck in place as she watched the alligator lumber towards her. By now it knew that it had missed and had stopped snapping aimlessly. It surveyed the surroundings and spotted Summer stuck in the mud. Its yellow eyes seemed to glow in the darkness of the swamp and as it opened its jaws wide, it seemed like it was grinning at her. Her voice caught in her throat and she could barely breathe; she was frozen with fear.

She wriggled franticly trying to extricate herself from the muck. Before the alligator got another step closer, Lochen jumped into the space between it and Summer, sliding across the mud and reeds. He came to a stop immediately under the alligator's gullet and thrust his knife up through the beast's lower jaw with such force that it slammed it up into the upper jaw. The blade of his knife pierced the soft tissue of the throat, slid through the tongue and wedged into the hard upper jaw, pinning the jaws shut. The alligator shook its head in anger, letting out a muffled roar. Lochen sat up with a look of satisfaction on his face. He had surprised even himself.

As the monster thrashed around trying to free its jaws, another swishing sound was heard. Lochen and Summer spun their heads in that direction to see a second, bigger alligator came up behind the first one. Its attention was focused in its partner, seemingly oblivious to the presence of Lochen and Summer. It only saw the first alligator defenseless and it detected the scent of the blood that dripped from the knife that had been wrenched from Lochen's hand. In spite of the twisting and jerking, the knife was still pinning the massive jaws shut.

In the blink of an eye, the second alligator attacked the first one. It sank its teeth into the flesh around the neck and clamped tightly shut. It then thrashed back and forth, slicing through tissue. As the two of them clawed each other, and lashed out with their mighty tails, Lochen pulled Summer free from the mud and slowly backed away. They inched their way backwards through the opening and back to the trail from which they had come.

Not looking where he was going, he stepped backwards into a small pool of mud and slime. He slipped and slid; falling farther backwards and immediately sank to his knees. As he tried to get a foothold and climb out, he sank even further. With every step, lifting one leg upward, he pushed himself further down with the other leg.

In a matter of seconds he was up to his waist and was continuing to sink. Still holding Summer in his hand, he opened it and pushed her away from him. She dropped to the ground a few feet away and stared at him, not yet comprehending what was happening. Lochen stopped struggling if only to slow down his descent into the mire.

"It's quicksand," he said more calmly than he felt. "Or quick mud, not that it matters much. The point is that I'm sinking and I can't yet feel anything solid beneath my feet to stop my sinking."

She still didn't understand what he was talking about. She had never heard of or experienced ground that sucked a person down.

"I think it would be most advisable if you sought help," he instructed a little more urgently. "Now would be good!"

She hesitated only a moment. Once the impact of what was happening sunk in, and realizing that there was nothing she could do to save him, she raced to catch up with the others.

Lochen slowly continued to sink into the quicksand. He kept as still as he could and at the same time kept his eyes on the battle between the two alligators. The one he had stabbed had finally lost the fight and was now dinner for the other. Lochen hoped that this would satisfy the hunger of the remaining alligator and that it wouldn't be interested in him as dessert. The sound of the feasting was almost as disturbing to him as his current plight.

For a second or two, he seemed to stop sinking, but then he dropped down further. As he sank lower and lower, he looked around for something to grab that would stop his descent. He spotted an old dead branch near his right. If he could grab the end of it he might be able to use it to hook on to some of the vines that were just out of his reach and pull himself free. He moved as if he was swimming, trying to float on the top of the mud, and trying to edge closer towards his right. When he was close enough and reached for the branch, a pair of eyes popped open and a pair of gleaming fangs snapped at his hand.

"I guess that won't exactly help," he said to himself, jerking his hand back and sinking another couple of inches deeper.

It seemed like an eternity since Summer had left him. The muck was over his chest and just under his arms. The only sounds he could hear were coming from the giant reptile that was still much too close, but for the moment was still dining on its partner. He couldn't detect any sounds of his friends returning to his rescue.

"I hope she can find the others all right," he thought. "And I hope they make it back here before it's too late. This is not how I expected things to end."

As he sunk lower and lower, he envisioned the sands in an hourglass as they neared the end. He knew that they moved no faster at the end of the hour than they did at the beginning of the hour; that it was only an illusion that they did so. Now he wasn't so sure. He felt as if he was sinking much faster than at the start, and that the sands of his life were sliding by at an alarming rate.

By now the slime was covering his mouth. Only the very top of his head and the tip of his nose were above the surface. He had resigned himself to the fact that he would not see the end of this quest. He felt a sudden rush of panic sweep over him as the top of his head dropped below the surface. One of his last thoughts was that he would never again see the rings around the planet Capurnica.

# Chapter twelve

After a while Sean, who had been at the end of the line, just ahead of Lochen, noticed that both Summer and Lochen were missing. He called ahead to Liam and the others to stop. They circled together and caught their breath, debating for a few minutes about whether they should stay where they were in the hopes that the missing two would catch up, or to go back and look for them. Liam was concerned that they may have taken one of several wrong turns and could be lost forever. If that was the case, they could search forever and never find them.

Solveig asked him, "What if they're waiting where they were so they won't get lost, hoping we'd come find them?"

As they were about to head back the way they had come, Summer came rocketing towards them, shouting loudly, not caring if she was overheard by wandering gargoyles.

"Help, help. Come quickly. Lochen fought off a giant lizard and he's sinking in the mud. Please hurry. I'll show you where!"

She spun around and headed back. The others ran frantically to keep up with her. When she arrived back where she had left Lochen, she saw that the one alligator was still eating its dead partner. It stopped gnawing, a large piece of raw meat dangling from its jaw. It glared at the interruption and uttered a low rumbling sound. Once it was satisfied that she was not there to steal its food, it returned to its meal,

Summer froze in the air, hovering near the pool of mud and staring back at the alligator. She was not sure whether it was a good sign or a bad one that the beast was still here and still eating. She was a little worried that it would try another attack, but if it hadn't been there she would probably have missed the spot where Lochen had fallen into the quicksand. She fluttered around and around, but didn't see him.

When the others finally caught up with her, they came to a quick stop, startled by the sight of the alligator. Sean readied his slingshot and Natalie and Stella drew their knives. The alligator once again stopped chewing and shifted slightly. It moved its body between its feast and the intruders, ready to defend or attack. For a few seconds, no one moved. Then Sean, Natalie and Stella inched between the pool of mud and the alligator, keeping their eyes on the beast, while it kept its eyes on them. Liam and Solveig searched the pool for a sign of Lochen, but could see nothing.

"Are you sure this is the spot?" asked Liam.

"Yes," shouted Summer, clearly distraught. "We heard a sound and crept through that break in the brush." She pointed through the opening towards the alligators.

"When we backed through, he slipped and fell in that pool or pond or whatever it is and started sinking."

As Lochen had sunk beneath the surface of the pond, he took what he was sure would be his final deep breath and turned his thoughts to his beloved stars and planets. He held his breath as long as he could. His lungs were burning. He had no idea how far beneath the surface he had sunk, and was certain he was lost. As he was about to let out his breath, he heard muffled sounds of shouts. He wasn't sure if it was a returning band of gargoyles or a rescue mission. He didn't much care which it was, although he thought he would much rather have his friends pull him free.

The thought of being eaten bit by bit was not particularly appealing, but in weighing the alternative to certain death beneath a layer of quicksand...he was becoming delirious, he knew: debating which manner of death would be preferable. He was on the verge of losing consciousness when he decided to take his chances and he raised his arm. Not knowing how far down he had sunk, he only hoped that his hand would break the surface.

Liam and Solveig were still looking around the pool of quicksand when suddenly, the surface of the pool was disturbed by a subtle ripple, and a set of fingertips appeared.

"Lochen," shouted Solveig. "Quickly; we need something to pull him free," she cried as she stepped towards the outreached hand.

Liam grabbed her and pulled her back.

"Be careful. We don't need two of you in there," he said.

Solveig was in a panic. She looked around for something for Lochen to grab on to. She shouted to the others to look around as well. She spotted some vines nearby and drew her knife to cut them free.

"Stop," shouted Liam. "Those are poisonous, and I have no cure for their venom. You'll both die if you try to use them to pull your Sorcerer free."

"Then find something in this godforsaken place that is NOT poisonous," she shouted.

Solveig thought she'd lose her mind. She saw Lochen's hand begin to drop below the surface. There had to be something. She and Liam were searching franticly. Even Sean had taken his eyes off the alligator to scan the surrounding area. There were thousands of vines and bushes, but nothing that was safe enough to use.

"This can't be happening," screamed Solveig.

And then, with barely a thought, she pulled her long red hair free from the back of her neck. In one quick motion she sliced her knife across it near the back of her head. Her fingers flew as she braided the strands into a rope and threw the end to Lochen's disappearing hand.

"Grab it, Lochen!" she shouted. "Reach out and grab it like you're reaching for the stars."

Lochen was close to blacking out. His lungs were burning with the air he held inside them. He thought he felt something soft strike his outreached fingertips, but he wasn't sure if it was real or if he only imagined it. It was as soft as silk. What could it be, he wondered. The last flickers of his conscious mind told him it didn't matter, to just grab it, which he did. As his fist closed around the hair, his arm dropped down towards his side. He nearly lost his grip on whatever he had grabbed, but it was tangled in his fingers.

He could hold his breath no longer, and the air escaped from his lungs, bubbling to the surface. As the bubbles rose, he felt himself being pulled upward. First his arm was raised, and then he felt his entire body moving upward. Am I going to heaven, he wondered. Will I see the planets and the stars? He felt the cooler air through the slime that covered his head followed by a hand wiping the muck away from his mouth. He sucked inward filling his burning lungs with a gasp of fresh air. It was still hot and humid air, but he couldn't recall anything tasting so sweet.

Some of the mud entered his throat and he began to cough. He was only barely aware of being turned onto his stomach and that his back was being pounded. The coughing subsided and he could feel that someone was pouring water over his mud caked head. When he was finally breathing normally and turned over to sit up, he opened his eyes. At first his vision was blurred, but as the images came into focus, he saw the tear filled eyes of his sister, his Princess. He immediately noticed the shortness of her hair. He looked into his hand and saw the deep red braid that had pulled him to safety.

"Your hair," he said in amazement. "Your Highness, you cut your hair."

It was all he could say.

"It seemed like a good idea at the time," she said. " And, anyway, it will grow back. I can always get new hair. I could never get a new Sorcerer."

He smiled at her and struggled to his feet. He poured some more water over himself to remove as much of the mud as he could, but this only seemed to make it worse. He glanced over to see the alligator still staring at all of them.

"Can you keep going?" Liam asked.

"Can't we let him rest?" asked Solveig.

"No," said Lochen. "I'm fine. Really. Liam's right. We should go."

"I agree," said Sean. "That alabaster is done eating and I think he's looking for dessert."

"I think you mean alligator," siad Liam, "But regardless, we're not out of reach of the gargoyles and night will be approaching soon. We have to keep going."

There was no more discussion and they took off, staying in a closer formation than before. Liam led them at a strenuous pace, repeatedly looking over his shoulder. Twice they had to stop to rest and both times he seemed more agitated than before. The others knew enough to trust his instincts and didn't argue when he pushed them almost mercilessly. It was dusk when they came upon a large clearing.

"We're not going to be able to go any further," he said, disappointed. "This will have to do."

He looked around at the surroundings. Within the clearing were about a dozen very tall trees. They had very few branches and shot straight up into the sky. Near the tops of three of them, barely visible against the darkening sky, were what looked to be large nests.

"Summer" Liam called. "Can you fly up near those nests and see if you notice any birds? Don't bother with the other trees. Those won't help us. Be very careful. Those are Blue Falcon nests, and even as fast as you are, you may not be able to outrun them. If there are no birds, then the nests are probably safe. If you see any nests with Falcons, or worse, if you see any eggs, get away quickly and quietly."

She understood and took off towards the top of the nearest tree. From the ground below, the others watched as she neared the first nest. She no sooner peeked over the top when she suddenly swooped down and away. She disappeared from sight briefly as a large talon appeared over the edge of the nest, followed by an even larger and more ominous beak. They saw her again as she approached the second nest in one of the neighboring tree. The same thing happened and she moved to the third nest. From there she dropped back down to ground level.

"The first two have Falcons in them, but that third one looked empty," she reported.

Liam showed everyone how to use the scales from the gargoyle skin leggings and foot ware to catch into the sides of the trees in order to climb to the top. For Sean this was just like home. He scampered up to the nest first and encouraged the others as they followed. Summer simply flew up and nestled in next to Sean. One by one, the others followed.

While they were doing that Liam went to the edge of the clearing to some tall grass. When he found what he was looking for, ran his hand along a piece of razor grass, opening a cut across his palm. He returned to the cluster of trees, and smeared the blood in both his hands. He then began to climb up the first tree that Summer had scouted. He went nearly to the top, but not quite all the way, then slid back to the ground and repeated this on the second tree Summer had surveyed.

When he was done, he wrapped the cut tightly in a scrap of cloth and made sure no blood seeped through. Then he climbed the third tree and rejoined the group in the nest.

"What was that all about?" Natalie asked him.

"I left the scent of my blood on those first two trees. If the gargoyles return, they'll follow that scent."

"Won't they also follow your scent up this tree?" asked Stella.

"It's not likely," he answered. "They're basically lazy. I'll be surprised if they even look to the second tree."

He went on to tell them that even with this precaution, it would be a good idea if they took turns standing guard. Nothing with gargoyles was predictable. He took the first shift and suggested that Lochen not stand guard, since he probably needed more rest after his ordeal. Lochen explained to him that he only needed to sleep an hour or two about once a week. He would be glad to keep each of the guards company.

"I would be glad to discuss some theories about the formation of the constellations, the creation of black holes, and the like," he said.

Solveig, who had heard this talk so many times before would have normally rolled her eyes and made some kind of disparaging remark.

However, as she reached back and felt the blunt edge where she had cut her hair, her heart swelled. She was so glad to have her brother safe and with her, that she looked forward to hearing him talk about his favorite topic once more.

"I'll take the second watch," she volunteered.

The night passed without incident. The lead sun had just begun to appear over the horizon, and the sky was still a light gray. Natalie was on guard duty. Lochen had been telling her some of the stories behind the various constellations in the night sky, when something caught her attention and she motioned him to be silent. Carefully they both crawled to the edge of the nest. They looked down into the clearing and then over at the two trees where Liam had placed a false scent.

Liam had been right. The gargoyles had followed them and come back in greater numbers. There looked to be about twenty of them gathered near the bottom of both of the other two trees. Some of them had already begun to climb towards the nests. Natalie crept over to each of the others, and, placing her hand over their mouths, gently woke each of them in turn. There was little else they could do for now but to watch.

Very quietly and very slowly several gargoyles inched their way up the two trees. Liam had also been right about what scent they would follow. None of them had bothered to even consider the tree Summer had identified as their refuge. As the first one reached the base of the nest, it settled itself in the supporting branches, making room for the gargoyle that was advancing right behind it. One by one, several of them climbed each of the trees and then waited for the others.

This pattern continued in both trees until there were about six of them positioned around the base of each nest. In the growing light, they could be seen gesturing to one another and then drawing long knives. As one in both of the two teams nodded, they all shoved their knives repeatedly up through the nest. Six long blades cut through the twigs and leaves of the nests and into the sleeping forms inside.

Instead of piercing the bodies of the travelers they had been chasing, their knives broke into the eggs that were being protected by the Falcons that were nesting there. The contents of the damaged eggs seeped through the crannies in the nests and the gaping holes made by the blades, and dripped on the heads of the attackers. As the realization of what was happening came to the Falcons that were covering the nests, they let out an ear piercing screech and flew out of the nests, circling the tops and dropping down below to see who or what had killed their eggs.

The gargoyles didn't immediately realize what they had done. The nests held the eggs of a pair of Falcon parents who now sought revenge. They watched stupidly as the birds circled and then began attacking the intruders. The Falcons were smarter, though, than the gargoyles. They attacked the ones further away from the nest first, leaving the ones above them no place to escape. They clawed and pecked, nipping at eyes and pulling at hands and feet.

One of the Falcons managed to pluck one of the gargoyles away from the tree and carried it off, dangling it by its ankle. The other birds seemed to know that the scales on the skin of the gargoyles were nearly impenetrable. They didn't attempt to gouge or cut them. They did, however, follow the lead of the one and pulled the gargoyles one by one away from the tree top and dropped them several hundred feet to the ground below. They fell on the others that were waiting at the bottom, staring up at the debacle.

Those that didn't fall were carried off to somewhere deep within the swamp. Liam guessed they would be fed to alligators whose teeth were strong enough to break through the scales, or they would be dumped in the quicksand pools where they would sink to the bottom, never to be rescued. The few that had remained at the base of the tree soon ran off. But the screams of the Falcons whose nests had been invaded, woke the other Falcon families in nearby nests. They joined the enraged birds and chased after the escaping gargoyles.

"I doubt that those gargoyles will ever get back to their base, and I don't think they'll be bothering us again," Liam told the others. "But I don't think we're safe even now."

"Are there more Falcons?" asked Stella.

In answer to her question he only said, "Worse."

He motioned to the distant sky that was now more visible since the lead sun had fully risen. Just over the horizon a massive black cloud was emerging. It was still too far off to hear the crashing thunder, but flickers of lightning flashes were visible. The Fury was clearly coming directly towards them.

They all quickly climbed down the tree and continued their trek. The terrain was gradually changing. It was apparent that they were finally leaving the swamp. Late in the day, they came upon a fast flowing stream.

"We can follow this up-stream for the next few days," announced Liam. "There are places we can use for shelter along the way. For a little while we shouldn't have to worry about being attacked, but that won't last long, even if we're able to keep ahead of that storm."

"Have you been this way before?" asked Natalie.

"No," he answered. "This is all new to me. But I think your magic powers will work. We're far enough from the Swamp that the spells that diminished your powers should no longer be effective."

"Won't that alert Ena Ray to our location?"

"It appears he already knows where we are," Liam said to her.

Over the next three days, no matter how fast a pace they set, the clouds of the storm seemed to keep getting closer. By the end of the second day, they could hear the booming thunder and it resonated even louder on the third day.

They had been following the same stream the entire way.  Now it was much deeper and much more turbulent. Just before midday the passage that ran along side of the stream became blocked with fallen trees and rocks.  Liam had to change course and the group went deeper into the surrounding woods, climbing well above the level of the stream.  The roaring of the water could still be heard, far below them.

This forest was much like the one Sean had grown up in.  He recognized some of the types of trees, although not all of them.  His mood swung back and forth between homesickness and exhilaration at being on familiar terrain, especially since they had moved away from the stream.  As late afternoon approached, he heard a rumbling sound not too far ahead of the group.

Slowly but surely, the sound got louder and louder.  They appeared to be heading straight for it.  Even before they got within sight, Sean knew what the sound was: a waterfall.  A sense of panic slowly began to seep into his consciousness. As they came through a thicket of trees and into a clearing they found themselves near the shore of the stream they had been following the previous three days.  Except now it was much wider, much deeper and the current was much faster.  Liam kept heading towards the water, and Sean began to get a weak feeling in his knees.  How had it gotten so close, he wondered.

"Where are we going?" he finally asked.

"To the edge of the waterfall," answered Liam.  "That's where the water is the shallowest and we can cross over on the rocks."

"Cross over?" asked Sean in disbelief, his voice almost an octave higher.

When the waterfall was in sight, he could see that it was almost a hundred foot drop to the reservoir below, which fed into the stream that had been their guide.  It was easy to see now why the stream was at their level when days before they had been climbing high above it.  Sean had no fear of heights, but the thought of crossing that water filled him with dread.

"I'll go first," volunteered Solveig. She hadn't forgotten Sean's bravery at jumping in the water to save her. She was well aware of his fear and his reluctance to show it.

"You can hold my hand as we cross. It would make me feel safer."

Sean just rolled his eyes. He knew Solveig was not afraid and that she had no concern for her safety. Her words were meant to console him. Part of him was dismayed at this thought, while part of him was glad for her offer. "Why is there always so much water?" he thought to himself.

"I'll go last to make sure everyone gets across safely," said Liam, and one by one, each of them began to step carefully on the slippery rocks that were closest to or above the surface. Although she was nervous, Solveig was more concerned about Sean. She thought to distract him by exaggerating her fears and she pretended to try to make a game of it, singing as she jumped from one stone to the next. She and Sean easily made it across, but nonetheless, she hoped they wouldn't have to do that again. One slip and it was a long way to the bottom.

"It's okay now," she told him as she pried her hand loose from his vise-like grip. "Thanks. I really felt safe."

"Whatevs," he said, somewhat embarrassed.

Next went Lochen, with Summer sitting on his shoulder. She could have easily flown across, but she sat with him whispering encouragement. He wasn't really nervous, and Summer was convinced of this. Her real concern was that he'd stop halfway across to attempt to calculate the speed of the water, the volume of the flow, the angle of the drop, the number of gallons per minute, or some other such nonsense. She wondered if he ever really thought of the dangers they faced without conducting some kind of mental analysis.

Stella crossed gingerly, slipping once and falling in to her waist. However, she managed to hold on to a rock that was jutting out of the water and she pulled herself back and across. Natalie, who had lived all her life in the sea crossed without mishap or concern. She literally danced across the stream and spun back to look as Liam began to cross.

"Show off," mumbled Sean.

As Liam was crossing, a bolt of lightning from the approaching storm flashed across the sky, splitting the air with a mammoth explosion of thunder. The suddenness of the sound and the sight made Liam slip and fall. He cracked his elbow on one of the large moss covered rocks, numbing his entire arm. He could feel the jolt all the way up to his shoulder and neck. He couldn't lift that arm and was unable to get a hand hold on anything. Before anyone knew what had happened, he quickly slid over the side, disappearing in the cauldron of churning water below.

As quickly as he disappeared, Natalie rushed back into the middle of the passage and before anyone could stop her, she dived over the falls into the reservoir, as graceful as a swan. She cut the water as cleanly as a knife, and then she, too, disappeared from sight. The rest of the group waited at the top breathlessly. The pair seemed to be underwater far too long.

Natalie had reacted without thinking of her own safety. Liam was a Pathfinder, but she sensed he was not much of a swimmer. He wasn't likely to have gone swimming too often in the Swamp. In a split second she had made the decision that she must do whatever she could to save his life. She plummeted down into the water, surprised as she hit how cold it was. This was so much different than the warm blue waters of the Cerulean Sea. This water was brown and murky, in addition to being ice cold. How could it be so cold when the rest of this place was so hot, she wondered.

Once beneath the surface, her eyes adapted quickly to the stream in spite of the darkness, and she began to search for Liam. She followed the natural current and soon she spotted a blurry image. She moved cautiously but quickly in that direction until she was close enough to know for sure it was Liam. She saw him tangled in the roots of the trees that lined the shore of the stream. She shot forward and cut him free with her knife.

As soon as she did, he was swept downstream. She stored her knife and took off after him. They both bobbed to the surface, gasping for air, but the strong current kept pulling them away from the falls. When she finally caught up to him, she wrapped one arm around his neck to hold his head above water and used the other arm to swim to shore. She eventually pulled him to the other side of the stream from where they had recently been, and lifted him out of the water.

He wasn't breathing and his skin had a gray waxy pallor to it. Natalie turned him on his stomach and pushed on his back, trying to clear his lungs of the water. Then she turned him back and began to resuscitate him, but he still wasn't breathing.

"Come on, breathe," she shouted as she pushed on his chest.

Then she remembered the special leaves in the pouch inside his shirt. She reached in and found it. Her fingers were numb, but she managed to untie the draw string and open it. Inside were several small leaves that were soaking wet and had a blue and green color to them. She was just about to put one in his mouth when she heard a light fluttering behind her. She reached for her knife and spun around ready to attack. She eased up a bit, put her knife away and turn to the leaves and to Liam, when she saw that it was Summer who had flown down to see what was going on.

"He's not breathing," said Natalie. "I remembered the leaves he gave to Stella. I thought they'd work with him.

Summer saw what Natalie was about to put into Liam's mouth. "Wait," she shouted. "The leaves he gave Stella were orange and yellow. Those are the wrong color."

"But they're wet. They may have changed color when they got soaked." Still, she searched him again, and found another pouch. Inside this one were other leaves, but they were a dull brown and a rusty gold color.

"Now what?" Natalie asked Summer.

"I don't know," Summer answered, "but we need to do something fast. He's still not breathing, and he's turning really gray."

Natalie looked at both leaves. She held the different leaves in her hands, closed her eyes and concentrated. She squeezed them tightly, wringing water from them. She glanced at them again to see no changes in the colors. There wasn't time to let the leaves dry out. Finally she decided to go with her instincts and pushed one of the blue and green leaves under Liam's tongue, and started working his jaw the same way he had done with Stella.

In a few seconds he started coughing and gasping for air. He looked at Natalie, and then down at her hands to the brown and gold leaves in one and the blue and green leaves in the other.

"Which one of those did you give me?" he asked, still catching his breath as he sat up and rubbed some warmth into his arms.

"This one," Natalie answered uncertainly, holding out the hand with the blue and green leaves in them.

He nodded, still coughing. "It's a good thing you didn't give me the other ones. I probably wouldn't be talking to you if you had. They're poisonous," he said between coughs. "How did you know which were the right ones?"

"I didn't," said Natalie. "I guessed."

He looked at her in surprise, coughed and sputtered, and said, "Lucky guess."

He got up and saw where they were. Turning to Summer, he said, "Go on back to the others and get them moving. All you have to do is keep the storm to their backs. I don't think it will be changing direction soon, so you should be all right, even if you don't know exactly where you're going. Natalie and I will catch up later down the trail, probably in a day or two. We're already on the right side of the stream; we just can't connect with you in any direct way, and you can't afford to wait for us. In fact, make sure they <u>don't</u> wait for us. Is that clear?"

Summer nodded that she understood. From his demeanor, she knew it would be pointless to try to change his mind.

"It should be safe to camp in the open, at least for tonight," he continued. "You can even light a fire. At this point whatever that storm is and whoever it's connected to, knows where we are. Besides, the fire will help keep any predators away." Anticipating her next question, he added, "And no, you won't have to worry about the gargoyles, at least not for a few days, and by then, we'll have caught up to you. Now get going."

Summer said she understood and flew back to the main group. Liam nodded to Natalie, thanked her for pulling him out of the water, and then led her into the woods.

# Chapter thirteen

"We'll have to run most of the way in order to catch up to them within the next two days," Liam told Natalie.

Natalie told him that was all right, but she thought to herself that he was probably exaggerating. There was no way they could run for two days, and besides, the others were only at the top of the waterfall. She and Liam hadn't floated that far away. How could it take two days of running to catch up? She decided to just let it pass for now, and with nothing more to say, they began.

In the meantime Summer had flown back and conveyed Liam's instructions to the others. They wasted no time, and quickly resumed their own journey forward. The storm had gotten closer, so it was much easier to see it and to keep it to their backs. Ahead of them was an open plain with low, rolling hills and a wide variety of trees and other vegetation. It was a pleasant relief from what they had just struggled through. There was no real path, but the traveling wasn't difficult. The terrain was open enough that they would be able to see anything or anyone that might be approaching.

Stella kept her eyes wide open for any sight of her Princess. She couldn't imagine why it would take so long for her and Liam to rejoin them. Aside from the drop on either side of the falls, which she thought would be easily navigated, she could see nothing that would create such a delay. As they continued on she noticed that the temperature had begun to drop. There was little wind, but the air seemed much cooler. The distant horizon looked gray and offered no clue as to what was ahead. She had to admit, though, that the cooler temperature was certainly welcome.

The terrain that Liam and Natalie were encountering was somewhat different. They had been running uphill since they started. After several hours Natalie's legs felt like rubber and her lungs were burning. They had been running through open fields with some small trees, but nothing else that broke up the monotony. She finally had to stop to rest. She was too winded to even call out. She just stopped and bent over with her hands on her knees.

Liam circled back, stopped for only a second to look at her. Without saying a word, he wandered off to look at some of the trees and shrubs nearby. Natalie turned her head without lifting it to watch as he walked away. Fine time to study the local plant life, she mumbled to herself, breathlessly. Soon he returned. He had cut a small piece of what looked like the bark from one of the trees.

"Here," he said. "Chew on this. It's OK to swallow, as long as you don't swallow the bark itself."

He didn't explain, but began running again. She looked at him in dismay.

"What?" she thought to herself, "I'm supposed to eat wood now? How's that going to make running any easier?"

She sniffed the small chunk of bark and jerked her head back, making a face at the rather unpleasant smell. She looked up to see that Liam hadn't waited for her. She was a bit peeved at him, but popped the bark into her mouth and began to chew on it. It tasted like strong soap and she almost spit it out; but before she did, she noticed that her legs felt better almost immediately. She kept chewing and within a minute or two the burning sensation in her lungs disappeared.

She began running again. If I can get past the awful taste and the burning sensation in my throat, she thought, this isn't so bad. The running didn't seem so painful any more, either. She picked up her pace until she finally caught up to Liam and asked him what it was.

"I don't know," he told her. "I just know it makes running easier."

She looked at him with a worried expression. Is he nuts, she asked herself. She wondered if he had any idea what this bark would do to her, especially when they finally stopped running. He's chewing something and he doesn't know what it is, she marveled, and what's worse – he gave some to me! In spite of her trepidation, she kept chewing the bark. She was amazed at how strong she felt. I could run for days, she thought – for weeks even.

She then asked him, "Why is it going to take two days to join up with the rest of the group. From where we got separated at the waterfall it was only about a hundred feet or so from the top to the bottom, and we went down stream no more than a couple hundred yards. Surely we could circle around and join up with them easily. It looks like we're going way out of our way. In fact," she looked around, "it looks like were going in almost the opposite direction.

"We are," he answered, and then said nothing more; he just kept running.

She was getting frustrated with his short answers and limited information. She sped up a bit and turned to face him, running backwards as she persisted in asking him why.

"There's a large field of dragon spadix between us and them. We need to keep as far away from that stuff as possible."

"What's dragon spadix?" she asked. "I don't see any dragons." She was still running backwards so she could face him.

"They're plants," he answered, "and are you going to run backwards all the way?"

"Plants?" she asked, ignoring his question about her running style. "What? Do they reach out and grab you?" she questioned sarcastically.

"Sort of," he said. "They have no roots, and they can move. The flowers look pretty, but they're dangerous. They can spray this stuff that sticks to your skin. It's like acid. It will eat away at you, and it gets worse if you put water on it, which is what people want to do to stop the burning. Eventually the acid will eat all the way through skin, muscle and bone, and melt a person down into a big glob of paste, which these plants feed on. So that's why we need to make a wide circle around them, and why you need to turn around."

Natalie was stunned, but she spun around and ran forward again. Was everything in this area dangerous? Then she recalled the stories about how the followers of Ena Ray had poisoned the land around them when they were imprisoned in the underworld.

"Is this still part of the poisoned land of your home?" she asked. "Is this stuff because of Ena Ray, too?"

Liam looked at her oddly before answering. "No. They're just nasty plants. Don't you have dangerous stuff in your world?"

She thought about that for a second. They had the "Dark Eyes" as well as numerous predatory fish and eels. "I suppose so," she answered.

"Did Ena Ray make them that way?"

"I guess not."

They continued on in silence after that. By late afternoon they had crested a long slow rising hill. Liam pointed to the horizon and told Natalie that the others were somewhere on the other side of the ridge, behind the horizon line. Then he dropped his arm a little and pointed to the field between the ridge and where they stood. The meadow looked like it was on fire. As far as she could see from left to right, it blazed with undulating colors of red, orange and yellow.

"It's beautiful," she said.

Liam looked at her oddly. "It's the field of dragon spadix," he told her. "We should be far enough away from it that the plants won't sense us and start moving this way. I hope the others steer clear of it. If they follow the direction I told them to go, they should be safe."

Suddenly it didn't look so beautiful and Natalie wondered if they would be able to circle it in only two days, it was so wide. As they stopped for the night, she noticed that it was still well before sunset. The days were getting longer.

- - - - - - - - - - - - - - - - - *** - - - - - - - - - - - - - - - - - -

On the other side of the ridge, Lochen suggested to the group that they, too, stop for the night. There was a small outcropping of rocks that would give them some shelter, although the weather wasn't a threat. He noticed that it was much cooler, but not yet uncomfortable. When Solveig asked him if it seemed that the days were getting longer, he told her that they were. As they moved closer to the northern axis, the twin suns would be visible in the sky for longer periods of time. Eventually, at least one of them would be in the sky at all times. Normally, she would have welcomed the thought of longer days, but now, with the sky filling with that ominous cloud, longer days didn't seem as welcome.

The next morning Summer was the first to rise. She looked back to see where the storm was so she could get a better gauge on the direction she needed to scout. She was taken aback at how close it was. Obviously it wasn't stopping to rest at night. She could now hear the rolling thunder and the cracks of lightning. Why hadn't we heard this during the night, she wondered. It seemed like the storm was trying to sneak up on them in the night. She didn't need to encourage the others to get going. They, too, could see and hear the oncoming storm.

As the day wore on everyone became aware of the gradual, but continual drop in the temperature. It was noticeably cooler since just that morning. The wind had also picked up, but it wasn't a gentle summer breeze any longer. It carried the frigid air of the polar regions with it. Lochen and Solveig were glad they had kept the remnants of their robes. Solveig cut some from hers to make a cloak for Summer. Lochen and Solveig, who were more accustomed to cooler temperatures, gave the remains to Stella and Sean to wear – at least for the time being.

"Won't you be cold?" asked Stella, who was already starting to shiver, just slightly.

"No; not yet," answered Solveig. "In our mountain castle the air is much cooler than what we've been traveling through lately. I guess our blood is a bit thicker."

"And as long as we keep up this pace, the walking will warm us, too," added Lochen. "I'm hoping that we won't be going too much further north, though. None of us have clothing for that."

Natalie and Liam noticed the cooler air, too. The fact that they spent their day running kept them warm enough so that they were unaffected by the increasing cold. Natalie was chewing the same piece of bark, which kept her legs fresh and her lungs filled. When they had stopped for the night, she had reached in to take the chunk of bark out of her mouth when Liam shouted at her to stop.

"Don't do that," he said. "It'll still be good tomorrow. In fact, it'll last several weeks," he said.

She looked at him in disbelief.

"I'm serious," he told her. "It won't get smaller or less powerful, unless you take it out of your mouth. So…don't take it out of your mouth."

"I'm supposed to sleep with it?" she asked incredulously.

"You can keep it under your tongue," he answered. "That will keep its power intact until you need it again."

"What if I swallow it?"

"You won't." He could see that she didn't believe him. "I can't explain it. You just have to trust me."

He had been right. She slept with it under her tongue and hadn't swallowed it. When she awoke the next morning it was lodged just where it had been when she fell asleep. She wasn't sure she believed it still had its original power, but she decided not to take it out of her mouth. Instead, she just kept it under her tongue.

When they had been running for a while, the fatigue she had experienced the day before quickly set in. She poked the piece of bark with her finger, moving out from under her tongue, and started chewing it again. Almost immediately she felt refreshed. She still wondered, though, if something bad was going to happen to her later on because of chewing a piece of tree bark. The bark had been a grayish black. She wondered what her tongue and teeth looked like.

I need to focus on something else, she told herself. I'm worried about what my mouth looks like when I should be worried about my friends. She gazed at the ridge off in the distance, and still saw the field of dragon spadix and wondered how much longer it would be until she saw the others.

Summer had just returned from her latest scouting trip.

"There doesn't seem to be any signs of danger ahead, but I also didn't see any signs of life - of any kind" she reported.

The scenery had already changed from the grassy fields to a more barren and rocky terrain. Summer told them that she was also seeing signs of frost on the ground. No one was surprised to hear that, although, in spite of anticipating this news, it was still disturbing to hear. The wind was getting colder and stronger. There was what looked like a mountain range just appearing over the horizon, but she thought they wouldn't reach that for another day or two.

Although no one mentioned it, they were all wondering what would happen if they got that far and still had not rejoined Natalie and Liam. Stella sensed the others' apprehension about this, and quietly expressed her own concerns about this to Lochen, who just dismissed her.

"They'll catch up or they won't," he said somewhat casually. When he saw her reaction to his comment, he continued. "There's nothing we can do either way. We don't know which way they are coming, so there's no way we can try to find them. And if we stop to wait for them, they may end up passing us and continue on hoping to catch up with us. Really, the best thing is for us to concentrate on moving forward and hoping we can find our way to the Crystal Citadel."

She knew he was right, but it made her angry that there was nothing she could do. Lochen could see that she wasn't satisfied with his answer.

"I have confidence in the Pathfinder," he said. "He found us in the middle of nowhere. He'll find us again."

By the time evening arrived Summer reported that there was nothing ahead that would provide them any shelter. Lochen thought that where they were was as good a place as any to camp for the night. Stella took one last glance to the left, not really expecting to see anything, but hoping, just the same. Some very faint movement caught her eye. At first she wasn't sure she really saw something, but she kept staring. It looked like a mirage at first, shimmering on the horizon. Then it became clearer. She saw a round object silhouetted against the sky bobbing up and down.

"Look," she announced loudly, "over there.'

She became apprehensive, thinking that this might be some new danger. However, as the figure got closer and more of it came up over the horizon, she recognized Liam's hat. But she saw only him coming towards them.

"It's Liam," she exclaimed. But where was Natalie?

Summer flew up next to her and hovered over her shoulder to look down her arm in the direction she was pointing. Once Summer spotted what Stella was looking at, she flew like a bullet in that direction. Even before she came back, Stella could see a second figure emerging.

Liam and Natalie slowed down as they approached a cheering welcome. Hugs and greetings were exchanged and when Lochen suggested that they camp for the night here, Liam looked back at the storm and told him they needed to go a bit further.

"Of course," said Lochen. "I defer to your judgment."

He looked at the wide grins on everyone's faces. It no longer mattered how tired everyone was. They were all together and safe – at least for the time being.

They kept moving forward with Liam in the lead marching rather quickly. In a very short time the ground below them had changed to ice. The transition had happened much more quickly than Liam had anticipated. The wind was blowing the loose bits of surface frost and it gave the appearance of a light snowstorm. No one complained, but Liam realized that they could go no further that evening. The problem was that there was no shelter ahead of them to protect them for the night. Lochen suggested that they could huddle together to keep warm, but it was Sean who suggested that they dig shallow trenches.

"They don't have to be too deep," he said. "They just have to be lower than ground level. That way the wind will blow over the top of us. We can line them up next to each other, too, and that will give us extra warmth."

"You don't live in this kind of climate," observed Lochen. "How did you come up with this idea?"

"I remember seeing some animals do this during a sand storm on a beach one time," he explained. "It just seemed like it would work here."

So they each carved out a narrow furrow in the ice and hunkered down for the night. Just as Sean had predicted, the wind eventually blew over them. At first, the wind just whipped around into the trenches. But before long, they were covered with a light layer of snow, which, surprisingly, made them even warmer than they had expected. By morning that light layer had gotten thicker and crusted over. When Sean popped his head up and looked around, he saw five snowy mounds. He had to look closely to see the sixth one where Summer was. He was feeling pretty good about his idea until he looked back towards the storm to find that it was filling nearly half the sky. The thunder was much more pronounced now. It had been muffled somewhat by the snow fall during the night, but there was no mistaking it now. The sporadic cracks of lightning were much closer and louder, too.

He called to the others to wake them and they immediately resumed their journey. There was no time or place to stop for a meal, so they drew from their limited provisions and some nuts and berries they had picked up along the way. The parts of the sky that weren't filled with the storm were filled with a white-gray mist. The twin suns were blurred by the mist and provided no warmth at all. The wind was still whipping snow and ice around and made walking more difficult. It also created drifts of snow that were knee deep or worse in most places.

"This is almost as bad as slogging through that mud," said Sean.

"Almost?" asked Natalie incredulously. "What could possibly make this not as bad?"

"It doesn't stick to my feet," Sean said as he raised one foot in the air and waved it ceremoniously.

That was just about the only advantage. The cold was beginning to sink into their bones, in spite of the exertion of walking, which was made all the more difficult by the wind that was pushing against them. It was almost impossible for Summer to fly very far. The wind buffeted her around so much that sometimes she found herself behind the others instead of in front of them. Ice began forming on her wings. She struggled to move them.

"There's not much point in having you try to scout ahead," Lochen told her. "And I'm afraid you'll lose sight of us and get blown off track trying to return. We can't afford to lose you," and without any further explanation, he swooped her up and nestled her in the folds of his hood. She might have complained about this before, but now she was grateful for the rest, the warmth, and the refuge.

By midday the storm had gotten uncomfortably and threateningly close. The rumbling thunder was a constant presence and the shock waves from the lightning strikes could be felt radiating through the ice beneath their feet. The wind seemed to be pushing them back more often than not. The clothing Liam had provided to them in the Swamp was ill suited for the freezing wind and snow. Even with the exertion of fighting the wind, they were beginning to suffer from hypothermia. In spite of the cold, Lochen refused to move Summer from his hood, as he still wore it behind his head, keeping her tucked away in the folds.

"There's no sense in both of us suffering," he argued. "I really won't be any warmer with my hood up, and you'll only freeze and get blown away."

Things were only getting worse. They had long passed the point of no return. Their exit was cut off. Their only option was to continue forward. By now the snow was hardening and in many sections they were crossing expanses of ice. At one point they came across a stretch of ice that was so slick, they couldn't get a footing against the wind. They had to detour around the span into drifts of snow where they at least could get some traction. For a while they had the wind to their backs and sides. Sometimes the gusts were so strong that they pushed the travelers down into the drifts.

All the time the storm kept getting closer and closer. It hadn't yet reached them, but that would only be a matter of time. The black clouds seemed to shift into the shape of a face of some unimaginable beast. It would rear its head back and then strike like a snake, shooting bolts of lightning down at the travelers. The electrical charges were nearly upon them. The wind and the snow had slowed them down so much that they felt like easy targets for the storm's rage. The snow was now waist deep or worse. The top layer was a hardened crust. Sometimes it was strong enough to hold them, but most often it crumbled under their weight, dropping them into deep drifts.

The swirling snow nearly blocked out the horizon making it difficult to distinguish the land from the sky. Even if they could see through the blizzard, there was nothing on the horizon for them to see beyond mountains and glaciers. Frost and ice had formed on their clothes and clung to their hair. Their faces burned with the cold. They no longer could feel their hands or feet. They were exhausted.

Liam had been a valiant trailblazer, but he was not accustomed to such cold, and was shivering uncontrollably. He no longer was able to walk in a straight line. Lochen moved to the front to help get him stable, and Liam only collapsed, pulling Lochen down with him. Without a word their march forward came to a halt. They were crowded together, more for comfort than for warmth. Each had come to the realization that they could go no further; that the storm would catch them.

Solveig finally gave voice to their plight. "Is this it? Is this what it's come to? We're giving in to the storm?"

She really didn't expect an answer, and she got none. The snow was beginning to drift around them, burying them in a heap of white.

Liam was still looking ahead. Between spasms he raised his hand, pointing into the distance ahead of them, and said, "Well, either the storm is going to get us, or that is."

They all looked into the blinding wind. At first none of them could see what he had spotted. They nearly dismissed it as a hallucination. And then one by one, they saw two bouncing objects just breaking through the mist. Sean fumbled for his slingshot, his fingers too numb to hold onto the stones he used for ammunition. They dropped from his hand and disappeared into the growing drift. He made a feeble attempt to find them, and then realized it was a futile effort.

He looked up at the oncoming two images. They were followed by a blur of white. There was an odd sound being carried by the wind and echoing off the churning snow and ice.

"What's that sound?" Stella croaked, her voice choked by the cold.

"You hear it, too?" asked Solveig. "I thought I was imagining it."

"It's a dog," said Lochen. "No, two dogs. They're barking."

"Wonderful," groused Sean. "I was just beginning to think things couldn't get worse. Now it looks like we're going to be eaten by dogs. I hope they like frozen Dozors."

The approaching dogs and whatever was right behind them were coming at a tremendous speed. Summer peeked her head out from Lochen's hood and looked back at the storm and then towards the approaching animals. It appeared to her as though the dogs would beat the storm, but not by much. The group wondered which fate would be worse.

The two bouncing objects were in fact giant dogs, but they were harnessed and were pulling an enormous sled. The white blur that had been following them turned out to be a giant covered in white fur. The dogs were barking excitedly, their large pink tongues flopping from one side of their mouths to the other. The one on the right was the bigger of the two, but not by much. It had short black and brown hair, a long tail curved up towards its large head, and one brown eye and one blue eye. As its head bobbed back and forth, the flashes of lightning turned the blue eye a deep red. Even Lochen had never seen anything quite like it. The other dog was smaller, but more muscular. It was covered with long black and white hair and a short, stubby tail on a wide butt.

By now their image was clearer, although still obscured somewhat by the blizzard. The dogs were pulling the giant on a large, long sled. The sled had long runners on either side and a small platform on the back on which the giant was standing. They were headed straight for the group and at the last minute the giant changed direction by pulling sharply on the reins. The sled swerved around the group, spraying snow up as it turned.

The giant quickly circled the travelers, and brought the sled to a stop, skidding right up next to them, positioning it between them and the approaching storm cloud.

The giant's head was covered by an enormous hood with white fur circling his round face. He leaned down, smiled at them and shouted, "I've been expecting you. You better get on the sled before it's too late."

He reached down to the sled, and with a flip of his wrist, pulled aside a large fur from the front of the sled. Without any further comment, he scooped them up one by one and placed them gently onto the sled. When they were all secured, he covered them over with the fur. He shouted a command to the dogs, and the sled took off like a rocket.

Almost immediately, the travelers began to feel warmer. At this point none of them cared if this giant was a friend or an enemy. All they could think of was being warm. Summer wriggled out of Lochen's hood and peeked out from under the pile of furs. She could just barely see past the giant to the storm, which was moving much faster – chasing them.

"Come on you two.  Faster than that or no treats for you," the giant shouted to the dogs.

Solveig was seated at the back part of the sled and was able to poke the top of her head above the fur covering.  She looked towards Summer and then turned to the front.  She could see the dogs pulling with all their might.  She looked behind her and just past the giant she saw the storm picking up speed.

"Am I just imagining things," she whispered to Summer, "or does it look like that storm is chasing us?"

"Definitely chasing," answered Summer.

The thunder was roaring louder than ever and the clouds seemed to be spitting lightning at the sled.  It struck the ground leaving blackened craters in its wake.  The images that the clouds took looked more and more like an angry beast.  It was becoming clear that the storm was a being and that being was mad.

"Move it, Kelsey Belsey, you fat old tub of lard," shouted the giant, and then, laughing added in a low singsong voice, "I'm not fat, I'm just big boned."  He was clearly mocking the dog.  "Faster, Rover, you lazy mutt," he kept up the playful taunting  "Are you going to let her beat you?"

It sounded like the giant thought this was some kind of game.  Solveig thought he must not know how dangerous that storm was.  When she turned her attention back towards the front, she saw a wall of ice quickly rising up before them.  They were headed straight at it.  She strained to see if there was an opening or some other kind of path ahead, but it was solid.  "Surely," she thought, "we'll turn off at the last minute."

But the sled kept going faster and faster and the wall kept getting higher and higher, and closer and closer.  When it was certain that they would crash into it, the giant raised his hand, pointed at the wall and shouted, "Open!"  With a flash the wall split open and the sled shot inside.  As soon as it had passed into the opening the giant shouted, "Close" and the wall crashed shut.  On the other side the storm crash against the wall.  But it couldn't penetrate.

The sled came to a stop and Solveig looked around.   They were inside a mammoth cavern.  Enormous icicles hung from the ceiling and there were giants everywhere.  What had they gotten into now, she wondered.

# Chapter fourteen

*T*he giant jumped off the sled and, instead of seeing to his passengers, ran to the two dogs who were shifting their glances between the passengers they had carried and the giant. He knelt down, released them from their harnesses and scooped them into his arms. Hugging and wrestling with them, he ruffled their ears and scratched their bellies. They barked loudly and nipped playfully at him and each other. They pushed him over and scrambled on top of him, licking and nipping.

"Good girl, Kelsey. And you, too, Rover. Yes, you're a good boy. Yes, yes, I've got treats for both of you." He gently pushed them away, and got up on his knees. He fumbled around, reaching into his pockets, and pulled out what looked like strips of meat. He held them in the air and commanded them both to sit. They did as instructed, cocking their heads and waiting expectantly. He tossed one to each dog, and they both ate them greedily. They finished them in an instant and then looked at the giant expectantly, wagging their tails and barking.

"No. That's it. No more," he said. "You'll get fat as sea lions, the both of you. And then who will pull my sled? Those worthless cats? I don't think so."

He ruffled their ears once more and then stood up and turned to the sled. He pulled the fur off the passengers and looked down at them, smiling. Solveig had never seen anyone so big. She wasn't sure if she should be frightened or relieved. In spite of his size, he didn't appear intimidating. He was covered from head to toe in white fur with only his round pink face peering out. His cheeks were bright red from the cold. Under the top of his hood, fair blond hair hung down over blue-gray eyes. When he smiled, which seemed to be all the time, his face split in a wide grin filled with sparkling white teeth and deep dimples appeared in both cheeks.

"Wow. You aren't exactly dressed for this kind of weather, are you," he said when he saw what they were wearing. "I'll make sure you get some better clothing. Oh, and yeah, I guess you could use some food and something to drink – something warm – I guess you don't want any iced tea." He laughed.

"Or maybe you do," he added as an afterthought. "I guess I shouldn't presume. Do you want something cold to drink?"

They all just stared at him and slowly shook their heads.

"No? OK. I didn't think so."

As he surveyed the group, his eyes stopped at Solveig.

"Oh, wow! What happened to your hair?" he asked her.

She raised her hand quickly to the back of her head. "Nothing," she answered defensively. She bent her head down a little and stole a glance towards Lochen.

"I like it like this," she said bit more stridently.

The giant became flustered. "Oh, yeah, I mean no. Of course. I mean it looks...ah, er... great...um...all...ah...ah...uneven like that." He quickly changed the subject, looking in every direction but back at Solveig. His face was beet red.

"My name is Quinn," he said, with his voice cracking just slightly. "I'm a Guardian of the Ice Kingdom. We're really glad you're here."

Before anyone could ask him what he meant, he lifted each of them out of the sled and invited them to follow him.

"Come on," he said. "Let me show you around while we get you some food and warm clothes."

He led them through several chambers deep inside the cavern. The entire system of chambers and passageways appeared to be carved into the ice. It was incredibly light throughout. Lochen was studying it as they walked along. The light from the suns must penetrate, refract and magnify through the ice, he thought. He wanted to ask Quinn about this, but he couldn't get a word in edgewise.

All along the way he chattered constantly, explaining to them who his people were, and what life was like in the Ice Kingdom. He told them that the Legends of the Ice Giants foretold of a great storm. He didn't know why the storm was coming now, but only that it was. Lochen tried to insert an explanation, but Quinn just kept talking. He told them that his people were responsible for guarding this ancient powerful sorcerer – some guy named Ena Ray. He had never met the person, himself.

"In fact," he said as he stopped in the middle of a long hallway, "I don't think anyone has actually seen him, but we know he's there. Oh, wow! I hope he's still there. Wouldn't that be a mess if he got out somehow?" He saw the looks of horror on their faces and quickly added, "No. Seriously, he's still there. We'd know if he wasn't. I guess everyone would know if he wasn't, wouldn't they?"

He told them what he knew about the exile and that it was as the result of some big flare up between him and an Enchantress and some other sorcerer. He looked at Stella and added unnecessarily, "Not you. It was another enchantress – a really old one. Well, I guess she wasn't old at the time, but she'd be really, really old now."

He told them that little was known about this other sorcerer, and he wasn't anywhere near here. None of his people knew where he was, just that he wasn't here. But his people knew the time would come when the spells that imprisoned Ena Ray would no longer hold him, and that heroic warriors from the different peoples of the world would come to recast the spells. The stars would tell them when to come and point the way.

"And sure enough," he said, "here you are!"

"But we're not heroic," said Sean. "And we're not warriors."

Quinn looked puzzled. "Well, yeah, you are! Didn't you make a dangerous journey to get here?" he asked.

"Well, yes, I guess so," answered Sean.

"And didn't you fight off all sorts of things?"

"Well, yes," Sean answered again. "But we're just...I don't know... ordinary?"

Quinn was shocked. "Ordinary?" he exclaimed. "You're far from ordinary. You're Legends!"

Before anyone could add to the debate, Lochen interjected, "Earlier you said you were expecting us. How could that be? Most of us didn't know each other until this journey began, and none of us knew where it would take us. How could you?"

"I just told you," answered Quinn, smiling broadly. "You're in our Legends. You are the Legends."

"I don't understand," said Lochen.

"Let me show you," and Quinn escorted them deeper into the cavern to a small chamber with a low rough ceiling – at least it seemed low for the giant. The light shining through from above gave the room an eerie blue-white glow. Once inside, Quinn waved his arm in a sweeping motion at several drawings, carved into one side of an ancient wall made from a large stone and smiled at them as if the drawings needed no further explanation.

"See?" he asked, smiling broadly.

The drawings were all rough engravings made centuries ago. They were almost childlike in their appearance and had been worn smooth over time; but they were still very distinctive. They were encompassed in a circle that was perfectly round and looked almost newly carved. Lochen stepped forward and placed his hand on the marks, touching each one separately. Then he ran his hand around the circle. Everyone was looking at the etchings on the cavern wall and watching Lochen. Finally he stepped back and turned to Quinn.

"These are clearly ancient carvings, but they obviously mean more to you than they do to us. I can't derive any meaning from them. I especially don't see any connection between these petroglyphs and any of us." He motioned to the carvings. I'm sorry," he shook his head regretfully. "I don't mean to offend or to belittle your legends. I just don't see any connection"

Quinn looked at them in disbelief. "Please, don't apologize. I just can't believe you don't see it. It's right there. Look."

He stepped up to the markings and began by pointing to the topmost one.

"See this? It's a star." It looked more like a simple triangle. "It represents someone in an honored position among their people," he continued. "The lines below this star represent the air. Together they stand for a princess of the air." He turned to Summer. "A faerie Princess."

215

Summer looked back at him in surprise. "But I don't live in the air, and neither does anyone in my village."

Quinn just smiled at her as he looked into the faces of each one of them. "Well, no, but from what I can see, you're the only one who can fly. Or did I miss something?"

When no one disagreed, he turned back to the drawings.

"This one on the bottom left," – another triangle – "represents another person in an honored position among people of the water. See these curving lines? Those are waves. And the third one represents one more person of honor; this one, on the bottom right, is from people of the mountains. See? These jagged lines under this star are a depiction of mountains."

He ran his finger from the first star to two other stars. The three symbols formed a large triangle. Like the waves under the top star that depicted waves of air, there were lines under the lower left star that gave the appearance of a curling wave of water, and under the other star on the lower right was a pair of lines that looked like uneven "M"s.

He turned back to the group, first to Natalie. "And you're a Princess of the sea sprites and you're a Princess of the mountain people," he said turning to Solveig. "See? It's really plain."

The all just looked at him blankly. So he continued the explanation.

"The air, the sea and the land. Don't you get it? They're the basic elements of the world. And each of them is connected to the other. Three elements and three princesses." He was beginning to feel like he was speaking to children, and trying hard not to get frustrated.

"OK, there's more. Look. These drawings on the inside of the larger triangle represent other elements that connect to the basic ones. Here," he pointed to one of the symbols inside the large outer triangle. It looked like a series of different-sized crooked lines that stretched up to the wavy lines he said represented the air.

"This tree reaches into the air. It draws life from the air." He turned to Sean. "It stands for the forest. That's where you live, right?"

He continued, pointing to another symbol close to the one that looked like waves. It looked like a tear drop with lines fanned around it.

"This one is the candle and the flickering flame. The sea would be dark without the light and the knowledge provided by an Enchantress. And see here?" He motioned to several circles, many of which looked only like chips or gouges in the stone. "The mountains are the highest points on our planet. They reach for the stars and planets beyond the sky." He looked to Stella and Lochen. "They symbolize the Enchantress of the sea sprites and an astronomer – the Sorcerer of the mountain people."

Before anyone could interrupt, he pointed to the arrow that was dead center in the drawings. "And this. It's not a weapon. It's a direction. It's the way shown by a Pathfinder, and it points to this, below it," he said as he pointed to the odd-shaped object at the bottom of the drawings.

"It's an ice shelf. That's where you are now. You've arrived. Just as the prophesies in  our legends predicted, and you're all here just in time to keep Ena Ray from escaping from his banishment."

Quinn was so passionate and convincing in his explanation it was hard to dispute him. Lochen stepped forward and looked at the drawings, studying them closely, again running his hands over the engravings, following the images from one to another. The others waited patiently for Lochen to comment, each of them sure that he would find some other, logical explanation. They all hated to burst Quinn's bubble. He had saved them from the storm and had been very congenial, but there was no way he could be right. Lochen finally stood up straight and turned back to the group.

"I have to admit, Quinn, that you made a very convincing argument. The marks do seem to parallel us and our objective."

But – everyone was waiting for him to say but and explain why it was all wrong. Lochen wrinkled his brow. They all looked at him expectantly: Quinn waiting for acknowledgment of the truth, the others waiting for a gentle, but decisive dismissal. Something was not quite right, Lochen thought to himself. Quinn's explanation didn't quite answer everything, but Lochen couldn't sort out what was missing. After a few minutes he seemed to come to some kind of resolution and continued.

"Well, then. We had better get going."

"What?" all the others nearly shouted.

Talking over one another, they each sputtered comments and questions.

"You can't be serious; those don't look like anything he said they were; he's really nice and I'm glad he saved us, but we don't know anything about him."

Lochen looked at them and asked, "If none of this is true, then how did he know who we are and where we come from? I'm not wearing a sign. Are any of you?"

His questions stunned them into silence. He used the silence to get back on track, and asked Quinn, "How do we get to the Crystal Citadel?"

Quinn looked at him in surprise. "I have no idea."

"But you said your people guard it," Lochen countered.

"Our people guard it, but that's because we guard the whole Ice Kingdom, and we know the Citadel is somewhere within the Kingdom. It's just that none of us knows where it is exactly or how to get into it. Don't worry, though; it's somewhere close – well sort of close."

Before anyone could re-assert any objections, Liam announced, "I know how to get there."

Quinn smiled broadly again. "I knew it. I knew it." He was nearly jumping with excitement and pointing at Liam. "OK, then. What can I do to help? Just tell me. Tell me what you need – clothes, weapons, transportation, whatever; just let me know. Ohhhh! I can't believe this is happening. I can't believe I'm seeing this. The LEGENDS! Oh, wow. Wait until I tell everybody!"

Everyone watched him do a little dance. They had resigned themselves to the fact that whether this so called legend was true or not, they would soon be moving on. Once Quinn settled down, Lochen asked him if he had access to any maps of the area. Quinn gave a little laugh.

"Maps? No. There aren't any maps of the Ice Kingdom. I know you didn't get to see much on the way in here, but take it from me: everything looks pretty much the same. Besides that, most of the things that, maybe, could be landmarks or guideposts or whatever, always get shifted around and moved. Sure, the main mountains don't move, but the glaciers change and the crevasses get covered up."

"Is there anything you can provide that would give us a clue as to the size and shape of this kingdom?" Lochen asked.

"Sure," he said. "I can draw the perimeter of the Ice Kingdom if that would help."

Lochen just told him to talk to Liam. It had been several days since he last slept and he needed a few hours to get refreshed. Quinn took him to a place where he could rest undisturbed and everyone else thought some rest would be good. He made sure they were all provided with some food and something to drink while new, warmer clothes were prepared for them. Quinn showed them where they would all meet once they had rested. They all left with Lochen while Liam and Quinn conversed.

219

Aside from Lochen, none of them slept. They were each exhausted, but now that they were so close, their minds were racing far too much to allow them to sleep. One by one, they arrived at the gathering place. Little conversation took place; each was lost in his or her own thoughts. A few hours later Lochen appeared, still looking worn out, but claiming that he was fully refreshed.

Quinn asked if they wanted any breakfast. They were now close enough to the axis of the planet that at least one of the twin suns was always in the sky, so it was difficult to know when morning was. It really didn't matter anymore. They were running out of time. None of them was hungry, but they thanked him for offering. Lochen informed them all that he had updated his calculations. He was certain that all the planets as well as the suns and Luna would be in alignment within the next two days. They had no time to waste.

"When did you do this so-called calculation?" asked Summer.

"While I was sleeping," Lochen answered matter-of-factly.

"While he was sleeping," shouted Quinn ecstatically. "Oh, wow. That's incredible. Do you do that all the time?"

"Yes," interjected Solveig. "Please don't encourage him."

Quinn led them to a spot near where they had entered the enormous cavern and showed them that he had his giant sled piled high with supplies, and his dogs, Kelsey and Rover were in their harnesses, eager to go for another run.

"OK," he said, "Based on what Liam told me, I pulled together everything you'll need for the rest of your expedition. Man! This is exciting. So what happens when you find the Crystal Citadel? I mean, what are you supposed to do?"

"We don't know," said Stella.

"In fact," added Summer, "on this whole journey we haven't known what we were supposed to do or where we were supposed to go next. Things just happened, and there seems to be some force that's guiding us."

Quinn just beamed. "Well, sure," he said. "It's just like in the prophesy."

"The prophecy that you all tell each other from those scratches on that rock?" asked Sean, apparently still in a state of denial.

Quinn smiled, "I knew you were just kidding me about those engravings. You knew all the time, didn't you?"

Sean just stared at him in disbelief. Is he for real, or is he making fun of me, he wondered.

"OK," Quinn went on. "The storm hasn't moved from the entryway. In fact, it's still pounding the wall we came through when we entered the Main Ice Hall. Whatever it is, it's really, really angry. It's probably better if we leave through another opening and steer well clear of the storm."

He made sure everyone was protected from the harsh weather and that his cargo was sufficiently secured, and then led everyone down a long passage to another opening. It looked like another solid wall of ice and rock. He snapped the reins and the dogs began to pull and bark at the same time. Quinn gave the sled a big push, running behind it until it picked up speed and then he jumped on the small platform at the back. They were headed straight for the wall. Just before it appeared certain they would crash into it, Quinn shouted, "Open" and a great fissure split down the center. The two halves swung open.

They burst into the open air and bright light like a shot. As soon as they were through, he shouted, "Close" without even looking behind him. Summer was looking past him and saw the two pieces shut, seamlessly. The sky was shimmering with the light from both suns. It bounced off the radiant white of the surrounding snow. Quinn had given everyone visors to shield their eyes. He had told the dogs to stay quiet until they were well away from the cavern. He wanted to put as much distance between his passengers and the storm as possible. They seemed to understand his instructions, and pulled the sled effortlessly in silence. Their barking had stopped almost immediately when he had commanded the wall to open and then shut behind them.

Lochen studied the position of the suns and determined that they had left before what was probably dawn. They traveled for several hours before Quinn stopped and gave Kelsey and Rover some treats he pulled from his pocket. They had been pulling a fully loaded sled all that time, but seemed as fresh as when they had started.

"They could go for hours – even days," said Quinn, "but I'd rather make sure they get some rest whenever we can."

He ruffled their fur as they ate quickly, lapping at him with their tongues between bites of whatever it was they were eating. He made sure everyone was warm and comfortable and asked Liam if they were still on the right course.

"You're heading in exactly the right direction," he told Quinn. He was fairly certain he knew where they were, but he also knew that his talents were unusual. He wondered if Quinn had the same talent. "Do you know how you're able to do that when everything around here looks the same?"

"No," answered Quinn. "But our people have lived here for hundreds of years. We can find our way around even in the dark season, when it's nighttime for several months. I'm not like you, though. I can't sense danger or find my way in areas other than the Ice Kingdom."

"You are more like me than you think," answered Liam.

Quinn laughed at that. "Maybe were related. Like brothers or cousins or something. Ha. Wouldn't that be a real hoot?"

They traveled most of the day and only saw a few animals off in the distance. The animals were covered in the same fur that Quinn was wearing. Sean asked him if those were the animals whose skins they were wearing. Quinn smiled widely and told him, yes they were; that those were polar oxen. They traveled in small herds and were tended to by some of his people.

"Wow," said Sean. "Those things are really big. What do you do with the rest of the body parts once they've been skinned?

Quinn looked at him slightly puzzled. "I don't understand. We just use their skins. We don't do anything with their bodies."

Sean looked at him with a shocked expression. "You mean you just skin them and leave the dead bodies to rot?"

Quinn looked shocked. "Dead bodies? We don't <u>kill</u> them," he nearly shouted. "We would <u>never</u> harm them. They provide us our clothing and materials for our boats and sails and our sleds and a bunch of other things. Why would we hurt them?"

Everyone was staring at him. In the short time they had been with him, they had never seen him so agitated. Then their eyes shifted to Sean.

Sean was a little nervous. "I'm sorry. I guess it's my turn to not understand. How do you get the skins off of them without..." he paused, searching for a delicate way to ask his question, "uhm...harming them?"

Quinn settled down, realizing that his passengers were apparently not familiar with polar oxen. "Oh. Well, they just shed their skins."

He relaxed visibly and then continued, "A few weeks after the dark season, the skins just peel off their bodies, fur and all, and are replaced by new fur covered skin from underneath. They're never in any pain."

As an afterthought, he added, "And I'm the one who should say I'm sorry. I didn't mean to shout. I just assumed you knew about our people and polar oxen."

Then he laughed and said, "Wow. You should have seen your face when I told you that we didn't kill them. You looked like you swallowed an arctic slug."

Sean laughed nervously. He had no idea what an arctic slug was or what it would taste like, and he had no interest in finding out. He was just happy to discover that the giant wasn't mad.

"Yeah, I'll bet." he responded, "And you should have seen your face. It looked like you just sat on a tree grub."

Quinn laughed. He had no idea what a tree grub was or what would happen if he sat on one, and, he was just as much not interested in finding out. Like Sean, he was happy that his outburst hadn't offended one of the Legends. His laughter caused Sean to laugh even harder, and soon they were both laughing uncontrollably and the others were just staring at them in puzzlement. Then the dogs started barking.

"OK.OK. Pipe down you two," Quinn shouted to the dogs between fits of laughter.

They were coming up to the edge of the land mass. Before them was a vast body of water with large chunks of ice floating in it. Some of the chunks were flat pieces that had broken off the ice shelf and others were immense icebergs of varying shapes. Quinn pulled the sled to a stop and began to untie the cargo.

"Can we help?" asked Lochen.

"No," said Quinn. "I've done this hundreds of times and it's probably easier for me to do it myself than explain it all to you."

He stopped and stood upright immediately. "I don't mean that you're stupid or wouldn't be able to figure it out…"

"We understand," Lochen assured him. "Don't worry. No one believes you think we're stupid."

He unwrapped several wooden poles and began fitting them together into a framework of some kind. Then he pulled out several very large pieces of oxen skin with the fur stripped off and woven together, and began to secure them around the frame. Soon it became clear that he was constructing some type of boat. He constructed three long narrow pods that were interconnected to each other like pontoons. The skins stretched completely around the frames of each of the pods with two small openings in the top. When he was done, he stepped back and looked proudly at this work.

"There you go," he said.

When everyone stood there looking from him to the pods and back, he added, "They're kayaks. You put them in the water and paddle to make them move. They'll take you where you need to go."

Sean looked at the pods, then out at the sea. "Oh great," he moaned. "More water."

Lochen looked at the pods and then turned to Quinn.

"I think you need one more. There's only room in these for the seven of us."

Quinn smiled again and answered, "Well, yeah. You only need room for the seven of you."

Lochen just looked at him, raising his eyebrows in a questioning look. Quinn continued, a bit nervously, "Well, I'm not going. I'm not one of the Legends. I'm just a Guardian in the Ice Kingdom."

Lochen looked at him closely. "You must go. You're a part of this quest. After all, it's written in your own legend."

# Chapter fifteen

Quinn's eyes opened wide and his mouth formed an almost perfect "O" of surprise.

"Oh, no. I can't go. I'm just a Guardian. I'm just..."

"Ordinary?" asked Solveig.

Quinn looked at each of them, all of whom had their eyes fixed on him. He was clearly uncomfortable with the thought of being held to the same level of honor as those in the legends.

"Yes," he finally answered. "I'm ordinary. I haven't journeyed untold distances to get here. I haven't faced any challenges. I'm not a hero or a warrior. I'm not one of the Legendaries."

"On the contrary," said Lochen. "As you were explaining to us when you described your ancient engravings, the one on the bottom is you."

"No," replied Quinn. "It's not me. It's the ice shelf."

"I think you are mistaken," Lochen told him. "All of the symbols represent individuals. That must also be true of the one at the bottom."

"No," he said, taking a step backwards, separating himself from the group. "It's an ice shelf. It represents the Ice Kingdom."

"I don't think so," said Lochen, "I think it is clear, even to you, that this symbol you have referred to as an ice shelf is in fact a guardian. It's not only a guardian to the Ice Kingdom, as you have said, but it's a guardian to the rest of the symbols. You're the guardian. You said it yourself. You are meant to join us. It's written in your own legend." He paused, and then said, "I understand that you might be afraid…"

"I'm not afraid," interrupted Quinn, standing more upright and taking a defiant step forward. He paced back and forth, clearly uncertain. "I just don't think I've done anything to deserve to join you."

Stella smiled at him and said, "Of course you did. You saved our lives. What more could be expected of you?"

Quinn thought a minute. He looked at each of them, waiting for someone to disagree with Lochen and Stella. When no one did, he sighed deeply, and then resigned himself to his new role. Without another word he rummaged around in the supplies on the sled and constructed one more boat, much larger than the others to accommodate his larger size. When he was done, there was nothing left of his sled. Everything was ready for them to set sail. He turned to his dogs, pulling their heads close to his body and giving them a hug.

"OK you two. This is as far as you go," he said as he held them tightly. They both sensed a change in his demeanor, dropped their tails and whimpered.

"None of that," he continued, clearing his throat. He stood up and looked down at them. "You know the way back. I expect you to go straight home. No side trips," he admonished them, pointing his finger at them. He turned them around and gave them a push in the direction of home.

"Get going."  But they refused to move.  They both barked and looked at him expectantly; waiting for him to lead them back.

"I'll be all right.  I'm with friends.  You need to go now."

And with that he turned back towards the water.  The dogs barked once more then turned away and took off like a shot, heading back the way they had come.  Quinn took a final look at them over his shoulder.  He missed them already, but he knew he had a more important task ahead of him.  He got the others situated in the pods on the edge of the shore.  The original three pods were lashed together like pontoons.

"This will help keep the kayaks more stable in case we run into any rough water," Quinn explained.  Sean just groaned.

The center one of the three pods was the largest and was set back from the others, which were attached with wooden poles Quinn had taken from the sides of the sled.  The other two pods were slightly forward and on either side.  Together they looked like a "V."  Natalie and Stella were placed in the one on the left: Stella in front and Natalie behind.  Lochen and Solveig were placed in the one on the right with Solveig in front and Lochen in the back.  Liam and Sean were placed in the center pod with Sean in front – groaning – and Liam in the back.  Summer was nestled in the front opening with Sean.  Quinn got into his kayak and showed them how to row and steer.  Then he pushed each of the crafts into the water, and then jumped into his own. He paddled quickly around the makeshift pontoon and led the way forward.

The water was as smooth as glass and littered with hundreds of pieces of ice that had broken off from the shelf or from glaciers.  Many of them were small and jagged, but others were enormous, towering over them like islands of white and gray.  At first Quinn had taken the lead, paddling his kayak with a long pole that had a wide blade at each end.  Sean and Liam each had smaller versions and had the chore of rowing the three pod pontoon.  But Quinn was so big and his strokes were so strong that he soon had moved far ahead of the others. He turned back when he heard them shouting for him.

"Slow down," shouted Sean. "You're getting too far ahead of us."

"We can't keep up, and he keeps splashing water on me," added Liam, who was suffering from Sean's difficulties in mastering the correct rowing technique.

As Quinn maneuvered his boat around and up to the others he could see that Sean and Liam were having some difficulty with the paddles. Liam was paddling valiantly, but Sean, who was crouched down as far as possible into his opening, was not only sending large sprays of water over his shoulders onto Liam, but was counteracting any progress Liam was making.

Quinn looked at Sean and said, "You need to be sitting up a little higher; otherwise your paddle doesn't get into the sea."

"That's all right," answered Sean, hunkering even lower in the kayak. "I'm fine where I am, as long as I don't have to look at it. I really don't like all that water."

Quinn thought a minute, then tied a line from the back of his kayak to the other pods and pulled them behind. Sean was glad he no longer had to raise his head above the edge of the pod and Liam was glad he wasn't going to get any more soaked than he already was. Soon they were out of sight of anything that looked like solid land.

They cut across the surface of the water with a speed that was surprising. All the time Quinn rowed and chatted effortlessly over his shoulder – not even aware or concerned if anyone heard him or was even listening. After several hours he headed for what looked like a shore. He rowed his kayak right up onto a shelf of ice, hopped out, pulled his kayak up, and then pulled the line attached to the other pods and dragged them onto the ice as well.

Lochen commented that it seemed like it was still early and wondered if Quinn just needed a rest.

"Oh, no," he answered. "I thought this would be a good place for us to make camp for the night."

The others looked around and saw nothing but a wide desolate expanse, and one of the two suns still blazing in the sky above. Quinn noticed the looks and their silence.

"We'll have to build a shelter," he explained.

When they were still silent and looking at the bleakness of their surroundings, he went on, "It's pretty simple. Really. I'll just cut pieces of ice from the edge of the shelf where it's only about a foot thick. I'll need to make a bunch of blocks to make a small igloo."

"What are you going to unglue?" asked Sean.

Quinn just laughed, "What a comedian. You're really funny."

He pulled a long saw from the inside of his kayak and began cutting large squares from the near edge of the shelf. The others still weren't sure what he was doing, but helped to slide the blocks away from the shore and over to the ridge that they used as a back wall to their igloo. The blocks were cut with beveled edges so that they fit neatly one on top of the other, gradually curving at the top. Quinn formed a narrow tunnel, big enough for him to crawl through while the others could walk hunched over. He removed the skins from the frames of the boats and added some furs that had been stored in the pods to make a dry floor to the enclosure. Once inside, he slid one more block into the entryway and in short order it was warm and comfortable inside.

"This is a really neat unglue," said Sean. Quinn just laughed.

Stella cast a spell on a small mound of ice once they were all inside, and it glowed brightly providing the group with light. Everyone's spirits were high – even Sean's since he was glad they were finally away from the water. Within minutes, the inside of the shelter was warm enough for them to take off their coats.

"In spite of the cold and the bareness," said Natalie, "I mean on the outside - the Ice Kingdom seemed to be a peaceful and really beautiful place."

Quinn agreed. "But don't be fooled" he cautioned them. "The weather can be very unpredictable and treacherous if you don't know what you're doing, and there are a few creatures that it would be - let's just say - advantageous to avoid."

He didn't go into detail and before long everyone had drifted off to sleep.

Early the next morning Stella sensed a presence outside their shelter. There had been no noise, but she felt a disturbance in the atmosphere that awakened her immediately. She woke Quinn who slowly and carefully moved the block in the opening and listened closely. He could hear a faint noise and motioned to Stella to keep as quiet as she could. He gently moved the block back in place and woke the others one by one, motioning to each the need for silence. When they were all awake he explained.

"I think there's a pack of glacier wolves nearby. We'll wait a while and then I'll go out and see if they're still around."

"Just wolves?" asked Sean. "After all the things we've battled we should be able to handle a few wolves."

"Well," said Quinn, "it's likely there are more than just a few. They usually travel in packs of about a dozen or so, and these aren't like most wolves. Food in these areas can be scarce. If they're this close to people, then they may be nearly mad with starvation, and possible rabid. They won't be turned away if attacked. In fact, they're likely to become more ferocious. Their teeth and claws are as sharp as knives. And they like to single out one member of a group and coordinate their attack. It's best if they think no one's here and they move on."

Before long, there was no need for Quinn to sneak out and see where the pack was. Everyone knew. They could hear growling and barking sounds as well as clawing and digging at the front of the entryway. The wolves picked up the scent of all of them from crawling through the tunnel that led to the interior of the igloo.

"They won't stop until they break through," said Quinn. "We're going to have to hope they stay occupied with trying to get in through the front so we can escape through the back."

"The back of what?" asked Natalie. "I thought this thing was built up against a mountain of some kind."

"Just watch," answered Quinn. "I picked this spot for a reason.

He began to carefully and quietly cut away at the ridge against which the igloo had been constructed. He was through in no time at all. Once the opening was large enough, he wiggled it free and poked his head out. It seemed to be clear on this side of the ridge. He asked Summer to fly out and up as high as she could before circling around to the front and scout their location. In a few short minutes she was back.

"There are about twenty of them," she reported. "Most of them are digging at the front of the tunnel. It's half gone, and falling apart. It won't be long before they have torn it away completely. The rest of them just seem to be watching or standing guard."

"Are they black or white?" he asked. "I hope they're black."

"Yes, they're black," she said. "Does that make a difference?"

"Yes. The black ones are glacier wolves, which is what I thought they were. White ones are arctic wolves. They usually travel alone."

"Wouldn't white ones be better?" asked Solveig. "If they travel alone, why would a crowd be better than one?"

"Because the one is much larger – I mean MUCH larger – and more dangerous."

"So why aren't they all digging to get in?" asked Liam.

"They need to have some to stand watch and guard against other predators who may want to take their food away."

"<u>Other</u> predators?" asked Summer. "You mean there's something out there that would attack that pack of wolves?"

"Yeah," he said, rather evasively. "A few things. Trust me. You don't want to run into them. The glacier wolves are bad enough."

He sent Summer out to keep an eye on the pack as one by one he began to lift the others out through the opening. When they were all out, he began to squeeze through the opening. Just as he was halfway through, Summer raced down to tell him that they were nearly through and he had to hurry. He wiggled more energetically, kicking and squirming through the hole, and just as the lead wolves clawed the block away from the opening, Quinn literally popped through the opening.

He scrambled to his feet and pulled a small object from inside his coat. It looked like small ax with a long sharp pointed end on the opposite side. He motioned for Liam to lead the group away from the wolves while Quinn covered their departure. He carefully backed step by step away from the igloo.

When the wolves broke past the final block and discovered that the shelter was empty they went into a frenzy, barking wildly and snapping at one another. The lead wolf let out a howl as he sensed the direction their prey had taken. The pack responded to his direction and took off.

By now Quinn was encouraging them all to run towards the water. Their boat frames were on the other side of the igloo, now out of reach to them. Besides, without the skins, which they had left behind, the frames were useless to them.

"Where are we going?" asked Lochen.

"Towards the water," Quinn answered. "We need to find a piece of glacier large enough to hold all of us, but one that's floating by itself near the shore. If we can find one close enough to jump to, the wolves won't come after us. They don't like the water."

"THEY don't like the water?" shouted Sean, panting. "Did you forget something? I'm not really keen on it either."

"Yeah," said Quinn, "but it beats getting eaten."

"I'm not so sure about that," grumbled Sean.

Quinn was searching frantically as he heard the barking and growling getting closer and closer. Finally he found what he was looking for and shouted to Liam, who headed for the floating platform.

Quinn stopped to turn and face the oncoming pack. The biggest wolf was in the lead, bearing down on Quinn, with his head down and his teeth flashing in the sunlight. He was several yards ahead of the rest of the pack and intent on being the first to this large target. Just as he jumped at Quinn's face, Quinn sidestepped and brought the pick-ax down in a slashing motion. He caught the wolf perfectly behind one ear, the pick piercing the soft flesh just behind the wolf's jaw and driving into its brain. The wolf was dead before it hit the ground. The others, however, were not fazed by this and kept up their charge.

From behind him Quinn heard a snap and a whiz. One of the closest wolves let out a yelp, fell to the ground and began clawing its own eye. Sean had come back to help Quinn and had placed a well-aimed stone into his victim's eye. Quinn shouted to him to get on the iceberg, but Sean stood his ground and fired off two more stones, each of which took down two of the attacking wolves. In spite of this their numbers were too great and they were coming too fast. They then suddenly shifted their attack. It looked like a swarm of bees. As if with one mind, the pack literally bypassed Quinn and headed for Sean.

Quinn spun around and chased after the pack, swinging his pick-ax and driving it into the hindquarters of a few of the wolves at the end of the charge. By now the others had circled Sean. One would snap at him and immediately fall back to one side, while another would do the same on the opposite side. Sean couldn't predict where the next attempt would come from and he couldn't get off enough shots to hold the wolves at bay.

The others hadn't noticed that Sean and Quinn had fallen behind them. As soon as they did, Natalie jumped off the ice float and ran back towards the attacking pack of wolves. She waved her hand and a rush of water drenched the wolves. That slowed them down, but didn't stop them. Unfortunately, it also distracted Sean for a few seconds.

In that time one of the wolves lunged at Sean. Lochen shot his arm forward and drove the wolf's head to the icy ground, burying it in the ice, but not before he cut into Sean's leg with one of his claws. The other wolves shook the water off and regrouped.

"Do that again," Solveig shouted to Natalie as Quinn picked Sean up in mid stride and ran towards the iceberg.

As he reached the others, all of whom had jumped off the iceberg to come to his aid, he positioned himself so that Natalie was somewhat behind him and the rest were slightly behind her. He turned back to the wolves and held his free arm out motioned everyone to stay behind him. The wolves had run after Quinn, but were now slowly advancing and surrounding the group. The wolves could smell the blood from Sean's wounded leg and were more ravenous than before.

"Even in this cold air that little bit of water won't slow them down" said Quinn. "They'll just shake it off. What good will it do to drench them again?"

"Just do it," Solveig said to Natalie. "Trust me."

Natalie waved her arm again and once more soaked the wolves in a downpour of water. But this time before they could shake it off, Solveig took a deep breath and blew. Her breath was like a freezing gale. The water covering the wolves froze instantly encasing them in a thick covering of crystal clear ice.

"Hurry," Solveig told Natalie. "That probably won't hold them long."

"Get back on the ice float," shouted Quinn. "We need to put some distance between us and them."

As he said this, the wolves were already starting to crack the ice coating. Their heads broke free first, followed by their shoulders and finally their legs. But by the time they could move freely, everyone had jumped onto the ice float and Quinn had pushed it from the shore. Two of the wolves thought they could jump the distance and leaped towards the float. Quinn met each of their attempts with a swift stroke of his pick-ax, sending them into the freezing cold water.

Before either one of them could return to the shore, the water had penetrated their fur. The weight was slowing them down. They were swimming frantically now, just to keep their heads above water, but the water was crystallizing and forming ice which weighed them down even further. Their heads bobbed under the water a few times and then disappeared altogether.

The small platform was floating further and further away from the pack. Some of them lingered, but most had already turned away in search of new prey.

"Why did you come back?" asked Quinn. "You were all safe."

"That's just the way we roll," said Solveig.

"We watch out for each other," said Natalie.

"And you're one of us," added Liam. "Oh, and you, too, Sean."

The all turned to look at Sean who was lying on his back near the back edge of the ice berg.

"That was close," Sean gasped.

The color had drained from his face. He was beginning to sweat, and his breathing was coming in short rapid gasps. Then his eyes rolled back in his head, his body went rigid and started to spasm.

"What's wrong with him?" asked Liam.

"He got scratched by one of the wolves," answered Quinn. "Their cuts can be fatal. We need to get help, but we're too far away from my people. We're going to have to go back"

Quinn was clearly upset. He knew how dangerous a wolf's cut could be and he was certain they were going to lose Sean.

Lochen asked him, "What caused this reaction?"

"I told you," said Quinn, his voice rising. "They're rabid. Their bites and cuts are fatal."

"Then we don't have enough time to go back to your people," Lochen said.

"We have to. There's nothing we can do here," Quinn shouted, clearly becoming panicked. He was holding his head in his hands and had a look of despair on his face.

Lochen spoke to Quinn in a low voice, slowly trying to calm him down and to get him to focus, "Do your people use the poison from these wolves for anything?"

Lochen grabbed Quinn's arms and turned the giant to face him.

"Look at me," he commanded in a stern voice.

When Quinn turned his attention to Lochen, he thought a minute and then answered, "Yes. When it's diluted and used in very small doses, it is used as a sleeping potion for when the village healer has to fix things like broken bones."

An anesthesia, Lochen thought, his mind working quickly. He considered the various poisons he was familiar with and focused on those that could be used as an anesthetic. He sat by himself mumbling, while the others looked at him expectantly. Summer was about to interrupt his thoughts, but Solveig stopped her.

"I've seen him like this before," she said. "He needs to be left alone so he can sort things out. He's working on a solution."

Sean's breathing was becoming more and more labored. He was alternating between barely moving and shaking uncontrollably. Quinn was distraught. He had seen this before. By now there was not much time left. He couldn't imagine that one of the Legends would die. He felt it was his fault. He hadn't acted fast enough.

Finally Lochen stood and announced, "We need the leaf of a Dulse plant"

Everyone looked at him blankly.

"We don't have any," wailed Quinn. "I told you! We have to go back! Those only grow at the bottom of the sea."

Without any further word Stella dove into the frigid water. Natalie shouted after her, but too late to stop her. The Enchantress knew well what this particular plant looked like and where it might be found. She forced herself to ignore the biting cold. It felt like thousands of needles being hammered into her body. Within seconds the light from above disappeared and the water was an inky black. She raised a hand before her and a beacon of light burst forward. She swam further and further towards the ocean floor. In the distance she could see sea creatures of varying sizes. Some were frightened away from the glowing light, while others were attracted to it. Ignoring them she scoured the rocks, sand

and ice of the bottom of the sea, keeping one eye out for the plant and another for Dark Eyes. Did they swim this far north, she wondered. She hoped not. Finally she found what she was looking for. She plucked a long broad leaf from underneath a rocky overhang, and darted for the surface.

She broke the water and climbed back onto the float. The others huddled around her to dry her off and warm her up. Solveig waived her hand and instantly dried her off. Stella handed the leaf to Lochen. It was a dull gray in color and had the texture of rubber covered in slime. He gave it back to her.

"You have to chew it," he said.

"Really? It looks disgusting."

"It has strange healing properties, but it must be ground into a paste and only by the person who pulled it from the sea. Try not to swallow any of it though. I'm not sure what it would do to you."

She looked at Sean and mumbled, "You owe me big time."

Hesitantly Stella bit off a piece of the leaf. It tasted worse than it looked. She had no worry about swallowing any of it. She could barely keep it in her mouth; the taste and texture were gagging her. She fought through her feelings of revulsion and kept chewing. Finally the leaf softened into a paste and she spit it out onto her hand.

"I hope this is good enough," she said. "I don't think I can take much more of it."

"I hope so too," answered Lochen as he smeared the paste onto Sean's open cut.

At first nothing happened. After a few minutes, the poultice began to change color, turning black. Then it began to sound like it was sizzling hot. Sean let out a yell. As Summer was about to reach for the paste and pull it off, Lochen stopped her.

"It's working," he said. "It's supposed to have that reaction."

It seemed like forever, but Sean's breathing finally returned to normal and the color came back in his cheeks.

"He'll probably sleep for a while," said Lochen, "but he should be all right."

"Yes," said Quinn, relieved. "I've seen this before. That's exactly what our Sage has done. You cured him. How did you know what to do?"

Before Lochen could answer, there was a loud thump from beneath their ice float.

"Did everyone else feel that?" asked Natalie.

Before anyone could answer, it was followed immediately by another, and then another. Each one was stronger than the one before. They were enough to knock everyone but Quinn off their feet. Lochen almost slid over the side. Solveig shot out an arm and grabbed his ankle, pulling him back towards the middle.

"What was that?" asked Solveig, as she scrambled to her knees.

"Something dangerous, I'll bet," said Liam, whose senses were reeling.

"I'm afraid I know," said Quinn. "Everyone get in the middle of the float. This is going to get rough."

# Chapter sixteen

The ice float shook with another jolt from beneath.

"What is it?" asked Natalie.

"Narwhals," said Quinn. "I hope there's just one of them."

"Why?" she asked.

"Because, if there's only one, it probably can't break through the bottom of this slab of ice."

"Probably?" everyone asked in unison.

For a second the beating against the ice stopped. Just then the creature broke through the surface of the water, bellowing furiously. Everyone skittered to the far side of the float. None of them but Quinn had ever seen anything so large. It was covered with sleek spotted fur and had large spiral tusks hanging down from the top of its mouth. In a split second, it crashed back into the water forcing a plume of spray high into the air that showered down on the ice float. Natalie had quickly waved her arm, covering everyone in a protective bubble to keep them all from getting soaked.

Quinn looked at the narwhal and then turned to the others and said, "Well there's only one. If there were more, they all would have jumped like that. That's the good news. The bad news is that it'll try to climb onto this float to get at us."

"That thing can climb out of the water?" Liam nearly shouted.

"Sure," said Quinn, "But they can't move so fast on land. Still, we have to be careful. They're tricky and they're nasty."

"Land?" asked Liam. "This isn't land we're on. It's a really, really tiny piece of frozen water! If Sean was awake, he'd be really, really...I don't know, but he wouldn't like it!"

They all backed even further away from the edge, and just in time. The narwhal again breached the surface, but this time made a diving bite at the nearest part of the float. His tusks rammed into the ice, breaking off a sizable chunk. The broken part slowly floated away, as the narwhal sunk below the surface of the water. He was moving too fast for anyone to cast a spell on him, and his movements were too unpredictable for anyone to be prepared in advance.

They stood huddled together, with Sean unconscious at their feet, waiting to see what would happen next. Nearly a minute dragged by while their eyes darted across the horizon searching for some kind of sign, and suddenly, the narwhal again broke the surface, dove towards the float and again rammed his tusks into the edge, breaking off another large piece. As everyone else backed further away, Lochen bent down and began making notations in the snow.

"What on earth are you doing?" asked Natalie.

Ignoring her question, he stood up and announced, "If it continues at that rate, I calculate that in about seven more bites, we'll be out of room." He turned to Quinn, "What happens then?"

"I expect we'll all get wet, and he'll want to eat us," Quinn answered and then smiled nervously. "I don't think it will come to that, though. He probably has one more bite and then the ice will be too thick for him to break it – at least in a single bite."

All their heads turned in a single motion to the bitten edge of the float, and then out to sea. Several of them had hands ready for some kind of spell – either offensive or defensive. They were too nervous to confer with one another. The narwhal repeated its attack and another large piece broke off and floated away. Several arms flailed and several spells were cast, but none found its mark. Part of the sea turned to a block of ice; another part shot up into the air and flew off, far into the distance, and yet another caught fire and quickly fizzled out.

"We should probably coordinate our efforts," said Lochen.

As he said this, Quinn took a few steps closer to the edge of the float.

"What are you doing?" asked Solveig.

"I've heard some of the elders talk about doing this," he said. "I've never seen it done, but it should work."

Without explaining further he watched as the narwhal rose up again and slammed down on the float. As Quinn had expected, it didn't break the ice this time. As it was sliding back into the water, Quinn rushed forward and shouted at it, waving his arms and taunting it.

"Are you crazy?" shouted Natalie, her hand ready with another spell.

"Just watch," he said.

This time the narwhal rose even higher, gyrating its massive tail to gain more elevation as it jerked its head down driving its tusks as hard as it could. Quinn jumped back out of reach of the two sharp, spiraled fangs that drove deep into the ice. Just as they struck the float, Quinn jumped on the top of the narwhal's head and drove the tusks deeper. Then he jumped again, pushing them as far as they would go. When the narwhal tried to lift its head, it discovered that it was stuck. It tried to shake its head back and forth, but was locked to the ice.

Solveig inched forward, ready to put her own spell on the beast, but Quinn stopped her.

"Don't," he said. "You might hurt it."

"Hurt it?" she was stunned. "It's trying to eat us and you're worried about hurting it?"

"It's only trying to eat us because it's hungry. It's not evil. Well, I suppose it's pretty mean, but it wouldn't try to eat us if it didn't need to. Besides, there's no telling what your spell will do to it. This is better. Trust me."

She looked at him for a second or two and then back at the narwhal. She stepped away and the others lowered their spell-ready hands.

The narwhal was clearly stuck. In anger and frustration it shook its massive body. Since the front end of its body was immobilized, the tail end began to heave. Quinn ran to the other end of the float and told Liam to stand there.

"Keep an eye on that coast line way off to the left. See it? We need to keep going parallel to it for a while. Just tell me when we have to steer right or left," he said.

Then he moved back near the head of the narwhal and waited for Liam's instructions, all the while shouting at the narwhal. With each shout the beast shook its tail, propelling the ice float forward. After a few minutes Liam shouted that they needed to go left. Quinn reached over and covered the narwhal's left eye. Since it couldn't turn its head, it shifted his body and in doing so, shifted the course of the ice float.

"That's far enough," shouted Liam.

Quinn uncovered the one eye and continued to taunt the narwhal.

"It's working," he shouted exuberantly.    "I can't believe it's really working."

They continued on this way for some time.  Eventually, the narwhal wore out and stopped thrashing.  Quinn knew at that point they would get no more help from the animal, and that it would no longer be a threat.  He reached under its upper lip and lifted the top of its mouth.  He gave a huge push and the tusks came free.  The narwhal slid off the float and dropped back into the water.  The float kept moving following the current of the sea as it swung along the coast.  It was less than half the size it was when they started and everyone hoped that they wouldn't see any more narwhals, or run into water warm enough to melt it.

As the day wore on Summer could see that the storm that had been chasing them all this time was again headed towards them.  She had nearly forgotten that the sky had been clear for a short while.  Whatever the storm was, it had apparently given up on trying to break through the ice wall.  It was spreading over the far edge of the polar sea, and gathering strength.  It was covering the horizon and seemed to be battering the sea.  A little while later she thought she noticed that the rocking of the ice float was a little more pronounced.  She looked at Stella and Natalie.  They returned her look and knew what was on her mind.  They both nodded.  They, too, had sensed a greater turbulence in the water.  There were large waves forming in the distance, gradually making their way towards the tiny shelf of ice.

Soon it had become very noticeable.  Large waves were appearing much closer.  Some of them were lapping at the edges of the float.  The distant storm was taking its rage out on the water, and there were no large landmasses to soften the sea or to deflect the waves.  The thunder was no longer a distant rumble.  It was growing into a roar.  The bolts of lightning that struck the water were like meteorites, creating splashes that soared nearly a hundred feet into the air and came crashing down with equal force. The waves created by this turmoil grew larger and larger. The ice float was being tossed from wave to wave like a cork.

Sean, who was still unconscious, slid from one side of the float to the other, with one friend after another clutching at him to keep him from flying over the side, while at the same time trying to keep themselves from plunging in. Only Quinn managed to keep his feet under him, riding the float like he was standing on a board balanced on a large ball. He shifted his weight from one side to the other. At the same time he would lunge and grab one or another of the travelers sliding across the float towards the roiling sea. Things only got worse. Each time one of them skidded across the berg, they smoothed the surface even more. It was gradually turning from a coarse snow covered plane to a very slippery sheet of ice.

The waves kept growing fiercer. When the float was at the top of one wave, it seemed like they were on the top of the tallest mountain. Then they would come surging down like the steepest roller coaster, leaving their stomachs high in the air. Sometimes the drop was so quick and so steep that they would be lifted off their feet only to come smashing down. At the bottom of the swells the rising waves towered above them, nearly blotting out the skies.

With each radical shift in position, all but Quinn slid from one side of the platform to the other, nearly getting swept into the sea. Somehow, Quinn managed to keep on his feet and not be affected by the increasing slickness of the surface. After a while, Summer spread her wings and raised herself up above the motion. She had to limit looking down at them, though, as their jerky movement was making her sea sick.

"Why aren't you sliding from side to side, too?" Summer shouted to Quinn, as she fluttered above her friends.

"Well," he said, looking at her and trying to hold on to everyone else, "first of all, I'm sort of used to this. And second of all, I guess it's because of the Reyther skin covering on my boots."

"What's Reyther skin?" she asked as the next wave shot the tiny berg of ice up into the air, slamming her down onto the surface.

"It's one of the sea creatures in these waters. Their skin is really rough. It can scrape the bottom of the hardest ice. It really digs in."

The wave dropped and Summer flew up high overhead. Quinn reached up and grabbed her before she got too far away.

"I guess I should have had got some boots with this stuff for everyone else," he said somewhat guiltily.

"You think?" Summer asked.

Quinn quickly bent down to keep the others from sliding off. By now they had all flattened themselves out as much as they could and interlocked their arms. It had helped to reduce some of their movement, but not all of it. Their body heat was warming the ice, making it more pliable and becoming even more slippery each time they slid across.

The current had increased dramatically. They were being washed quickly into an expanse of ice debris. Some of the other ice floats were small and were either pushed aside, or broke up into even smaller pieces. Others were much larger. As if the rising and falling wasn't bad enough, they began to slam into these other large chunks of ice. Each time they struck one of these mountains of ice, another piece of their small floating island chipped and broke off. What the narwhal couldn't do, the sea was taking care of much faster and more efficiently.

After only a few collisions, the float had been reduced to a size barely big enough to hold all of them. Liam had been keeping an eye on where they were headed. He had been interlocked with Stella and Natalie, and he pulled them in as close as he could.

"Hold on," He shouted to all of them. "Quinn! Grab Summer and get down as flat as you can."

Without questioning the direction, Quinn scooped Summer into his hand and tucked her close to his side. The next wave lifted them high into the air. They hovered there for a second or two, and then the wave and their much diminished transport plummeted downward. This time, though, the wave splashed onto the shore of a new, much larger and much more solid ice shelf. The float landed with a teeth-rattling crash and then skidded several hundred feet across the ice, spinning in circles as it did. It came to a halt with a loud crack against a crest in the ice on a large drift of snow and broke completely apart, depositing everyone unceremoniously in a pile.

When it came to a stop, Sean opened his eyes and looked around.

"Why is everything upside down?"

"It's you that's upside down," clarified Summer as she crawled out from under Quinn's arm.

"Oh," he said as he righted himself. "Are we on land?"

"Yes," said Quinn.

"Good," answered Sean as he sat up and looked at the clump of goo on his leg. "I'm glad we didn't have to travel on the water again."

Natalie was about to fill him in, but Solveig touched her arm and just shook her head.

"I think we're here," said Liam.

"I just said that," noted Quinn. "We're on land. We've landed."

"No," said Natalie. "I think we're at the Crystal Citadel."

Everyone looked around. Their surroundings didn't look much different than they had ever since they reached the Ice Kingdom – except for the water, of course. None of them saw anything that looked like a citadel, in spite of the fact that none of them knew what a citadel would look like.

"Are you sure?" asked Quinn.

"Yes, I'm pretty sure," answered Natalie. "It just feels different."

"I can feel a difference, too," said Summer and Solveig almost at the exact same time, as they looked at each other.

Stella closed her eyes for a second and placed her hands on the ground. When she opened them, she turned to Lochen and said, "Yes, it's here."

"I agree," he said. "We only need to find a way in."

Lochen looked around. He didn't see anything that even remotely looked like a citadel or any kind of entryway. He studied the terrain, taking in the shapes of the ice peaks and the mounds and drifts around them. Still, he couldn't get a clue as to where to turn next.

He turned to Liam, "Can you sense which way to go?"

"No, not any more," he said. "It's like a switch was thrown. I can't tell where we're supposed to go." He looked around. "In fact, I can't feel where we are or anything else like I used to. It's like I was blindfolded once we landed here. I'm not even certain we're in the right place, but I trust that the sensations the rest of you are feeling are accurate. The only sense I'm getting is that we shouldn't be here."

"That's probably a good indicator that we're in the right place," Lochen said.

He looked around at the surroundings once more to see if there was anything that would confirm his and Liam's suspicions. They were running out of time and couldn't afford to waste it on a wrong "hunch," but couldn't break his mental impasse.  As he always did when he came upon a problem he couldn't solve, he looked to the stars.

The others watched him expectantly; each eager for action, but sharing his concern about making a wrong decision.  He raised his head and studied the heavens.  He had never seen them from this position before, and at first he couldn't get his bearings.  Then he looked for Luna and saw it barely over the horizon just beyond the jagged crest of the ice ledge in front of them.

Luna had been the first celestial body he had studied and it has always served as a starting point for him.  From there he looked for first one then another constellation he knew.  He couldn't see them due to the light of the trail sun, so he turned his attention to the planets.

He spotted Hermes and Athena, almost directly in line with Luna to the right.  He raised his hand to follow their direction.  Gradually he could make out the other planets to the left.  From this angle they were in what seemed to be a haphazard arrangement, but he knew that from another angle they were in a nearly perfect line.

Suddenly it struck him.  He recognized the pattern of the planets as seen from this location.  He turned to Sean and asked him for his armband.  Sean took it off and handed it to Lochen.  Lochen then turned to Summer.

"May I trouble you again for that stone from your neck?" he asked.

"Of course," she said, untying it and handing it to him.

He placed into the indentation in the armband as he had done before.  Then he twisted the inner band, lining up those symbols with the ones on the outer band.  As the bands rotated they expanded.  When the symbols were matched up, he gave the band to Stella and asked her to put it on.

"But face Luna" he told her as he positioned her in the right direction and Stella settled the band on her head.

As the band slipped into place on Stella's head, her eyes shut, her body went rigid, and she went into a trance-like state. The symbols on the band began to glow and a beam of light shot from the triskelion directly towards Luna. The light expanded until the entire area in front of them was glistening. Then a beam of light bounced back from Luna and illuminated a gateway in the ice crest immediately before them.

"There it is," shouted Lochen. "We've found it. We've found it."

Stella's body relaxed and she opened her eyes. She reached up to take the band off, but Lochen stopped her.

"We may need it to keep the gateway open, and there may be other things that will be visible to us only if you are wearing it."

"All right," she said, lowering her hands from the band.

They all moved towards the image of the gateway. It was there and not there at the same time – almost like a projected picture on the face of the ice crest. Even as they got closer the opening remained only an apparition. Standing immediately before it they all paused. There was no change in the wall of ice and stone. The image of the opening still only looked like it was projected. Nothing happened.

"I think we should go in," said Natalie.

"You mean just keep walking into that wall of ice?" asked Solveig incredulously.

"Yes," answered Natalie. "I think we'll be able to pass through to the other side."

Even though the others were not as confident as she was, no one voiced any objection. At the same time, no one took a step forward. Natalie thought to herself, this was my idea, I guess I better put my money where my mouth is. She reached her arm out to brace herself as she took a long step and passed through the wall. Even though the others saw this happen right before their own eyes, they were still hesitant to follow. As a single body, though, they all stepped towards the wall, raising their arms out as Natalie had done, bracing for the hard cold surface. They were all surprised when nothing happened.

"It's like passing out of our bubble back home," announced Stella. And it was.

The wall of ice was extremely thick, but the passage from the outside to the inside was like walking through a thin veil of water. They suddenly found themselves inside a large open area. The light that had led the way illuminated the inside. Crystals of ice hung from the ceiling and jutted from the walls. The floor was a smooth clear pathway.

"So, what now?" asked Quinn.

"Your guess is as good as any of ours," said Solveig.

He was about to point out once again that they were the Legends, but then thought better of doing so. They might point out once again that he was now one of them, and he didn't have any ideas.

"Well, we know from which way we've come," said Lochen, "so logically, forward seems the best option. I don't believe anyone is going to come and guide us.

Still uncertain of what they were supposed to do or where they were supposed to go, they slowly and hesitantly moved forward. Sean turned around to look back at the passageway through which they had come. It was gone. There was no indication whatsoever that there had been an opening. A sense of foreboding settled over him. He was about to say something, but noticed that everyone was already moving forward.

"I wish I had something to leave as a trail," he mumbled.

Only Summer heard him. She turned back at the sound of his voice and saw the worried look on his face.

"Look on the bright side," she said, trying to lift his spirits. "No water."

He looked around at all the ice and with no change of expression, said, "Unless all this melts. Then we're in real trouble."

The path wound narrowly through the crystals and beneath the stalactites, twisting and turning. There were often side paths on either side of the main route. Most of them were very narrow or the openings were very low. They all stopped at the first juncture that presented several passable and similar options.

"It's a labyrinth," commented Lochen.

He turned to Liam. "Can you tell which path is the correct one?"

"No," he said. "I told you. I've lost that ability. I'm not even sure which way we've come. I have no idea which way we go."

"I know," said Quinn. Something from his early childhood memories had been awakened. He was soon flooded with the recollection.

Before anyone could ask he said, "From the earliest time I can remember, every baby and child in the Kingdom was taught this rhyme. None of us knew what it really meant. It was just some old nonsense story that had been handed down from generation to generation, mostly to amuse the little ones. But it describes a journey through a forest of ice and the turns to take or to avoid in order to reach the end.

'In the land of ice there is a way

With many paths that go astray.

Learn the course from start to end

Or with dangers great you will contend.

Four counts left then one to right

Keep your goal well in sight.'

And it goes on like that for several verses.  The description in the rhyme is probably about this place and the path through the maze."

He saw a look of uncertainty on their faces.

"Probably?" asked Sean.  "I'd feel a little better if you were a little more certain."

"Well, yeah, I guess," stammered Quinn.  Then he straightened his shoulders and said more confidently, "No.  I mean, yes.  Yes this IS the place and the rhyme IS about this maze."

"What?" asked Sean.  "NOW you're certain?  I don't know if any of you realized, but the way we came in isn't there anymore."

"What do you mean?" asked Solveig.  "It was a wall.  How could it not be there anymore?"

"It's there," answered Sean.  "It's the image that Stella's band – my band – you know what I mean – the image that was on the wall when we came in.  That's what's gone."

"Please trust me.  I know I'm right," Quinn pleaded.

"Of course, you're right" said Lochen.  They all jerked their heads in his direction.  "I don't think any of us has a better idea of how to negotiate this maze.  Liam got us most of the way purely on our faith in him.  Quinn has gotten us to this point.  If we can't trust him, I'm certainly open for hearing other options.  But I must remind you, in a short while – a VERY short while – all this debate will become academic."

Everyone was silent.  Hearing no objections or alternate theories on which way to go, Lochen nodded to Quinn and motioned for him to take the lead.  With that Quinn looked at the various paths, silently recited the nursery rhyme and then led the way.

The paths twisted back and forth so often no one was able to keep track of where they were going or from where they had just come. Some of the turns Quinn took seemed like they were clearly the wrong choices. He had to stoop down so far, that he was duck walking through some of them. The entire cavern was absolutely and eerily silent.

The wind and noises from outside were completely absent. They had diminished shortly after they had crossed into the cave, but the silence now was unnerving. The interior of the citadel was dimly lit from some unknown source. The light that had guided them in and lit the initial cavern had faded away. Now, instead, the source seemed to be following or associated with each of them. There was an odd glow or aura around each of them that, collectively, brightened the area around them. Beyond their small circle the light faded. Actually, it was more like the light was smothered by the darkness.

Several times each of them had tried to cast a spell to generate more light, but it seemed that their powers were being blocked. Even Summer's sprinkling of faerie dust had no effect. Periodically, Lochen would turn to Liam with an inquisitive look. He didn't have to ask. Liam knew he wondered if his navigational abilities had returned. He only shook his head in response.

The further they traveled along the path the thicker the darkness became. The crystals that surrounded them were lit only by the reflection of the globe of light that circled the group. The turns became harder to see, but somehow Quinn knew exactly where they were and walked with confidence as he mumbled the ancient rhyme. Lochen only hoped he remembered all of it, and that he remembered the verses correctly.

# Chapter seventeen

The deeper they crept into the labyrinth, the more oppressive the darkness became. It enveloped them like a dank musty old blanket. The light that had surrounded them had gradually dimmed the further they went. The darkness wasn't the only change they noticed. The air was becoming thicker – staler. It left an acrid, metallic taste in their mouths as they breathed.

They all also detected a pervasive odor that got stronger the further they went. It smelled like rotting garbage. As if this wasn't bad enough, they started to hear the faint sound of breathing. At first, most of them thought that their ears were playing tricks on them or that the sound was just an echo of their shuffling along the path. But then it grew more audible. It had a raspy sound to it. Each of their senses was being assaulted.

Finally Quinn stopped his recitation and stopped walking. The others stopped, too, crowding around him.

"What's wrong?" asked Stella.

"The rhyme is over," he told everyone, his voice croaking. "I don't know where to go from here."

Even in the thickening darkness they could see a look of concern on his face. The directions from his fabled rhyme had ended, but the path had not.

Sean stepped forward. "Maybe we should just keep following this path. Can you see if there are any turn offs ahead?"

"If I stand up straight, I can barely see you," responded Quinn; but he inched his way ahead and the others followed closely behind him.

They were almost feeling their way along, it had gotten so dark. Even as close to the ground as Summer was, she could not see any further intersections. She fluttered up slowly and bumped into the cavern ceiling just inches above Quinn's head. She hadn't been able to see the ceiling, it had gotten so dark, or the ice had turned black. She wasn't sure which. The ice seemed to sting, too.

"Ouch," she yelped as a spark flew from where she hit the ice. She warned the others, "Be careful about touching this ice. It burns."

Feeling an overwhelming need to find out for himself, Sean placed his hand against the wall.

"Yeow, that hurt," he shouted, pulling his hand back.

"What?" asked Summer, "you didn't believe me?"

"Quiet," whispered Lochen. "It's probably not in our best interest to announce our arrival; especially since we can't see where we are."

It had taken several minutes to go a short distance. They were inching their way along. After a few more yards, they felt like they were passing through the same kind of opening they crossed when they first entered the citadel. It was like walking through a light film of water, but even lighter – more like spider webs. Summer quickly ran her hands over her body to wipe them off, but nothing was there.

Once they all passed through the film, the glow around them slowly broadened. It was enough for them to see they were now in what seemed to be a large alcove. Quinn was still in the forefront with the others nearly cowering behind him. The smell was almost unbearable. The odor of rotting garbage was the same, but there was an additional scent that was overly sweet and metallic. Lochen went rigid.

"Blood," he whispered. "I smell blood."

As he uttered these words, the sound of the breathing changed. There was a sharp sound as if someone was quickly breathing in.

A low, booming, gravelly voice bellowed, "Who dares enter my world?"

The sound penetrated each of them. The pitch tingled deep inside their ears, chilling them to their very core. When no one answered, the voice boomed again, even louder, resonating off the walls.

"I command you! Present yourself!"

Again, no one dared make a sound. It was impossible for them to know where the voice came from, as it echoed. No one moved. The speaker took in a deep ragged and wheezing breath, and let out a roar.

"I am Ena Ray, the all powerful. No one can hide from me. Present yourself."

While his words were still bouncing off the walls and buzzing in their ears, a loud crack split the fetid air and the entire chamber began to glow with a swirling dull gray-green light. A wave of stench struck them as if it was a solid object. As they swallowed, a cloying taste stuck in their throats. Their skin prickled as something charged the air around them.

A formless cloud of black slowly became visible in a corner of the cavern. It was so black it seemed to absorb any light that was near it. It was distinguishable only because of the absence of any shadows or lines that were evident elsewhere in the cavern.  In the center of the cloud two burning coals appeared that seemed to serve as eyes.  They scanned the chamber and fixed on the intruders.

It glared at them and snarled like a trapped animal.  They all knew they had discovered the Crystal Citadel.  They knew they had been seeking the entity before them, but none of them had ever actually expected to come face to face with Ena Ray.  Nor had they any idea of what he would look like.  They looked at each other with growing fear; hiding behind Quinn's outstretched arms, as if he could protect them.  Quinn was unable to take his eyes off the evil before them, and none of them was sure what was supposed to happen now.

The images of the storm and the villagers that had been turned to stone ran through Summer's mind.  She felt a wave of depression settle over her.  How were they ever going to get this…thing…to stop the storm and change her people back?  She quietly moved up onto Lochen's shoulder.  Part of her wanted to confront this monster, but part of her was frightened to be seen.

Solveig and Lochen were pressed close behind Quinn, both hidden by Quinn's expansive coat.  Natalie and Stella held each other tightly behind them.  Sean, who had been at the end of the line had pulled out his slingshot and some stones and was ready to step out from behind Quinn and fire off at the formless creature.  Lochen motioned to him to stay behind them all.

The image facing Quinn appeared to shift slightly forward to get a better look at him, but didn't move from its spot in the small crevice in which it had been hovering.  The coals flared and the grating voice reverberated in the small space.  The light that emanated from the coals swept over Quinn.  He could feel it as it washed from his head to his feet, stinging as it went.

"One from the Ice Kingdom, I see. Probably a Guardian. Did you lose your way?" the voice sneered.

Quinn stood stark still, his arms remained outstretched. He didn't know what to say, so he said nothing. He was beginning to tremble. Think happy thoughts, he told himself repeatedly. He thought of Kelsey and Rover and the people in the Ice Kingdom. The black cloud from which the voice emanated billowed and expanded, but didn't move any closer. Swirls of deep red bubbled up from inside the core of blackness. It inhaled sharply, making a sound like fingernails on a chalkboard. A wave of stench blew in Quinn's direction.

"Yes, that's right," mocked the voice, "think happy thoughts. Think about your dogs. The dogs I will feed to wolves, bit by bit. Think about your precious Ice Kingdom, which I will melt into the sea."

Quinn was startled to hear his thoughts violated by this creature. He wanted to say something to shut the voice up, but words escaped him. The others, too, were stunned silent and huddled closer together.

"You dare to stand before me like a giant lump of dirt?" The voice nearly screamed the question at Quinn.

The suddenness of the reproach startled Quinn.

"I'm not a lump of dirt," he shouted back defiantly. "I am Quinn, Guardian of the Ice Kingdom. I am here to see that you are never freed. You will never touch my dogs. You will never harm my kingdom. You will never leave here."

Solveig started to peek around from behind Quinn, but Lochen grabbed her arm to stop her. He raised a finger to his lips to motion her to keep quiet and then to stay put. She didn't know why he wanted her to do this, but she knew enough to trust him.

Lochen thought to himself, "Ena Ray doesn't know the rest of us are here. For some unknown reason, he can't sense our presence." He wasn't sure if that was important or not, but he thought it best to keep their enemy uninformed for the time being. He caught the attention of the others and motioned for them to huddle closer and to keep out of sight.

For several uncomfortable seconds neither Quinn nor Ena Ray spoke. The only sound that could be heard was the wheezing intake of air into the cloud mass. Finally Ena Ray broke the silence.

"You don't know what to do," Ena Ray said. "The great Guardian of the Ice Kingdom has come to stop the return of the almighty Ena Ray," he laughed, "and he doesn't have a clue how to do that."

The blackness began to take some kind of amorphous shape. It reminded Quinn of a cloud, only black. The shape of the cloud began to change and coalesce. The top puffed up and reared back. It almost looked like a giant swarm of wasps forming into a single unit, buzzing loudly to intimidate its enemy. Then, like a wasps, it shot forward and the voice emitted a raspy buzz.

"You ignorant piece of nothing. You can't stop me. You can't keep me here. You're too late. My powers have already created the storm that has laid waste to the inferiors of this world. I have moved that storm great distances without even leaving this prison. The planets will be aligned within the hour and I will be free. Once I am free, my army will be freed from their underworld prison. I will return stronger than ever, and you will be the first person I crush into dust."

How can he control the storm but not free himself, wondered Lochen. There's something more here that is happening – some other power at work.

The top of the cloud was leaning forward, pointed directly at Quinn, but it still had not moved from its spot in the small grotto in which it had first appeared. Lochen had been trying to catch unseen glimpses of the image. He needed to see more than his position would allow. His powers had been hindered since they all had entered the citadel, so a simple spell to hide himself was out of the question. Besides, he thought, a spell might just do the opposite and alert Ena Ray to his presence.

Quinn lowered his arm slightly for just a second. The movement exposed a bit more of the grotto to Lochen's field of vision. He could see a faint jagged line along the floor between the cloud and where Quinn stood. It looked like a break in the ice. A crevasse, maybe, he wondered. But surely Ena Ray could easily jump over it. Lochen wondered why he didn't – or couldn't. It might be part of the spell that kept Ena Ray captive, Lochen concluded. It might also prevent anyone from crossing the other way.

"You won't get past me," shouted Quinn bravely. "There's no other way out, and I'll do everything in my power to make sure you stay locked in here, even if it costs me my life."

Ena Ray began to laugh, but his laugh was not filled with mirth. It was contemptuous of Quinn and his brave stance.

"The cost of your life is a certainty," he laughed. "You have no idea how to stop me. Your mere presence is not enough. And you have no clue as to the key to my captivity. I can read it in your thoughts. I can read your fear. Nothing about you is hidden from me."

He's told us more than he intended, thought Lochen. The key. Of course. At that comment Lochen knew what needed to be done. The mysteries of the ancient tales and documents became clear. He took Stella's hand and stepped out from behind Quinn. One by one the others followed his lead.

"He may not know," said Lochen, "but I do."

There was a startled silence, and then the voice began to laugh again, but Lochen detected a lessening of confidence and bravado, "Well, well; what an assortment of nobodies and misfits. I defeated the greatest leaders in the known world and this is what has come to stop me now?" His laughter grew louder and bounced off the walls.

"You're the hope of mankind? Your magic won't work in here, and even if it did, it wouldn't be powerful enough to overcome me."

"We don't need magic to deal with you," answered Lochen calmly. "And we don't need to overcome you."

He moved Stella to the front of the small group. The band she still wore on her head began to pulsate; the triskelion in the center began to glow and then shot a ray of light towards the corner in which the cloud that was Ena Ray had been imprisoned for a thousand years.

"An Enchantress!" screeched Ena Ray. "And a piece of the pendant."

His voice betrayed his fear and hatred. He had spotted the stone in the headband Stella wore. A raw screech pierced the air. The cloud shape that Ena Ray had taken compressed itself into a small compact undulating mass near the floor. Above it suspended in the air was a glowing circle of light: a tiny band. It was barely visible, looking more like a pinhole of light.

"There's the key," said Lochen.

The cloud laughed again, trying to regain composure. "So, you've discovered the key. You still can't reach it."

"What is it?" whispered Stella.

"It's part of the spell that has imprisoned him," answered Lochen. "It's also the key to releasing him. And, if it's what I think it is, it may also be his connection to the storm – maybe even how he controls it. We need to get it."

"I'm not afraid of him," proclaimed Quinn, as he took a step around Stella and began to move towards the band.

"No," shouted Lochen, as he grabbed Quinn's arm and pulled him back.

As soon as the band had become visible and started to glow, the line along the floor that Lochen had noticed earlier was more visible. The light from the band illuminated the line, casting shadows that gave it form — and depth. It wasn't just a line. It was a wide chasm, far too wide for any of them, even Quinn to jump across. The width had been hidden by the darkness and the angle at which Lochen had seen it.

Summer could get across. The thought crossed everyone's mind at nearly the same time. She was still hidden from Ena Ray's view or consciousness. In stopping Quinn, Lochen had raised his hand. He hoped Summer understood that he was also motioning for her to stay hidden. Something still didn't seem right about that chasm.

There was a very low sound, barely noticeable, that seemed to be coming from the fissure. Lochen looked around and found a small piece of ice nearby. He picked it up and tossed it over the crevice. Before it got to the other side it was sucked instantly downward.

It was a vortex. That was one more part of the enchantment that kept Ena Ray prisoner, Lochen realized. That probably explained why he never moved any closer when confronting Quinn. He'd be sucked deep into the core of the planet.

"Oh, please, let him come. By all means," Ena Ray said, mocking Quinn's bravado. "I would be greatly entertained to watch him vanish into that abyss." His voice rattled with a mirthless laugh. "So you see. You may know where the key is, but you'll never reach it in time — if at all. The planets will be aligned very soon now. When that happens, that chasm will close, the spell will be broken, my body will be returned to me, and you will be my first victims."

The embers glowed more intensely as he stared at Stella, and said, "I'll save the little enchantress for last and take back that stone."

"Take back?' Lochen wondered to himself. Pieces of an ancient puzzle were starting to fall into place. He would have to solve that later. Right now, there was a more immediate dilemma facing them.

All during the time Ena Ray was surveying the group before him he had failed to notice Summer, who, because of her size, was hidden from view. She had been hovering over Lochen's shoulder, behind Quinn. After tossing the piece of ice over the chasm, Lochen had stepped back and had given her a very secretive glance.

Without a word or any further suggestion or encouragement she concentrated hard. She changed her appearance, becoming nearly clear so she could blend into the ice that coated the walls and ceiling of the cave. Then she readied herself, and flew like an eagle up past the chasm, wavering only slightly as she passed over it, straight up to the circle of light.

As she grabbed it in her hands, she felt a jolt run up her arms, and her brain was flooded with images. Her entire body went rigid for just a second, until she was able to pull the band back from its position immediately above the black cloud of Ena Ray. Just as quickly she hurled it down towards Quinn. All this had happened so fast and so unexpectedly that it was over before anyone knew it had begun.

Ena Ray could feel the movement of the band, and raised himself up. The force of his energy shot to the ceiling of his side of the cavern, nearly crushing Summer. She barely escaped, nearly tumbling across the abyss as she swooped down safe behind Quinn's shoulder, to the sound of Ena Ray as he let out a cry of horror.

"NO!" he shouted. "That's mine. It's mine, mine!"

Quinn acted reflexively as his hand shot out and caught the circle. It felt hot in his hand, but it didn't burn. Not having the magical powers of the others, the band didn't have the same effect on him as it had on Summer, but he could still feel the power.

He brought it down and opened his hand so that Lochen and the others could see it. It was tiny, but began to expand and enlarge before their eyes. In seconds, Quinn needed both hands to hold it. As they all examined it, it looked to be divided into eight equal segments, each of

265

which was moving in an odd and irregular motion. Inside the band the light churned and swirled, blending different colors. Beneath the colors Lochen could see various markings.

"Look here, Quinn" he motioned. "The markings on the separate sections of the band appear to be the same as those that had been etched into the walls in the chamber of your Kingdom."

"You're right," answered Quinn. "See? There's the sea, and there's the mountains," he said as he pointed to the individual markings.

"Stella," said Lochen. "Move over here. Natalie, you move next to Solveig."

He immediately positioned each of his companions around the circle to match up with their marking.

"Now, place your hands on the band," he instructed.

As they placed their hands on the radiating light, their segment stopped spinning with a click that sounded like the tumblers of a lock falling into place. One by one, they each felt a jolt run through their bodies. Even those who had no magical powers knew something magical was happening.

Stella was most affected. Her head jerked back as images flooded her mind. Lochen touched her forehead with his fingertip, which was enough to clear her mind. He then placed his hands on the band - the last to do so. When his segment locked into place, everything started to spin.

"We're moving," said Solveig in surprise. She could feel the power of the band releasing immense energy pulses.

"No," said Natalie, looking at the walls of the cavern, "we're not moving. Everything else is."

She was right. The walls of the room surrounding them became distorted, twisting in a spiral. The image of Ena Ray again puffed itself to its full height and howled with rage.

"NO!" he shouted. "You can't do this. That band is mine. You can't leave me here! My army will hunt you down. There is no place that will be safe for you."

He continued to shout threats, although his voice seemed to be moving farther and farther away. The stalactites and ice crystals stretched and spun. The entire room twisted around them faster and faster, becoming a blur. The wind created by the movement howled like a siren. It was like being in the eye of a tornado. They were in the center of a calm breeze, but everything immediately surrounding them was chaos.

The last thing they heard was the pained voice of Ena Ray screaming, "You're too late" and then there was a flash of light and everything disappeared.

The spinning had made them all feel dizzy and they had closed their eyes. As the sounds died away, they each noticed a radical change in the atmosphere. The frigid air of the Ice Kingdom was gone. It had been replaced by the heat of the desert. One by one, each of them gradually opened their eyes. All but Quinn expected to see the arid sands of the Devil's Desert. He, though, was totally unfamiliar with heat of this intensity, and was reluctant to open his eyes to find out what it was.

They were no longer in the Crystal Citadel.

"We're underground," said Sean, which prompted Quinn to pop open his eyes.

All around them were deep ravines filled with smoke and burning lava. There were walls of fire almost everywhere they looked. They were at the end of a long narrow peninsula with no way out. They surveyed their surroundings. At the other end of the long, narrow ledge on which they had landed, they could see two steel doors with strange markings on them.

"This doesn't seem like an improvement," said Sean. "Where are we?"

"I know," said Liam, excitedly. His powers had returned; he knew where they were, where they had to go, and where the dangers were. "We're at the portal to the underworld."

"Wonderful," said Sean. "We went from one hole in the ground to another. What are we supposed to do here?

They each still had their hands on the circle. It was still pulsating, but it was slowly beginning to shrink in size. Their attention was diverted to the sounds of banging on the steel doors. Solveig turned in their direction and could see that they were starting to move.

"Whatever we're going to do, we'd better hurry," she said.

Stella shouted, "We need to get the circle to the door."

No one questioned her command. In the center of each of the doors was what looked like a handle. When the doors were closed the two handles formed a circle, but that circle was starting to separate. Quinn kept one hand on the circle and with his other arm he scooped up everyone else and bolted towards the door. With his enormous stride he covered the distance in eight quick steps. He threw his body against the opening door, slamming it shut. The banging on the other side intensified. Someone or something was trying to get out.

"I can't hold it closed for long," he said. "What do we do now?"

"Put the band around those handles," Stella told him.

Quinn looped the band over the top of the handles. At first the band hung loosely, but it was continuing to contract in size. A sudden surge on the other side pushed the doors apart very slightly, knocking the band off one of the handles. Quinn dug his heels into the ground and pushed with all his strength, keeping the door shut as he worked the circle over the handles. He managed to push the band over the last part of the handle as it kept shrinking. Finally, everything snapped into place, but nothing happened.

The pounding on the other side became more furious. They could all hear deep growls and screams that made their ears hurt. Quinn kept trying to dig his heels in farther and farther as he pushed against the door, but he was losing ground. The circle was being jarred loose.

"Place your hands on your markings," shouted Stella.

"Won't that make us disappear again?" asked Liam.

"No," she said. "It should lock the doors."

"I hope you're right," said Sean as he moved in underneath Lochen to place his hands on the tree markings.

"So do I," said Stella, as she did the same.

Quinn could no longer hold the door shut. He had to turn his body in order to reach the band. He waited until the others were all in place, and then he quickly turned, releasing his hold on the door and put his hands in position.

The segments remained locked in place, but the lines separating them disappeared. The colors inside the band began to race around beneath their hands and they blurred into a blinding white light. The circle melted the handles, sealing them together and locking the doors. A burning light moved from the handles up and down the seam of the door, welding it shut.

When the melting was finished the circle shrunk into the tiny ring it had been when it hung over the form of Ena Ray, settling into a depression where the handles had once been. The markings remained intact, but were so small that they were nearly invisible. Once that happened, there was a final flash.

The last thing they all saw was that blinding flash of light, and the last thing they heard over the agonizing screams on the other side of the door was an ear splitting crash.  Then everything went black.

# Chapter eighteen

Quinn felt like he had rolled down the side of a mountain in the middle of an avalanche.  He was confused and his mind was spinning.  He was awake, but his eyes were closed.  He wasn't sure where he was and he wasn't sure he wanted to open his eyes to find out.

The last thing he recalled was being in a place that was hotter than anything he could have imagined.  He just couldn't recall where that was.  He remembered pushing against something, but he couldn't remember what.  He was filled with a sense of dread, but he didn't know why.

His left cheek was wet.  Something was pressed up against the side of his face.  He slowly opened his left eye.  Right in front of him was this large black object.  Above it were these two brown orbs and below it was this large pink thing that ran across his cheek, getting it wet.

He shut his eye and jerked his head away, scrambling back from whatever the object was.  When he opened it again he found Rover nestled next to him, licking his cheek.  He spun his head away before the dog could take another lap and came nose to nose with another black object to his right.  Above this one were one brown orb and one blue orb and another large pink tongue stroking his other cheek. He bolted upright to a sitting position.

"Kelsey," he shouted as he turned back to his left. "Rover! What are you doing here?"

He quickly spun his head, looking from left to right. He was in his own room at home, under a layer of fur. He jumped up and ran outside. The dogs cocked their heads and looked quizzically at him.

"I'm home," he announced. "How did that happen?"

He walked around outside his home and saw his friends and neighbors acting like they did before the arrival of the Legendaries, none of whom was anywhere to be found. Was it all a dream, he wondered. He looked at his hands, still tingling from the band. No, he thought. It wasn't a dream; it was real. It had happened. He looked everywhere for signs of his friends. They were nowhere to be found, and no one knew what he was talking about.

Finally, he attached the dogs to their harnesses and took them and his sled to the ice wall. He hesitated for only a second, and then commanded the door way to be opened. Once on the other side, he half expected to see that the storm had advanced and was now covering the sky. Instead he was met with an intense bright blue expanse, broken only by the twin suns high in the sky. The air was crisp and fresh. He took in a deep breath. It felt better than he ever remembered.

The wind was gentle and clear, and the dogs barked in anticipation, eager to be on the run. He looked around, completely puzzled, wondering what he was supposed to do. Nothing, he concluded. I really have nothing to do.

Finally he then said to the dogs, "Let's go south this time. I'd like to see how far we can go. We might meet some interesting people."

And with that he gave them the signal and they took off like a shot.

- - - - - - - - - - - - - - - - - \*\*\* - - - - - - - - - - - - - - - - -

Deep in the Venomous Swamp Liam was having a similar awakening. He sat up from his bed and took a deep breath. Something was different, but at the same time nothing was different. He was back home. He had no idea how he had gotten here or when. He was wearing some strange clothes. Where did I get these, he wondered. As he got changed, he surveyed his array of weapons. He started to strap them on, but hesitated. He sensed no danger nearby. In fact, he sensed no danger at all.

Puzzled, he went outside and found his boat still up against the dock where he had left it – how long ago? He wasn't sure. The air seemed fresher, and it wasn't as humid as it normally was. In fact, it was downright pleasant. Just as he was about to step into his boat, he saw a strange flower growing near the shoreline.

He had never seen one like this before. It had pale yellow star-like petals. He hesitated for a second bending down to examine the bud more closely. He couldn't recall any plant in the swamp that wasn't poisonous or dangerous in some way, but he sensed no danger from this plant. He took a chance and leaned over to sniff the center of the blossom. It had a pleasant aroma that seemed to shift between a gentle sea breeze, mountain air, and a sandy shore.

Very unusual, he thought. I seem to recall that aroma from...where, he wondered...someplace nice was all he could bring to mind. He climbed into his boat and dropped the sail. He untied the lines and took his seat at the wheel. He was thinking about the mapping he had been doing – when? He wasn't sure.

That was weird, he said to himself. He couldn't recall when or why he had stopped the detailed mapping of the Swamp. His initial instinct was to go downstream, towards the west, but something compelled him to change his mind.

"I think I'll go north," he said to no one in particular. "At least to begin with. I might meet someone interesting and maybe together we'll explore some other places...maybe to the south."

Natalie rolled over onto her back and stretched. With a start she sat up opening her eyes wide. Her first thought was, "Where is Stella?" She looked around and found herself in bed. She climbed out and, as she began to look for her clothes, realized that she was already dressed. She was wearing some kind of white fur.

"Where did these come from," she said out loud to no one.

Without giving it much more thought, she stepped out her door and onto the balcony at the side of her palace. Below she could see hundreds of her subjects scurrying about. They were preparing for the weekly fair. Had the storm passed them over? She looked for signs of her companions, but could see nothing that told her where they were.

"I need to find my Enchantress," she said aloud.

"Yes, your Highness," called a voice from the other side of the room. One of her ladies in waiting had answered. She walked into Natalie's room and stared at the odd clothing her Princess was wearing. Saying nothing, she left in search of Stella.

Stella was sitting in the Sanctorum. When the lady in waiting arrived, she stopped, startled to see the Enchantress in the same odd clothing as the Princess, sitting in a trance-like state. She stood at the edge of the Sanctorum, uncertain what to do. Before she could collect her thoughts, the Enchantress spoke.

"I know, the Princess wants to see me," she told the lady in waiting.

It was not unusual for the Enchantress to know what someone was going to say before they said it, but the lady in waiting was startled just the same. As Stella stood up, the lady's eye was caught by the unusual headband that the Enchantress was wearing. She had never seen her wear such an object before.

Finding her voice she stammered, "That's a beautiful band you're wearing. And what an unusual stone. Where did you get it, if I may ask?"

Stella raised her hand to her head and felt the band, surprised that it was still on her head.

"I got it from some friends. A long time ago, I think," she answered, "but I only just found it again."

The lady in waiting just looked at her oddly.

Then Stella said, walking past the lady in waiting, "Prepare the guest quarters. I think we'll be needing them soon."

"Are we expecting guests," asked the lady.

"I don't know," said Stella. "I think so."

She then went off to see Natalie. When she arrived, before she could say anything Natalie told her she wanted her opinion on something.

"I think I'd like to move our people to the surface," she said. "I was thinking of finding a nice island somewhere between the shore and the forest."

Stella smiled. "I think that would be nice. I think it would also be nice to reach out to the peoples in those areas and to extend our friendship."

Natalie smiled back at her. "I agree. What would I do without you?"

------------------ *** ------------------

Solveig was aroused from her distant thoughts by the sound of the maid bringing in a service of tea.

"Good morning, Princess," she said. "I thought you would like some tea."

"Yes," said Solveig. "Thank you."

As the maid was leaving, Solveig stopped her.

"How long have we been gone?" she asked the maid.

"Gone, your Highness?" asked the maid. "I'm not sure what you mean."

"Gone," repeated Solveig. "The Sorcerer and I. How long were we gone?"

"I'm sorry, your Highness," answered the maid, clearly puzzled. "I wasn't aware that either of you had left the castle."

Solveig wrinkled her brow, but didn't say anything.

"Will there be anything else, Your Highness?" the maid asked.

Solveig just dismissed her and went in search of Lochen. She crossed the courtyard in the middle of the castle grounds and saw her people going about their daily business as usual. She looked up to the sky and saw an intense bright blue expanse, broken only by the twin suns high in the sky. She gave the storm only a passing thought as she continued. She found Lochen in his planetarium. He was sorting through papers and books, tossing some aside and piling others into an old leather case.

"Are you going somewhere?" she asked.

Without looking up he answered, "I thought I should like to see the rings of Capurnica once more. It's something I told myself I needed to do."

"And when did you come to this decision," she said, sounding a bit annoyed.

At that he looked up at her.

"Your hair," he said in an amazed voice.

Solveig reached up, expecting to feel jagged edges. She couldn't explain why she had this expectation, but she did. Instead she felt the long red strands down to the center of her back. Her eyes shot back to his with the unspoken question of "How?" Lochen just looked back at her and shook his head slowly.

"You expected the same thing, didn't you?" she asked, knowing she didn't have to explain her odd comment.

"Yes," he said, "but for the life of me, I can't explain why."

He returned to his desk, rummaging around for something undefined. Solveig watched for a few seconds more.

"I understand how much you'd like to go," she finally said, "but I ask that you delay your trip for a little while."

"As you wish," he answered. He stood up straight and turned to her and asked, "But why?"

"I'd like to leave our mountain and visit the forest and the shore below. After that I think I'd like to go north. I'm not sure why, but I'd like to see who we meet. Would you join me?"

Lochen thought for a minute. He looked back at his solar maps and then down at the papers and charts he had been packing.

"I suppose I could wait a little while before going back to Capurnica," he said. "And it might be nice to meet some new people."

------------------ *** ------------------

Sean was aroused by the sounds of people arguing. He jumped up and reached for his slingshot. When he had his senses fully about him, he recognized the noises. It was the lodge chiefs debating over some trivial matter, as usual. When he jumped up with his sling shot in hand, the arguing stopped. Everyone looked at him in wonder.

"What's the matter, Sean?" asked one of the chiefs. "Have the faeries stolen your thoughts?"

All the others laughed.

"It would be good if you could stay awake in our meetings," another one said.

Sean just looked around at them.

"Where is your armband?" a third one asked. "Have you lost it again?"

He reached to his arm. The band was gone.

"And what animal did you capture to find those clothes?"

He started to say something, but then thought it better to just keep quiet. Without a word he left the lodge chiefs. As he walked around the lodge he was greeted by his friends. He looked at them as curiously as they looked at him. They all seemed to be all right. No one had been turned to stone.

He realized that he didn't hear the sound of thunder or the crash of lightning. He looked to the sky, expecting to see the black clouds of the approaching storm. He was somewhat taken aback when, instead, he saw an intense bright blue expanse, broken only by the twin suns high in the sky.

"I wonder if others see the same sky?" he asked himself aloud.

A passing neighbor commented to him, "What others? Are you talking to yourself again, Sean? The faeries must have stolen your thoughts."

"The faeries," thought Sean. "Summer!"

He wondered if she was all right and if she knew what had happened. He ran off to their meeting place in the side of the cliff. As he approached the crest he noticed that nothing had changed. The line of rocks at the top was still there. He scrambled down to the opening and crawled in. It was just as it had always been. What was going on? He sat down, hugged his knees and waited, hoping she would come soon.

- - - - - - - - - - - - - - - - - \*\*\* - - - - - - - - - - - - - - - - -

Summer felt like she was floating on the gentle currents of air. It must be night time, because everything was dark. She shifted her position slightly and suddenly had the sensation she was falling. She was diving downward head first, unable to stop herself. Just as she opened her mouth to scream, her eyes opened and she saw the ground rushing up at her.

She landed face first, her open mouth filling with sand from the shore on which she landed. Sputtering, she rolled over and sat up. Nothing hurt but her dignity. She looked up and saw a large Banchu leaf bobbing up and down. Above the leaf instead of a sky blackened by the storm that had been chasing her for far too many days, she saw an intense bright bue expanse, broken only by the twin suns high in the sky.

She must have fallen asleep on the leaf and when she moved, she had fallen off. Storm, she thought immediately. Rubbing her head, she wondered, was that all a dream? As she tried to recall details, they became fuzzier and fuzzier.

Nearby two little ones from the village were laughing at her. She reddened slightly and stood up, dusting herself off. Then it hit her. She snapped her head up and turned to the two small faeries who were laughing and pointing at her. They were all right. They weren't stone statues. She rushed into the village and all around her she saw the normal morning activities. Everything had returned to normal.

She stopped one of the elders who was passing by.

"How did this happen?" she asked him.

He looked at her quizzically. "How did what happen?" he asked.

"How was the spell broken?" she persisted. "How did everyone get changed back to normal?"

"I don't know what you mean, Princess," he answered.

"Everyone had been turned to stone," she nearly shouted. "How did they get turned back to normal? Who did it? When did it happen?"

Had the spell just worn off by itself, she wondered. Had the terrible journey she had undertaken been unnecessary? She was torn between competing emotions of anger and joy. The elder pulled his arm from her grasp and began to move away from her.

"I think you were asleep in the sun a little too long," he told her. "You have been dreaming."

"No," she said defensively. "There was a storm. It turned everyone to stone, and I…I. I did something."

She was really confused now. Was it a dream? Had any of it happened? Had any of WHAT happened? Sean would know. She raced to their secret meeting place. When she arrived she found him hunched in the backmost part of the cave, almost as if he was hiding.

"Are you all right?" she asked when she saw him.

"Yes," he said a little too forcefully. "No. I don't know. The lodge chiefs think nothing happened. They think I was day dreaming."

"I know. I got the same reaction. Were we dreaming? How could you and I both have the same dream?"

Sean answered, "Well my armband is gone, and I didn't lose it like the chiefs think. I see your locket is gone, too. If I remember right, you never took it off, so it's not likely you lost it any more than I lost my band. And what are we wearing? We weren't dreaming. I'm sure of it."

For the first time, she noticed she was wearing some odd white fur. Now she was really confused. After a few minutes of silence, they came to the realization that it didn't matter if any of the others knew what had happened or not. They were all safe. Summer went to the front of the cave and peered out.

"Well, since everything here seems to be all right," she said as she turned back and looked at Sean, "what do you think of taking a little trip? I was thinking about crossing the forest to see what's on the other side. What do you think?"

The idea appealed to Sean. He smiled broadly and said, "I'd like that. You never know who you might meet."

He didn't even mention that he hoped they didn't have to travel near any water.

# ABOUT THE AUTHOR

Ricvhard Reda spent most of his life working for various agencies and Departments in the Federal Government.  He believes this gave him a solid foundation for writing fantasy and fiction.  He lives with his wife in Manassas, Virginia, where he retired – the first time.

The *Quest of Eight* series originated as bed time stories for his grandchildren.  As the grandchildren got older and the bed time stories got longer, it was suggested to him that he write them down.  So he did.  One, however, was not enough.  Follow the saga in *Part Two: In Search of the Alchemist.*